The Strange Case of Cavendish

Randall Parrish

Alpha Editions

This edition published in 2024

ISBN : 9789362999931

Design and Setting By
Alpha Editions
www.alphaedis.com
Email - info@alphaedis.com

As per information held with us this book is in Public Domain.
This book is a reproduction of an important historical work. Alpha Editions uses the best technology to reproduce historical work in the same manner it was first published to preserve its original nature. Any marks or number seen are left intentionally to preserve its true form.

Contents

CHAPTER I THE REACHING OF A DECISION .... - 1 -

CHAPTER II THE BODY ON THE FLOOR .... - 5 -

CHAPTER III MR. ENRIGHT DECLARES HIMSELF .... - 9 -

CHAPTER IV A BREATH OF SUSPICION .... - 14 -

CHAPTER V ON THE TRACK OF A CRIME .... - 18 -

CHAPTER VI AT STEINWAY'S .... - 21 -

CHAPTER VII MISS DONOVAN ARRIVES .... - 27 -

CHAPTER VIII A GANG OF ENEMIES .... - 32 -

CHAPTER IX A NIGHT AND A MORNING .... - 38 -

CHAPTER X AT A NEW ANGLE .... - 43 -

CHAPTER XI DEAD OR ALIVE .... - 49 -

CHAPTER XII VIEWED FROM BOTH SIDES .... - 56 -

CHAPTER XIII THE SHOT OF DEATH .... - 63 -

CHAPTER XIV LACY LEARNS THE
   TRUTH ....- 69 -

CHAPTER XV MISS LA RUE PAYS A
   CALL ....- 76 -

CHAPTER XVI CAPTURED..- 83 -

CHAPTER XVII IN THE SHOSHONE
   DESERT ....- 90 -

CHAPTER XVIII IN MEXICAN POWER ....- 97 -

CHAPTER XIX WESTCOTT FINDS
   HIMSELF ALONE ....- 104 -

CHAPTER XX TO COMPEL AN
   ANSWER..- 110 -

CHAPTER XXI THE MARSHAL PLAYS
   A HAND ....- 117 -

CHAPTER XXII THE ROCK IN THE
   STREAM ....- 124 -

CHAPTER XXIII THE ESCAPE ....- 131 -

CHAPTER XXIV THE CAVE IN THE
   CLIFF ....- 138 -

CHAPTER XXV IN THE DARK
   PASSAGE..- 144 -

CHAPTER XXVI THE REAPPEARANCE
   OF CAVENDISH ....- 149 -

CHAPTER XXVII A DANGEROUS
   PRISONER ....- 156 -

CHAPTER XXVIII WITH BACK TO THE
    WALL ....- 164 -

CHAPTER XXIX A NEEDLE IN A
    HAYSTACK ....- 172 -

CHAPTER XXX ON THE EDGE OF THE
    CLIFF ....- 180 -

CHAPTER XXXI WITH FORCE OF
    ARMS ....- 189 -

CHAPTER XXXII IN THE TWO CABINS ....- 197 -

CHAPTER XXXIII THE REAL MR.
    CAVENDISH ....- 203 -

CHAPTER XXXIV MISS DONOVAN
    DECIDES ....- 209 -

CHAPTER I
THE REACHING OF A DECISION

For the second time that night Frederick Cavendish, sitting at a small table in a busy café where the night life of the city streamed continually in and out, regarded the telegram spread out upon the white napery. It read:

Bear Creek, Colorado, 4/2/15.

FREDERICK CAVENDISH,
  College Club,
    New York City.

Found big lead; lost it again. Need you badly.

WESTCOTT.

For the second time that night, too, a picture rose before him, a picture of great plains, towering mountains, and open spaces that spoke the freedom and health of outdoor living. He had known that life once before, when he and Jim Westcott had prospected and hit the trail together, and its appeal to him now after three years of shallow sightseeing in the city was deeper than ever.

"Good old Jim," he murmured, "struck pay-dirt at last only to lose it and he needs me. By George, I think I'll go."

And why should he not? Only twenty-nine, he could still afford to spend a few years in search of living. His fortune left him at the death of his father was safely invested, and he had no close friends in the city and no relatives, except a cousin, John Cavendish, for whom he held no love, and little regard.

He had almost determined upon going to Bear Creek to meet Westcott and was calling for his check when his attention was arrested by a noisy party of four that boisterously took seats at a near-by table. Cavendish recognised the two women as members of the chorus of the prevailing Revue, one of them Celeste La Rue, an aggressive blonde with thin lips and a metallic voice, whose name was synonymous with midnight escapades and flowing wine. His contemptuous smile at the sight of them deepened into a disgusted sneer when he saw that one of the men was John Cavendish, his cousin.

The two men's eyes met, and the younger, a slight, mild-eyed youth with a listless chin, excused himself and presented himself at the elder's table.

"Won't you join us?" he said nervously.

Frederick Cavendish's trim, bearded jaw tightened and he shook his head. "They are not my people," he said shortly, then retreating, begged, "John, when are you going to cut that sort out?"

"You make me weary!" the boy snapped. "It's easy enough for you to talk when you've got all the money—that gives you an excuse to read me moral homilies every time I ask you for a dollar, but Miss La Rue is as good as any of your friends any day."

The other controlled himself. "What is it you want?" he demanded directly: "Money? If so, how much?"

"A hundred will do," the younger man said eagerly. "I lost a little on cards lately, and have to borrow. To-night I met the girl——"

Frederick Cavendish silenced him and tendered him the bills. "Now," he said gravely, "this is the last, unless—unless you cut out such people as Celeste La Rue and others that you train with. I'm tired of paying bills for your inane extravagances and parties. I can curtail your income and what's more, I will unless you change."

"Cut me off?" The younger Cavendish's voice took on an incredulous note.

The other nodded. "Just that," he said. "You've reached the limit."

For a moment the dissipated youth surveyed his cousin, then an angry flush mounted into his pasty face.

"You—you—" he stuttered, "—you go to hell."

Without another word the elderly Cavendish summoned the waiter, paid the bill, and walked toward the door. John stared after him, a smile of derision on his face. He had heard Cavendish threaten before.

"Your cousin seemed peeved," suggested Miss La Rue.

"It's his nature," explained John. "Got sore because I asked him for a mere hundred and threatened to cut off my income unless I quit you two."

"You told him where to go," Miss La Rue said, laughing. "I heard you, but I don't suppose he'll go—he doesn't look like that kind."

"Anyhow, I told him," laughed John; then producing a large bill, cried: "Drink up, people, they're on me—and goody-goody cousin Fred."

When Frederick Cavendish reached the street and the fresh night air raced through his lungs he came to a sudden realisation and then a resolution. The realisation was that since further pleading would avail nothing with John Cavendish, he needed a lesson. The resolution was to give it to him.

Both strengthened his previous half-hearted desire to meet Westcott, into determination.

He turned the matter over in his mind as he walked along until reflection was ended by the doors of the College Club which appeared abruptly and took him in their swinging circle. He went immediately to the writing-room, laid aside his things and sat down. The first thing to do, he decided, was to obtain an attorney and consult him regarding the proper steps. For no other reason than that they had met occasionally in the corridor he thought of Patrick Enright, a heavy-set man with a loud voice and given to wearing expensive clothes.

Calling a page boy, he asked that Enright be located if possible. During the ensuing wait he outlined on a scrap of paper what he proposed doing. Fifteen minutes passed before Enright, suave and apparently young except for growing baldness, appeared.

"I take it you are Mr. Cavendish," he said, advancing, "and that you are in immediate need of an attorney's counsel."

Cavendish nodded, shook hands, and motioned him into a chair. "I have been called suddenly out of town, Mr. Enright," he explained, "and for certain reasons which need not be disclosed I deem it necessary to execute a will. I am the only son of the late William Huntington Cavendish; also his sole heir, and in the event of my death without a will, the property would descend to my only known relative, a cousin."

"His name?" Mr. Enright asked.

"John Cavendish."

The lawyer nodded. Of young Cavendish he evidently knew.

"Because of his dissolute habits I have decided to dispose of a large portion of my estate elsewhere in case of my early death. I have here a rough draft of what I want done." He showed the paper. "All that I require is that it be transposed into legal form."

Enright took the paper and read it carefully. The bulk of the $1,000,000 Cavendish estate was willed to charitable organisations, and a small allowance, a mere pittance, was provided for John Cavendish. After a few inquiries the attorney said sharply: "You want this transcribed immediately?"

Cavendish nodded.

"Since it can be made brief I may possibly be able to do it on the girl's machine in the office. You do not mind waiting a moment?"

Cavendish shook his head, and rising, the attorney disappeared in the direction of the office. Cavendish heaved a sigh of relief; now he was free, absolutely free, to do as he chose. His disappearance would mean nothing to his small circle of casual friends, and when he was settled elsewhere he could notify the only two men who were concerned with his whereabouts—his valet, Valois, and the agent handling the estate. He thought of beginning a letter to John, but hesitated, and when Enright returned he found him with pen in hand.

"A trifling task," the attorney smiled easily. "All ready for your signature, too. You sign there, the second line. But wait—we must have witnesses."

Simms, the butler, and the doorman were called in and wrote their names to the document and then withdrew, after which Enright began folding it carefully.

"I presume you leave this in my care?" he asked shortly.

Cavendish shook his head: "I think not. I prefer holding it myself in case it is needed suddenly. I shall keep my rooms, and my man Valois will remain there indefinitely. Now as to your charges."

A nominal sum was named and paid, after which Cavendish rose, picked up his hat and stick and turned to Enright.

"You have obliged me greatly," he smiled, "and, of course, the transaction will be considered as strictly confidential." And then seeing Enright's nod bade him a courteous "Good night."

The attorney watched him disappear. Suddenly he struck the table with one hand.

"By God!" he muttered, "I'll have to see this thing a little further."

Wheeling suddenly, he walked to a telephone booth, called a number and waited impatiently several moments before he said in intense subdued tones: "Is this Carlton's Café? Give me Jackson, the head-waiter. Jackson, is Mr. Cavendish—John Cavendish—there? Good! Call him to the phone will you, Jackson? It's important."

CHAPTER II
THE BODY ON THE FLOOR

The early light of dawn stealing in faintly through the spider-web of the fire-escape ladder, found a partially open window on the third floor of the Waldron apartments, and began slowly to brighten the walls of the room within. There were no curtains on this window as upon the others, and the growing radiance streamed in revealing the whole interior. It was a large apartment, furnished soberly and in excellent taste as either lounging-room or library, the carpet a dark green, the walls delicately tinted, bearing a few rare prints rather sombrely framed, and containing a few upholstered chairs; a massive sofa, and a library table bearing upon it a stack of magazines.

Its tenant evidently was of artistic leanings for about the room were several large bronze candle-sticks filled with partially burned tapers. A low bookcase extended along two sides of the room, each shelf filled, and at the end of the cases a heavy imported drapery drawn slightly aside revealed the entrance to a sleeping apartment, the bed's snowy covering unruffled. Wealth, taste and comfort were everywhere manifest.

Yet, as the light lengthened, the surroundings evidenced disorder. One chair lay overturned, a porcelain vase had fallen from off the table-top to the floor and scattered into fragments. A few magazines had fallen also, and there were miscellaneous papers scattered about the carpet, one or two of them torn as though jerked open by an impatient hand. Still others lying near the table disclosed corners charred by fire, and as an eddy of wind whisked through the window and along the floor it tumbled brown ashes along with it, at the same time diluting the faint odour of smoke that clung to the room. Back of the table a small safe embedded in the wall stood with its door wide open, its inner drawer splintered as with a knife blade and hanging half out, and below it a riffle of papers, many of them apparently legal documents.

But the one object across which the golden beams of light fell as though in soft caress was the motionless figure of a man lying upon his back beside the table near the drapeless window. Across his face and shoulders were the charred remains of what undoubtedly had been curtains on that window. A three-socketed candle-stick filled with partially burned candles which doubtless had been knocked from the table was mute evidence of how the tiny flame had started upon its short march. As to the man's injuries, a blow from behind had evidently crushed his skull and, though the face was seared and burned, though the curtain's partial ashes covered more than a half of it, though the eye-lashes above the sightless eyes were singed and the trim beard burned to black stubs, the face gave mute evidence of being that of Frederick Cavendish.

In this grim scene a tiny clock on the mantel began pealing the hour of eight. As though this were a signal for entrance, the door at the end of the bookcase opened noiselessly and a man, smooth faced, his hair brushed low across his forehead, stepped quietly in. As his eyes surveyed the grewsome object by the table, they dilated with horror; then his whole body stiffened and he fled back into the hall, crashing the door behind him.

Ten minutes later he returned, not alone, however. This time his companion was John Cavendish but partially dressed, his features white and haggard.

With nervous hands he pushed open the door. At the sight of the body he trembled a moment, then, mastering himself, strode over and touched the dead face, the other meanwhile edging into the room.

"Dead, sir, really *dead?*" the late comer asked.

Cavendish nodded: "For several hours," he answered in an unnatural voice. "He must have been struck from behind. Robbery evidently was the object—cold-blooded robbery."

"The window is open, sir, and last night at twenty minutes after twelve I locked it. Mr. Cavendish came in at twelve and locking the window was the last thing I did before he told me I could go."

"He left no word for a morning call?"

Valois shook his head: "I always bring his breakfast at eight," he explained.

"Did he say anything about suddenly leaving the city for a trip West? I heard such a rumour."

"No, sir. He was still up when I left and had taken some papers from his pocket. When last I saw him he was looking at them. He seemed irritated."

There was a moment's silence, during which the flush returned to Cavendish's cheeks, but his hands still trembled.

"You heard nothing during the night?" he demanded.

"Nothing, sir. I swear I knew nothing until I opened the door and saw the body a few moments ago."

"You'd better stick to your story, Valois," the other said sternly, "The police will be here shortly. I'm going to call them, now."

He was calm, efficient, self-contained now as he got Central Station upon the wire and began talking.

"Hello, lieutenant? Yes. This is John Cavendish of the Waldron apartments speaking. My cousin, Frederick Cavendish, has been found dead in his room and his safe rifled. Nothing has been disturbed. Yes, at the Waldron, Fifty-Seventh Street. Please hurry."

Perhaps half an hour later the police came—two bull-necked plain-clothes men and a flannel-mouthed "cop."

With them came three reporters, one of them a woman. She was a young woman, plainly dressed and, though she could not be called beautiful, there was a certain patrician prettiness in her small, oval, womanly face with its grey kind eyes, its aquiline nose, its firm lips and determined jaw, a certain charm in the manner in which her chestnut hair escaped occasionally from under her trim hat. Young, aggressive, keen of mind and tireless, Stella Donovan was one of the few good woman reporters of the city and the only one the *Star* kept upon its pinched pay-roll. They did so because she could cover a man-size job and get a feminine touch into her story after she did it. And, though her customary assignments were "sob" stories, divorces, society events and the tracking down of succulent bits of general scandal, she nevertheless enjoyed being upon the scene of the murder even though she was not assigned to it. This casual duty was for Willis, the *Star's* "police" man, who had dragged her along with him for momentary company over her protest that she must get a "yarn" concerning juvenile prisoners for the Sunday edition.

"Now, we'll put 'em on the rack." Willis smiled as he left her side and joined the detectives.

A flood of questions from the officers, interspersed frequently with a number from Willis, and occasionally one from the youthful *Chronicle* man, came down upon Valois and John Cavendish, while Miss Donovan, silent and watchful, stood back, frequently letting her eyes admire the tasteful prints upon the walls and the rich hangings in the room of death.

Valois repeated his experience, which was corroborated in part by the testimony of John Cavendish's valet whom he had met and talked with in the hall. The valet also testified that his employer, John Cavendish, had come home not later than twelve o'clock and immediately retired. Then John Cavendish established the fact that ten minutes before arriving home he had dropped Celeste La Rue at her apartment. There was no flaw in any of the stories to which the inquisitors could attach suspicion. One thing alone seemed to irritate Willis.

"Are you sure," he said to Cavendish, "that the dead man is your cousin? The face and chest are pretty badly burned you know, and I thought perhaps——"

A laugh from the detectives silenced him while Cavendish ended any fleeting doubts with a contemptuous gaze.

"You can't fool a man on his own cousin, youngster," he said flatly. "The idea is absurd."

The crime unquestionably was an outside job; the window opening on the fire-escape had been jimmied, the marks left being clearly visible. Apparently Frederick Cavendish had previously opened the safe door—since it presented no evidence of being tampered with—and was examining certain papers on the table, when the intruder had stolen up from behind and dealt him a heavy blow probably, from the nature of the wound, using a piece of lead pipe. Perhaps in falling Cavendish's arm had caught in the curtains, pulling them from the supporting rod and dragging them across the table, thus sweeping the candlestick with its lighted tapers down to the floor with it. There the extinguished wicks had ignited the draperies, which had fallen across the stricken man's face and body. The clothes, torso, and legs, had been charred beyond recognition but the face, by some peculiar whim of fate, had been partly preserved.

The marauder, aware that the flames would obliterate a portion, if not all of the evidence against him, had rifled the safe in which, John testified, his cousin always kept considerable money. Scattering broadcast valueless papers, he had safely made his escape through the window, leaving his victim's face to the licking flames. Foot-prints below the window at the base of the fire-escape indicated that the fugitive had returned that way. This was the sum of the evidence, circumstantial and true, that was advanced. Satisfied that nothing else was to be learned, the officers, detectives, Willis, and Miss Donovan and the pale *Chronicle* youth withdrew, leaving the officer on guard.

The same day, young John, eager to be away from the scene, moved his belongings to the Fairmount Hotel, and, since no will was found in the dead man's papers, the entire estate came to him, as next of kin. A day or two later the body was interred in the family lot beside the father's grave, and the night of the funeral young John Cavendish dined at an out-of-the-way road-house with a blonde with a hard metallic voice. Her name was Miss Celeste La Rue.

And the day following he discharged Francois Valois without apparent cause, in a sudden burst of temper. So, seemingly, the curtain fell on the last act of the play.

CHAPTER III
MR. ENRIGHT DECLARES HIMSELF

One month after the Cavendish murder and two days after he had despatched a casual, courteous note to John Cavendish requesting that he call, Mr. Patrick Enright, of Enright and Dougherty, sat in his private office on the top floor of the Collander Building in Cortlandt Street waiting for the youth's appearance. Since young Cavendish had consulted him before in minor matters, Mr. Enright had expected that he would call voluntarily soon after the murder, but in this he was disappointed. Realising that Broadway was very dear to the young man, Enright had made allowances, until, weary of waiting, he decided to get into the game himself and to this end had despatched the note, to which Cavendish had replied both by telephone and note.

"He ought to be here now," murmured Mr. Enright sweetly, looking at his watch, and soon the expected visitor was ushered in. Arising to his feet the attorney extended a moist, pudgy hand.

"Quite prompt, John," he greeted. "Take the chair there—and pardon me a moment."

As the youth complied Enright opened the door, glanced into the outer room, and gave orders not to be disturbed for the next half-hour. Then, drawing in his head, closed the door and turned the key.

"John," he resumed smoothly, "I have been somewhat surprised that you failed to consult me earlier regarding the will of your late cousin Frederick."

"His—his will!" John leaned forward amazed, as he stared into the other's expressionless face. "Did—did he leave one?"

"Oh! that's it," the attorney chuckled. "You didn't know about it, did you? How odd. I thought I informed you of the fact over the phone the same night Frederick died."

"You told me he had called upon you to prepare a will—but there was none found in his papers."

"So I inferred from the newspaper accounts," Enright chuckled dryly, his eyes narrowing, "as well as the information that you had applied for letters of administration. In view of that, I thought a little chat advisable—yes, quite advisable, since on the night of his death I did draw up his will. Incidentally, I am the only one living aware that such a will was drawn. You see my position?"

Young Cavendish didn't; this was all strange, confusing.

"The will," resumed Mr. Enright, "was drawn in proper form and duly witnessed."

"There can't be such a will. None was found. You phoned me shortly before midnight, and twenty minutes later Frederick was in his apartments. He had no time to deposit it elsewhere. There is no such will."

Enright smiled, not pleasantly by any means.

"Possibly not," he said with quiet sinister gravity. "It was probably destroyed and it was to gain possession of that will that Frederick Cavendish was killed."

John leaped to his feet, his face bloodless: "My God!" he muttered aghast, "do you mean to say——"

"Sit down, John; this is no cause for quarrel. Now listen. I am not accusing you of crime; not intentional crime, at least. There is no reason why you should not naturally have desired to gain possession of the will. If an accident happened, that was your misfortune. I merely mention these things because I am your friend. Such friendship leads me first to inform you what had happened over the phone. I realised that Frederick's hasty determination to devise his property elsewhere was the result of a quarrel. I believed it my duty to give you opportunity to patch that quarrel up with the least possible delay. Perhaps this was not entirely professional on my part, but the claims of friendship are paramount to mere professional ethics."

He sighed, clasping and unclasping his hands, yet with eyes steadily fixed upon Cavendish, who had sunk back into his chair.

"Now consider the situation, my dear fellow. I have, it is true, performed an unprofessional act which, if known, would expose me to severe criticism. There is, however, no taint of criminal intent about my conduct and, no doubt, my course would be fully vindicated, were I now to go directly before the court and testify to the existence of a will."

"But that could not be proved. You have already stated that Frederick took the will with him; it has never been found."

"Quite true—or rather, it may have been found, and destroyed. It chances, however, that I took the precaution to make a carbon copy."

"Unsigned?"

"Yes, but along with this unsigned copy I also retain the original memoranda furnished me in Frederick Cavendish's own handwriting. I believe, from a legal standpoint, by the aid of my evidence, the court would be very apt to hold such a will proved."

He leaned suddenly forward, facing the shrinking Cavendish and bringing his hand down hard upon the desk.

"Do you perceive now what this will means? Do you realise where such testimony would place you? Under the law, providing he died without a will, you were the sole heir to the property of Frederick Cavendish. It was widely known you were not on friendly terms. The evening of his death you quarrelled openly in a public restaurant. Later, in a spirit of friendship, I called you up and said he had made a will practically disinheriting you. Between that time and the next morning he is murdered in his own apartments, his safe rifled, and yet, the only paper missing is this will, to the existence of which I can testify. If suspicion is once cast upon you, how can you clear yourself? Can you prove that you were in your own apartments, asleep in your own bed from one o'clock until eight? Answer that."

Cavendish tried, but although his lips moved, they gave utterance to no sound. He could but stare into those eyes confronting him. Enright scarcely gave him opportunity.

"So, the words won't come. I thought not. Now listen. I am not that kind of a man and I have kept still. No living person—not even my partner—has been informed of what has occurred. The witnesses, I am sure, do not know the nature of the paper they signed. I am a lawyer; I realise fully the relations I hold to my client, but in this particular case I contend that my duty as a man is of more importance than any professional ethics. Frederick Cavendish had this will executed in a moment of anger and devised his estate to a number of charities. I personally believe he was not in normal mind and that the will did not really reflect his purpose. He had no thought of immediate death, but merely desired to teach you a lesson. He proposed to disappear—or at least, that is my theory—in order that he might test you on a slender income. I am able to look upon the whole matter from this standpoint, and base my conduct accordingly. No doubt this will enable us to arrive at a perfectly satisfactory understanding."

The lawyer's voice had fallen, all the threat gone, and the younger man straightened in his chair.

"You mean you will maintain silence as to the will?"

"Absolutely; as a client your interests will always be my first concern. Of course I shall expect to represent you in a legal capacity in settling up the estate, and consequently feel it only just that the compensation for such services shall be mutually agreed upon. In this case there are many interests to guard. Knowing, as I do, all the essential facts, I am naturally better prepared to conserve your interests than any stranger. I hope you appreciate this."

"And your fee?"

"Reasonable, very reasonable, when you consider the service I am doing you, and the fact that my professional reputation might so easily be involved and the sums to be distributed, which amount to more than a million dollars. My silence, my permitting the estate to go to settlement, and my legal services combined, ought to be held as rather valuable—at, let us say, a hundred thousand. Yes, a hundred thousand; I hardly think that is unfair."

Cavendish leaped to his feet, his hand gripping his cane.

"You damned black———"

"Wait!" and Enright arose also. "Not so loud, please; your voice might be heard in the outer office. Besides it might be well for you to be careful of your language. I said my services would cost you a hundred thousand dollars. Take the proposition or leave it, Mr. John Cavendish. Perhaps, with a moment's thought, the sum asked may not seem excessive."

"But—but," the other stammered, all courage leaving him, "I haven't the money."

"Of course not," the threat on Enright's face changing to a smile. "But the prospects that you will have are unusually good. I am quite willing to speculate on your fortunes. A memoranda for legal services due one year from date—such as I have already drawn up—and bearing your signature, will be quite satisfactory. Glance over the items, please; yes, sit here at the table. Now, if you will sign that there will be no further cause for you to feel any uneasiness—this line, please."

Cavendish grasped the penholder in his fingers, and signed. It was the act of a man dazed, half stupefied, unable to control his actions. With trembling hand, and white face, he sat staring at the paper, scarcely comprehending its real meaning. In a way it was a confession of guilt, an acknowledgment of his fear of exposure, yet he felt utterly incapable of resistance. Enright unlocked the door, and projected his head outside, comprehending clearly that the proper time to strike was while the iron was hot.

Calling Miss Healey, one of his stenographers, he made her an official witness to the document and the signature of John Cavendish.

Not until ten minutes later when he was on the street did it occur to John Cavendish that the carbon copy of the will, together with the rough notes in his cousin's handwriting, still remained in Enright's possession. Vainly he tried to force himself to return and demand them, but his nerve failed, and he shuffled away hopelessly in the hurrying crowds.

CHAPTER IV
A BREATH OF SUSPICION

As Francois Valois trudged along the night streets toward his rooming house his heart was plunged in sorrow and suspicion. To be discharged from a comfortable position for no apparent reason when one contemplated no sweet alliance was bad enough, but to be discharged when one planned marriage to so charming a creature as Josette La Baum was nothing short of a blow. Josette herself had admitted that and promptly turned Francois's hazards as to young Cavendish's motives into smouldering suspicion, which he dared not voice. Now, as he paused before a delicatessen window realising that unless he soon obtained another position its dainties would be denied him, these same suspicions assailed him again.

Disheartened, he turned from the pane and was about to move away, when he came face to face with a trim young woman in a smart blue serge. "Oh, hello!" she cried pleasantly, bringing up short. Then seeing the puzzled look upon the valet's face, she said: "Don't you remember me? I'm Miss Donovan of the *Star*. I came up to the apartments the morning of the Cavendish murder with one of the boys."

Valois smiled warmly; men usually did for Miss Donovan. "I remember," he said dolorously.

The girl sensed some underlying sorrow in his voice and with professional skill learned the cause within a minute. Then, because she believed that there might be more to be told, and because she was big-hearted and interested in every one's troubles, she urged him to accompany her to a near-by restaurant and pour out his heart while she supped. Lonely and disheartened, Valois accepted gladly and within half an hour they were seated at a tiny table in an Italian café.

"About your discharge?" she queried after a time.

"I was not even asked to accompany Mr. Frederick's body," he burst out, "even though I had been with him a year. So I stayed in the apartment to straighten things, expecting to be retained in John Cavendish's service. I even did the work in his apartments, but when he returned and saw me there he seemed to lose his temper, wanted to know why I was hanging around, and ordered me out of the place."

"The ingrate!" exclaimed the girl, laying a warm, consoling hand on the other's arm. "You're sure he wasn't drinking?"

"I don't think so, miss. Just the sight of me seemed to drive him mad. Flung money at me, he did, told me to get out, that he never wanted to see me again. Since then I have tried for three weeks to find work, but it has been useless."

While she gave him a word of sympathy, Miss Donovan was busily thinking. She remembered Willis's remark in the apartments, "Are you sure of the dead man's identity? His face is badly mutilated, you know"; and her alert mind sensed a possibility of a newspaper story back of young Cavendish's unwarranted and strange act. How far could she question the man before her? That she had established herself in his good grace she was sure, and to be direct with him she decided would be the best course to adopt.

"Mr. Valois," she said kindly, "would you mind if I asked you a question or two more?"

"No," the man returned.

"All right. First, what sort of a man was your master?"

Valois answered almost with reverence:

"A nice, quiet gentleman. A man that liked outdoors and outdoor sports. He almost never drank, and then only with quiet men like himself that he met at various clubs. Best of all, he liked to spend his evenings at home reading."

"Not much like his cousin John," she ventured with narrowing eyes.

"No, ma'am, God be praised! There's a young fool for you, miss, crazy for the women and his drinking. Brought up to spend money, but not to earn any."

"I understand that he was dependent upon Frederick Cavendish."

"He was, miss," Valois said disgustedly, "for every cent. He could never get enough of it, either, although Mr. Frederick gave him a liberal allowance."

"Did they ever quarrel?"

"I never heard them. But I do know there was no love lost between them, and I know that young John was always broke."

"Girls cost lots on Broadway," Miss Donovan suggested, "and they keep men up late, too."

Valois laughed lightly. "John only came home to sleep occasionally," he said; "and as for the women—one of them called on him the day after Mr. Frederick was killed. I was in the hall, and saw her go straight to his door—

like she had been there before. A swell dresser, miss, if I ever saw one. One of those tall blondes with a reddish tinge in her hair. He likes that kind."

Miss Donovan started imperceptibly. This was interesting; a woman in John Cavendish's apartment the day after his cousin's murder! But who was she? There were a million carrot-blondes in Manhattan. Still, the woman must have had some distinguishing mark; her hat, perhaps, or her jewels.

"Did the woman wear any diamonds?" she asked.

"No diamonds," Valois returned; "a ruby, though. A ruby set in a big platinum ring. I saw her hand upon the knob."

Miss Donovan's blood raced fast. She knew that woman. It was Celeste La Rue! She remembered her because of a press-agent story that had once been written about the ring, and from what Miss Donovan knew of Miss La Rue, she did not ordinarily seek men; therefore there must have been a grave reason for her presence in John Cavendish's apartments immediately after she learned of Frederick's death.

Had his untimely end disarranged some plan of these two? What was the reason she had come in person instead of telephoning? Had her mysterious visit anything to do with the death of the elder Cavendish?

A thousand speculations entered Miss Donovan's mind.

"How long was she in the apartment?" she demanded sharply.

"Fifteen or twenty minutes, miss—until after the hall-man came back. I had to help lay out the body, and could not remain there any longer."

"Have you told any one else what you have told me?"

"Only Josette. She's my *fiancée*. Miss La Baum is her last name."

"You told her nothing further that did not come out at the inquest?"

Valois hesitated.

"Maybe I did, miss," he admitted nervously. "She questioned me about losing my job, and her questions brought things into my mind that I might never have thought of otherwise. And at last I came to believe that it wasn't Mr. Frederick who was dead at all."

The valet's last remark was crashing in its effect.

Miss Donovan's eyes dilated with eagerness and amazement.

"Not Frederick Cavendish! Mr. Valois, tell me—why?"

The other's voice fell to a whisper.

"Frederick Cavendish, miss," he said hollowly, "had a scar on his chest—from football, he once told me—and the man we laid out, well, of course his body was a bit burned, but he appeared to have no scar at all!"

"You know that?" demanded the girl, frightened by the import of the revelation.

"Yes, miss. The assistant in the undertaking rooms said so, too. Doubting my own mind, I asked him. The man we laid out had no scar on his chest."

Miss Donovan sprang suddenly to her feet.

"Mr. Valois," she said breathlessly, "you come and tell that story to my city editor, and he'll see that you get a job—and a real one. You and I have started something, Mr. Valois."

And, tossing money to cover the bill on the table, she took Valois's arm, and with him in tow hurried through the restaurant to the city streets on one of which was the *Star* office, where Farriss, the city editor, daily damned the doings of the world.

That night when Farriss had heard the evidence his metallic eyes snapped with an unusual light. Farriss, for once, was enthusiastic.

"A great lead! By God, it is! Now to prove it, Stella"—Farriss always resorted to first names—"you drop everything else and go to this, learn what you can, spend money if you have to. I'll drag Willis off police, and you work with him. And damn me, if you two spend money, you've got to get results! I'll give you a week—when you've got something, come back!"

CHAPTER V
ON THE TRACK OF A CRIME

In the city room of the *Star*, Farriss, the city editor, sat back in his swivel chair smoking a farewell pipe preparatory to going home. The final edition had been put to bed, the wires were quiet, and as he sat there Farriss was thinking of plunging "muskies" in Maine streams. His thoughts were suddenly interrupted by a clatter of footsteps, and, slapping his feet to the floor, he turned to confront Willis and Miss Donovan.

"Great God!" he started, at their appearance at so late an hour.

Miss Donovan smiled at him. "No; great luck!"

"Better than that, Mr. Farriss," echoed Willis. "We've got something; and we dug all week to get it."

"But it cost us real money—enough to make the business office moan, I expect, too," Miss Donovan added.

"Well, for Pete's sake, shoot!" demanded Farriss. "Cavendish, I suppose?"

The two nodded. Their eyes were alight with enthusiasm.

"In the first place," said the girl, with grave emphasis, "Frederick Cavendish did not die intestate as supposed. He left a will."

Farriss blinked. "By God!" he exclaimed. "That's interesting. There was no evidence of that before."

"I got that from the servants of the College Club," Willis interposed. "The will was drawn the night before the murder. And the man that drew it was Patrick Enright of Enright and Dougherty. Cavendish took away a copy of it in his pocket. And, Mr. Farriss, I got something else, too—Enright and young John Cavendish are in communication further. I saw him leaving Enright's office all excited. Following my hunch, I cultivated Miss Healey, Enright's stenographer, and learned that the two had an altercation and that it was evidently over some document."

Farriss was interested.

"Enright's in this deep," he muttered thoughtfully, "but how? Well—what else?"

Stella Donovan began speaking now:

"I fixed it with Chambers, the manager of the Fairmount, to get Josette La Baum—she's Valois's *fiancée*, you remember—into the hotel as a maid. Josette 'soaped the keyhole' of the drawers in John Cavendish's rooms there. I had a key made from the soap impression, and from the contents of the correspondence we found I learned that Celeste La Rue, the blonde of the Revue, had got some kind of hold on him. It isn't love, either; it's something stronger. He jumps when she holds the hoop."

"La Rue's mixed up in this deeply, too," Willis cut in. "Neither one of us could shadow her without uncovering ourselves, so we hired an International operative. They cost ten dollars a day—and expenses. What he learned was this—that while she was playing with young Cavendish and seeing him almost daily, the lovely Celeste was also in communication with—guess who!"

"Enright?" Farriss ventured.

"Exactly—Enright," he concluded, lighting his half-smoked cigarette.

"Well," the city editor tapped his desk; "you two have done pretty well, so far. You've got considerable dope. Now, what do you make of it?"

He bent an inquiring gaze on both the girl and the youth.

"You do the talking, Jerry," Miss Donovan begged Willis; "I'm very tired."

Willis was only too eager; Willis was young, enthusiastic, reliable—three reasons why the *Star* kept him.

"It may be a dream," he said, smiling, "but here is the way I stack it up. The night after he quarreled with John, Frederick Cavendish called in Enright and made a will, presumably, cutting John off with practically nothing.

"Immediately after Frederick's departure, Enright calls Carbon's Café and talks to John Cavendish, who had been dining there with Celeste La Rue.

"It is reasonable to suppose that he told him of the will. Less than five hours afterward Frederick Cavendish is found dead in his apartments. Again it is reasonable to suppose that he was croaked by John Cavendish, who wanted to destroy the will so that he could claim the estate.

"These Broadway boys need money when they travel with chorines. Anyhow, the dead man is buried, and John starts spending money like water. One month later he receives a letter—Josette patched the pieces together—asking him to call at Enright's office.

"What happened there is probably this: Young Cavendish was informed of the existence of the will, and it was offered to him at a price which he couldn't afford to pay—just then.

"Perhaps he was frightened into signing a promise to pay as soon as he came into the estate—tricked by Enright. Enright, as soon as he heard no will had been found in Frederick's effects, may have figured that perhaps John killed him, or even if he did not, that, nevertheless, he could use circumstances to extract money from the youngster, who, even if innocent, would fear the trial and notoriety that would follow if Enright publicly disclosed the existence of that will.

"John Cavendish may be innocent, or he may be guilty, but one thing is certain—he's being badgered to death by two people, from what little we know. One of them is the La Rue woman; the other is Enright.

"Now I wonder—Mr. Farriss, doesn't it occur to you that they may be working together like the woman and the man in the Skittles case last year? You remember then they got a youngster in their power and nearly trimmed him down to his eye-teeth!"

Farriss sat reflecting deeply, chewing the stem of his dead pipe.

"There's something going on—that's as plain as a red banner-head. You've got a peach of a start, so far, and done good pussyfooting—you, too, Stella—but there's one thing that conflicts with your hypothesis——"

The two leaned forward.

"Valois's statement that he was almost positive that the dead man was not Cavendish," the city editor snapped.

"I now believe Valois is mistaken, in view of developments," said Willis with finality. "So does Stella—Miss Donovan, I mean. Remember the body was charred across the face and chest—and Valois was excited."

Farriss was silent a moment.

"Stick to it a while longer," he rapped out; "and get La Rue and Cavendish together at their meeting-place, if you can discover it."

"We can!" interjected Willis. "That's something I learned less than an hour ago. It's Steinway's Café, the place where the police picked up Frisco Danny and Mad Mike Meighan two years ago. I followed them, but could not get near enough to hear what they said."

"Then hop to it," Farriss rejoined. "Stick around there until you get something deeper. As for me—I'm going home. It's two o'clock."

CHAPTER VI
AT STEINWAY'S

It was the second night after Farriss had given them his instructions that Miss Donovan and Willis, sitting in the last darkened booth in Steinway's Café, were rewarded for their vigil. The booth they occupied was selected for the reason that it immediately joined that into which Willis had but three days before seen Cavendish and the La Rue woman enter, and now as they sat toying with their food, their eyes commanding the entire room, they saw a woman swing into the café entrance and enter the booth directly ahead of them.

"La Rue!" whispered Willis to Miss Donovan.

Ten minutes later a young man entered the café, swept it quickly with his eyes, then made directly for the enclosure occupied by his inamorata. The man was Cavendish.

In the booth behind. Miss Donovan and Willis were all attention, their ears strained to catch the wisps of conversation that eddied over the low partition.

"Pray for the orchestra to stop playing," whispered Miss Donovan, and, strangely enough, as she uttered the words the violins obeyed, leaving the room comparatively quiet in which it was not impossible to catch stray sentences of the subdued conversation.

"Well, I'm here." It was John's voice, an ill-humoured voice, too. "But this is the last time, Celeste. These meetings are dangerous."

"Yes—when you talk so loud." Her soft voice scarcely reached the listeners. "But this time there was a good reason." She laughed. "You didn't think it was love, did you, deary?"

"Oh, cut that out!" disgustedly. "I have been foolish enough to satisfy even your vanity. You want more money, I suppose."

"Well, of course," her voice hardening. "Naturally I feel that I should share in your good fortune. But the amount I want now, and must have to-night—to-night, John Cavendish—is not altogether for myself. I've heard from the West."

"My God! Has he been located?"

"Yes, and is safe for the present. Here, read this telegram. It's not very clear, but Beaton wants money and asks me to bring it."

"You? Why does he need you?"

"Lack of nerve, I guess; he's out of his element in that country. If it was the Bowery he'd do this sort of job better. Anyhow, I'm going, and I want a roll. We can't either of us afford to lie down now."

Cavendish half smothered an oath.

"Money," he ejaculated fiercely. "That is all I hear. Enright has held me up something fierce, and you never let me alone. Suppose I say I haven't got it."

"Why, then, I'd laugh at you, that's all. You may not love me any more, my dear, but surely you have no occasion to consider me a fool. I endeavour to keep posted on what the court is doing in our case; I am naturally interested, you know. You were at the Commercial National Bank this afternoon."

"How the devil did you know that?"

"I play my cards safe," she laughed mirthlessly. "I could even tell you the size of your check, and that the money is still on your person. You intended to place it in a safe-deposit box and keep it hidden for your own use."

"You hellion, you!" Cavendish's voice rose high, then later Miss Donovan heard him say more softly: "How much do you want?"

"Ten thousand. I'm willing enough to split fifty-fifty. This Colorado job is getting to be expensive, deary. I wouldn't dare draw on you through the banks."

Miss Donovan had only time to nudge Willis enthusiastically before she overheard the next plea.

"Celeste, are you trimming me again?"

"Don't be a fool!" came back in subdued tones. "Do you think that telegram is a fake? My Gawd—that is what I want money for! Moreover, I should think you would be tickled, Johnnie boy, to get me out of town—and the price is so low."

In the back booth Willis muttered:

"God, things are going great." Then he bent his ear to sedulous attention and again he could hear the voice of Cavendish.

"You've got to tell me what you're going to do with the money," it said.

The La Rue woman's answer could not be heard; evidently it was a whispered one, and therefore of utmost importance. Came a pause, a clink of glasses, and then a few straggling words filtered over the partition.

"Isn't that the best way?" Celeste La Rue's voice was easily recognisable. "Of course it will be a—well, a mere accident, and no questions asked."

"But if the man should talk!"

"Forget it! Ned Beaton is an oyster. Besides, I've got the screws on him. Come on, Johnnie boy, don't be a fool. We are in this game and must play it out. It has been safe enough so far, and I know what I am doing now. You've got too much at stake to haggle over a few thousand, when the money has come to you as easily as this has. Why, if I'd breathe a word of what I know in this town——"

"For God's sake, not so loud!"

"Bah! No one here is paying any attention to us. Enright is the only one who even suspicions, and his mouth is shut. It makes me laugh to think how easily the fools were gulled. We've got a clear field if you will only let me play the game out in my own way. Do I get the money?"

He must have acceded, for his voice no longer rose to a high pitch. Presently, when the orchestra began playing again. Miss Donovan and Willis judged the pair were giving their attention to the dinner. Finally, after an hour had passed, Cavendish emerged from the booth, went to the check-room, and hurriedly left the café. Waiting only long enough to satisfy herself that Cavendish was gone, Celeste La Rue herself emerged from the booth and paused for a moment beside its bamboo curtains. Then turning suddenly, she made her way, not toward the exit of the café, but to another small booth near the check-room, and into this she disappeared.

But before she had started this short journey, a yellow piece of paper, closely folded, slipped from her belt where it had been tucked.

"It's the telegram! The one of which they were speaking." Miss Donovan's voice whispered dramatically as her eyes swept the tiny clue within their ambit.

Willis started. He almost sprung from the booth to pick it up, but the girl withheld him with a pressure of the hand.

"Not yet," she begged. "Wait until we see who leaves the other booth into which La Rue just went."

And Willis fell back into the seat, his pulse pounding. Presently, with startled eyes, they beheld Celeste la Rue leave the booth, and then five minutes later a well-dressed man, a suave, youthful man with a head inclined toward baldness.

"Enright!" muttered Willis.

"Enright," echoed Miss Donovan, "and, Jerry, our hunch was right. He and La Rue are playing Cavendish—and for something big. But now is our time to get the telegram. Quick—before the waiter returns."

At her words Willis was out of the booth. As Miss Donovan watched, she saw him pass by the folded evidence. What was wrong? But, no—suddenly she saw his handkerchief drop, saw him an instant later turn and pick it up, and with it the telegram. Disappearing in the direction of the men's room, he returned a moment later, paid the check, and with Miss Donovan on his arm left the café.

Outside, and three blocks away from Steinway's, they paused under an arc-light, and with shaking hands Willis showed her the message. There in the flickering rays the girl read its torn and yet enlightening message.

lorado, May 19, 1915.

him safe. Report and collect. come with roll Monday sure 've seen papers. Remember Haskell.

NED.

"It's terribly cryptic, Jerry," she said to the other, "but two things we know from it."

"One is that La Rue's going to blow the burg some day—soon."

"The other, that 'Ned' is Ned Beaton, the man mentioned back there in Steinway's. Whatever his connection is, we don't know. I think we had better go to Farriss, don't you?"

"A good hunch," Willis replied, taking her arm. "And let's move on it quick. One of us may have to hop to Colorado if Farriss thinks well of what we've dug up."

"I hope it's you—you've worked hard," said Miss Donovan.

"But you got the big clue of it all—the telegram," gallantly returned her companion, as he raised his arm to signal a passing cab which would take them to the Star office.

Once there, in their enthusiasm they upset the custom of the office and broke into Farriss's fullest hour, dragged him from his slot in the copy desk and into his private office, which he rarely used. There, into his impatient ears they dinned the story of what they had just learned, ending up by passing him the telegram.

For a mere instant he glanced at them, then his lips began to move. "Beaton—Ned—Ned Beaton—Ned Beaton," he mused, and then sat bolt upright in his chair, while he banged the desk with a round, hard fist.

"Hell's bells!" he ejaculated. "You've run across something. I know that name. I know the man. Ned Beaton is a 'gun,' and he pulled his first job when I was doing 'police' in Philadelphia for the *Record*. Well, well, my children, this is splendid! And what next?"

"But, Mr. Farriss, where is he?" put in Stella Donovan. "Where was the message sent from? Colorado, yes, but where in Colorado? That's the thing to find out."

"I thought it might be the last word in the message—Haskell," ventured Willis.

Mr. Farriss paused a moment, then,

"Boy!" he yelled through the open door.

"Boy, get me an atlas here quick, or I'll hang your hair on a proof-hook!"

A young hopeful, frightened into frenzy, obeyed with alacrity, and Farriss, seizing the atlas from his hand, thumbed it until he found a map of Colorado. Together the three pored over it.

"There it is!" Stella Donovan cried suddenly. "Down toward the bottom. Looks like desert country."

"Pretty dry place for Celeste," laughed Willis. "I might call her up and kid her about it if——"

Farriss looked at him sourly. "You might get a raise in salary," he snapped sharply, "if you'd keep your mind on the job. What you can do is call up, say you're the detective bureau, and ask carelessly about Beaton. That'll throw a scare into her. You've got her number?"

"Riverside 7683," Willis said in a businesslike voice. "The Beecher apartments. I'll try it."

He disappeared into the clattering local room, to return a moment later, white of face, bright of eye, and with lips parted.

"What's the dope?" Farriss shot at him.

"Nothing!" cried the excited young man. "Nothing except that fifteen minutes ago Celeste La Rue kissed the Beecher apartments good-bye and, with trunk, puff, and toothbrush, beat it."

"To Haskell," added the city editor, "or my hair is pink. And by God, I believe there's a story there. What's more, I believe we can get it. It's blind chance, but we'll take it."

"Let Mr. Willis——" began Miss Donovan.

"Mind your own business, Stella," commanded Farriss, "and see that your hat's on straight. Because within half an hour you're going to draw on the night cashier for five hundred dollars and pack your little portmanteau for Haskell."

Willis's face fell. "Can't I go, too?" he began, but Farriss silenced him on the instant.

"Kid," he said sharply but kindly, "you're too good a hound for the desert. The city needs you here—and, dammit, you keep on sniffing."

Turning to the unsettled girl beside him, he went on briskly:

"Work guardedly; query us when you have to; be sure of your facts, and consign your soul to God. Do I see you moving?"

And when Farriss looked again he did.

CHAPTER VII
MISS DONOVAN ARRIVES

When the long overland train paused a moment before the ancient box car that served as the depot for the town of Haskell, nestled in the gulch half a mile away, it deposited Miss Stella Donovan almost in the arms of Carson, the station-agent, and he, wary of the wiles of women and the ethics of society, promptly turned her over to Jim Westcott, who had come down to inquire if the station-agent held a telegram for him—a telegram that he expected from the East.

"She oughtn't to hike to the Timmons House alone, Jim," Carson said. "This yere is pay-day up at the big mines, an' the boys are havin' a hell of a time. That's them yellin' down yonder, and they're mighty likely to mix up with the Bar X gang before mornin', bein' how the liquor is runnin' like blood in the streets o' Lundun, and there's half a mile between 'em."

In view of these disclosures, Miss Donovan welcomed the courteous acquiescence of Westcott, whom she judged to be a man of thirty-one, with force and character—these written in the lines of his big body and his square, kind face.

"I'm Miss Stella Donovan of New York," she said directly.

"And I," he returned, with hat off in the deepening gloom, "am Jim Westcott, who plugs away at a mining claim over yonder."

"There!" laughed the girl frankly. "We're introduced. And I suppose we can start for the Timmons House."

As her words trailed off there came again the sound of yelling, sharp cries, and revolver shots from the gulch below where lights twinkled faintly.

Laughing warmly, Westcott picked up her valise, threw a "So-long" to Carson, and with Miss Donovan close behind him, began making for the distant lights of the Timmons House. As they followed the road, which paralleled a whispering stream, the girl began to draw him out skilfully, and was amazed to find that for all of his rough appearance he was excellently educated and a gentleman of taste. Finally the reason came out.

"I'm a college man," he explained proudly. "So was my partner—same class. But one can't always remain in the admirable East, and three years ago he and I came here prospecting. Actually struck some pay-dirt in the hills yonder, too, but it sort of petered out on us."

"Oh, I'm sorry." Miss Donovan's condolence was genuine.

"We lost the ore streak. It was broken in two by some upheaval of nature. We were still trying to find it when my partner's father died and he went East to claim the fortune that was left. I couldn't work alone, so I drifted away, and didn't come back until about four months ago, when I restaked the claim and went to work again."

"You had persistence, Mr. Westcott," the girl laughed.

"It was rewarded. I struck the vein again—when my last dollar was gone. That was a month ago, I wired my old partner for help, but——" He stopped, listening intently.

They were nearing a small bridge over Bear Creek, the sounds of Haskell's revellers growing nearer and louder. Suddenly they heard an oath and a shot, and the next moment a wild rider, lashing a foaming horse with a stinging quirt, was upon them. Westcott barely had time to swing the girl to safety as the tornado flew past.

"The drunken fool!" he muttered quietly. "A puncher riding for camp. There will be more up ahead probably."

His little act of heroism drew the man strangely near to Miss Donovan, and as they hurried along in the silent night she felt that above all he was dependable, as if, too, she had known him months, aye years, instead of a scant hour. And in this strange country she needed a friend.

"Now that I've laid bare my past," he was saying, "don't you think you might tell me why you are here?"

The girl stiffened. To say that she was from the New York *Star* would close many avenues of information to her. No, the thing to do was to adopt some "stall" that would enable her to idle about as much as she chose. Then the mad horseman gave her the idea.

"Oh!" she exclaimed, "I forgot I hadn't mentioned it. I'm assigned by *Scribbler's Magazine* to do an article on 'The Old West, Is It Really Gone?' and, Mr. Westcott, I think I have a lovely start."

A few moments later she thanked Providence for her precaution, for her companion resumed the story of his mining claim.

"It's mighty funny I haven't heard from that partner. It isn't like him not to answer my wire. That's why I've waited every night at the depot. No, it's not like 'Pep,' even if he does take his leisure at the College Club."

Miss Donovan's spine tingled at the mention of the name: "Pep," she murmured, trying to be calm. "What was his other name?"

"Cavendish," Westcott replied. "Frederick Cavendish."

A gasp almost escaped the girl's lips. Here, within an hour, she had linked the many Eastern clues of the Cavendish affair with one in the West. Was ever a girl so lucky? And immediately her brain began to work furiously as she walked along.

A sudden turn about the base of a large cliff brought them to Haskell, a single street running up the broadening valley, lined mostly with shacks, although a few more pretentious buildings were scattered here and there, while an occasional tent flapped its discoloured canvas in the night wind. There were no street lamps, and only a short stretch of wooden sidewalk, but lights blazed in various windows, shedding illumination without, and revealing an animated scene.

They went forward, Westcott, in spite of his confident words, watchful and silent, the valise in one hand, the other grasping her arm. The narrow stretch of sidewalk was jammed with men, surging in and out through the open door of a saloon, and the two held to the middle of the road, which was lined with horses tied to long poles. Men reeled out into the street, and occasionally the sharp crack of some frolicsome revolver punctuated the hoarse shouts and bursts of drunken laughter. No other woman was visible, yet, apparently, no particular attention was paid to their progress. But the stream of men thickened perceptibly, until Westcott was obliged to shoulder them aside good-humouredly in order to open a passage. The girl, glancing in through the open doors, saw crowded bar-rooms, and eager groups about gambling tables. One place dazzlingly lighted was evidently a dance-hall, but so densely jammed with humanity she could not distinguish the dancers. A blare of music, however, proved the presence of a band within. She felt the increasing pressure of her escort's hand.

"Can we get through?"

"Sure; some crowd, though. 'Tisn't often as bad as this; miners and punchers all paid off at once." He released her arm, and suddenly gripped the shoulder of a man passing. He was the town marshal.

"Say, Dan, I reckon this is your busy night, but I wish you'd help me run this lady through as far as Timmons; this bunch of long-horns appear to be milling, and we're plum stalled."

The man turned and stared at them. Short, stockily built, appearing at first view almost grotesque under the broad brim of his hat, Stella, recognising the marshal, was conscious only of a clean-shaven face, a square jaw, and a pair of stern blue eyes.

"Oh, is that you, Jim?" he asked briefly. "Lord, I don't see why a big boob like you should need a guardian. The lady? Pardon me, madam," and he touched his hat. "Stand back there, you fellows. Come on, folks!"

The little marshal knew his business, and it was also evident that the crowd knew the little marshal. Drunk and quarrelsome as many of them were, they made way—the more obstreperous sullenly, but the majority in a spirit of rough good humour. The time had not come for war against authority, and even the most reckless were fully aware that there was a law-and-order party in Haskell, ready and willing to back their officer to the limit. Few were drunk enough as yet to openly defy his authority and face the result, as most of them had previously seen him in action. To the girl it was all terrifying enough—the rough, hairy faces, the muttered threats, the occasional oath, the jostling figures—but the two men, one on each side of her, accepted the situation coolly enough, neither touching the revolver at his belt, but, sternly thrusting aside those in their way, they pressed straight through the surging mass in the man-crowded lobby of the disreputable hotel.

The building itself was a barnlike structure, unpainted, but with a rude, unfinished veranda in front. One end contained a saloon, crowded with patrons, but the office, revealed in the glare of a smoky lamp, disclosed a few occupants, a group of men about a card-table.

At the desk, wide-eyed with excitement, Miss Donovan took a service-worn pen proffered by landlord Pete Timmons, whose grey whiskers were as unkempt as his hotel, and registered her name.

"A telegram came to-day for you, ma'am," Peter said in a cracked voice, and tossed it over.

Miss Donovan tore it open. It was from Farriss. It read:

If any clues, advise immediately. Willis digging hard. Letter of instruction follows.

FARRISS.

The girl folded the message, thrust it in her jacket-pocket, then turning to the marshal and Westcott, gave each a firm hand.

"You've both been more than kind," she said gratefully.

"Hell, ma'am," Dan deprecated, "that warn't nothin'!" And he hurried into the street as loud cries sounded outside.

"Good night, Miss Donovan," Westcott said simply. "If you are ever frightened or in need of a friend, call on me. I'll be in town two days yet, and after that Pete here can get word to me." Then, with an admiring, honest gaze, he searched her eyes a moment before he turned and strolled toward the rude cigar-case.

"All right, now, ma'am?" Pete Timmons said, picking, up her valise. The girl nodded, and together they went up the rude stairs to her room where Timmons paused at the door.

"Well, I'm glad you're here," he said, moving away. "We've been waitin' for you to show. I may be wrong, ma'am, but I'd bet my belt that you're the lady that's been expected by Ned Beaton."

"You're mistaken," she replied shortly.

As she heard him clatter down the stairs, Miss Stella Donovan of the New York *Star* knew that her visit would not be in vain.

CHAPTER VIII
A GANG OF ENEMIES

The miner waited, leaning against the desk. His eyes had followed the slender figure moving after the rotund Timmons up the uncarpeted stairs until it had vanished amid the shadows of the second story. He smiled quietly in imagination of her first astonished view of the interior of room eighteen, and recalled to mind a vivid picture of its adornments—the bare wood walls, the springless bed, the crack-nosed pitcher standing disconsolate in a blue wash-basin of tin; the little round mirror in a once-gilt frame with a bullet-hole through its centre, and the strip of dingy rag-carpet on the floor—all this suddenly displayed by the yellowish flame of a small hand-lamp left sitting on the window ledge.

Timmons came down the stairs, and bustled in back of the desk, eager to ask questions.

"Lady a friend o' yours, Jim?" he asked. "If I'd a knowed she wus comin' I'd a saved a better room."

"I have never seen her until to-night, Pete. She got off the train, and Carson asked me to escort her up-town—it was dark, you know. How did she like the palatial apartment?"

"Well, she didn't say nothin'; just sorter looked around. I reckon she's a good sport, all right. What do ye suppose she's come yere for?"

"Not the slightest idea; I take it that's her business."

"Sure; but a feller can't help wonderin', can he? Donovan," he mused, peering at the name; "that's Irish, I take it—hey?"

"Suspiciously so; you are some detective, Pete. I'll give you another clue—her eyes are Irish grey."

He sauntered across to the stove, and stood looking idly at the card-players, blue wreaths of tobacco smoke circling up from the bowl of his pipe. Some one opened the street door, letting in a babel of noise, and walked heavily across the office floor. Westcott turned about to observe the newcomer. He was a burly, red-faced man, who had evidently been drinking heavily, yet was not greatly under the influence of liquor, dressed in a checked suit of good cut and fashion, but hardly in the best of taste. His hat, a Stetson, was pushed back on his head, and an unlighted cigar was clinched tightly between his teeth. He bore all the earmarks of a commercial traveller of a certain sort—a domineering personality, making up by sheer nerve what he might lack in brains. But for his words the miner would have given the fellow no further thought.

"Say, Timmons," he burst forth noisily, and striding over to the desk, "the marshal tells me a dame blew in from New York to-night—is she registered here?"

The landlord shoved the book forward, with one finger on the last signature.

"Yep," he said shortly, "but she ain't the one you was lookin' for—I asked her that, furst thing."

"Stella Donovan—huh! That's no name ever I heard; what's she look like?"

"Like a lady, I reckon; I ain't seen one fer quite a spell now."

"Dark or light?"

"Waal, sorter medium, I should say; brown hair with a bit o' red in it, an' a pair o' grey eyes full of fun—some girl, to my notion."

The questioner struck his fist on the wood sharply.

"Well, what the devil do you suppose such a woman has come to this hole clear from New York for, Timmons? What's her game, anyhow?"

"Blessed if I know," and the proprietor seated himself on a high stool. "I didn't ask no questions like that; maybe the gent by the stove there might give yer all the information yer want. He brought her up from the dapoo, an' kin talk English. Say, Jim, this yere is a short horn frum New York, named Beaton, an' he seems ter be powerfully interested in skirts—Beaton, Mr. Jim Westcott."

The two men looked at each other, the miner stepping slightly forward, and knocking the ashes out of his pipe. Beaton laughed, assuming a semblance of good nature.

"My questions were prompted solely by curiosity," he explained, evidently not wholly at ease. "I was expecting a young woman, and thought this new arrival might prove to be my friend."

"Hardly," returned Westcott dryly. "As the landlord informed you, Miss Donovan is a lady."

If he expected this shot to take effect he was disappointed, for the grin never left Beaton's face.

"Ah, a good joke; a very good joke, indeed. But you misunderstand; this is altogether a business matter. This young woman whom I expect is coming here on a mining deal—it is not a love affair at all, I assure you."

Westcott's eyes sparkled, yet without merriment.

"Quite pleased to be so assured," he answered carelessly. "In what manner can I satisfy your curiosity? You have already been informed, I believe, that the person relative to whom you inquire is a Miss Stella Donovan, of New York; that she has the appearance and manners of a lady, and possesses brown hair and grey eyes. Is there anything more?"

"Why, no—certainly not."

"I thought possibly you might care to question me regarding my acquaintance with the young woman?" Westcott went on, his voice hardening slightly. "If so, I have not the slightest objection to telling you that it consists entirely of acting as her escort from the station to the hotel. I do not know why she is here, how long she intends staying, or what her purpose may be. Indeed, there is only one fact I do know which may be of interest to you."

Beaton, surprised by the language of the other, remained silent, his face turning purple, as a suspicion came to him that he was being made a fool of.

"It is this, my friend—who she is, what she is, and why she happens to be here, is none of your damn business, and if you so much as mention her name again in my presence you are going to regret it to your dying day. That's all."

Beaton, glancing about at the uplifted faces of the card-players, chose to assume an air of indifference, which scarcely accorded with the anger in his eyes.

"Ah, come now," he blurted forth, "I didn't mean anything; there's no harm done—let's have a drink, and be friends."

Westcott shook his head.

"No, I think not," he said slowly. "I'm not much of a drinking man myself, and when I do I choose my own company. But let me tell you something, Beaton, for your own good. I know your style, and you are mighty apt to get into trouble out here if you use any Bowery tactics."

"Bowery tactics!"

"Yes; you claim to live in New York, and you possess all the earmarks of the East-Side bad man. There is nothing keeping you now from roughing it with me but the sight of this gun in my belt, and a suspicion in your mind that I may know how to use it. That suspicion is correct. Moreover, you will discover this same ability more or less prevalent throughout this section. However, I am not looking for trouble; I am trying to avoid it. I haven't sought your company; I do not want to know you. Now you go back to your bar-room where you will find plenty of your own kind to associate with. It's going to be dangerous for you to hang around here any longer."

Beaton felt the steady eyes upon him, but was carrying enough liquor to make him reckless. Still his was naturally the instinct of the New York gunman, seeking for some adventure. He stepped backward, feigning a laugh, watchful to catch Westcott off his guard.

"All right, then," he said, "I'll go get the drink; you can't bluff me."

Westcott's knowledge of the class alone brought to him the man's purpose. Beaton's hand was in the pocket of his coat, and, as he turned, apparently to leave the room, the cloth bulged. With one leap forward the miner was at his throat. There was a report, a flash of flame, the speeding bullet striking the stove, and the next instant Beaton, his hand still helplessly imprisoned within the coat-pocket, was hurled back across the card-table, the players scattering to get out of the way. All the pent-up dislike in Westcott's heart found expression in action; the despicable trick wrought him to a sudden fury, yet even then there came to him no thought of killing the fellow, no memory even of the loaded gun at his hip. He wanted to choke him, strike him with his hands.

"You dirty coward," he muttered fiercely. "So you thought the pocket trick was a new one out here, did you? Come, give the gun up! Oh! so there is some fight left in you? Then let's settle it here."

It was a struggle between two big, strong men—the one desperate, unscrupulous, brutal; the other angry enough, but retaining self-control. They crashed onto the floor, Westcott still retaining the advantage of position, and twice he struck, driving his clenched fist home. Suddenly he became aware that some one had jerked his revolver from its holster, and, almost at the same instant a hard hand gripped the neck-band of his shirt and tore him loose from Beaton.

"Here, now—enough of that, Jim," said a voice sternly, and his hands arose instinctively as he recognised the gleam of two drawn weapons fronting him. "Help Beaton up, Joe. Now, look yere, Mr. Bully Westcott," and the speaker shook his gun threateningly. "As it happens, you have jumped on a friend o' ours, an' we naturally propose to take a hand in this game—you know me!"

Westcott nodded, an unpleasant smile on his lips.

"I do, Lacy," he said coolly, "and that if there is any dirty work going on in this camp, it is quite probable you and your gang are in it. So, this New Yorker is a protégé of yours?"

"That's none of your business; we're here for fair play."

"Since when? Now listen; you've got me covered, and that is my gun which Moore has in his hand. I cannot fight you alone and unarmed; but I can talk yet."

"I reckon yer can, if that's goin' ter do yer eny good."

"So the La Rosita Mining Company is about to be revived, is it? Eastern capital becoming interested. I've heard rumours of that for a week past. What's the idea? struck anything?"

Lacy, a long, rangy fellow, with a heavy moustache, and a scar over one eye, partially concealed by his hat brim, grinned at the others as though at a good joke.

"No, nuthin' particular as yet," he answered; "but you hev', an' I reckon thet's just about as good. Tryin' ter keep it dark, wasn't yer? Never even thought we'd caught on."

"Oh, yes, I did; you flatter yourselves. I caught one of your stool-pigeons up the gulch yesterday, and more than ten days ago Moore and Edson made a trip into my tunnel while I happened to be away; they forgot to hide their trail. I knew what you were up to, and you can all of you look for a fight."

"When your partner gets out here, I suppose," sneered Lacy.

"He'll be here."

"Oh, will he? Well, he's a hell of a while coming. You wired him a month ago, and yer've written him twice since. Oh, I've got the cases on you, all right, Westcott. I know you haven't got a cent left to go on with, and nowhere to get eny except through him." He laughed. "Ain't that right? Well, then, yer chances look mighty slim ter me just at present, ol'-timer. However, there's no fight on yet; will yer behave yerself, an' let this man Beaton alone if I hand yer back yer gun?"

"There is no choice left me."

"Sure; that's sensible enough; give it to him, Moore."

He broke the chamber, shaking the cartridges out into his palm; then handed the emptied weapon over to Westcott. His manner was purposely insulting, but the latter stood with lips firmly set, realising his position.

"Now, then, go on over thar an' sit down," continued Lacy. "Maybe, if yer wait long enough, that partner o' yours might blow in. I got some curiosity myself as to why that girl showed up ter-night under yer guidance, an' why yer so keen ter fight about her, Jim; but I reckon we'll clear that up ter-morrow without makin' yer talk."

"You mean to question Miss Donovan?"

"Hell, no; just keep an eye on her. 'Tain't likely she's in Haskell just fer the climate. Come on, boys, let's liquor. Big Jim Westcott has his claws cut, and it's Beaton's turn to spend a little."

Westcott sat quietly in the chair as they filed out; then took the pipe from his pocket and filled it slowly. He realised his defeat, his helplessness, but his mind was already busy with the future.

Timmons came out from behind the desk a bit solicitous.

"Hurt eny?" he asked. "Didn't wing yer, or nuthin'?"

"No; the stove got the bullet. He shot through his pocket."

"Whut's all the row about?"

"Oh, not much, Timmons; this is my affair," and Westcott lit his pipe with apparent indifference. "Lacy and I have got two mining claims tapping the same lead, that's all. There's been a bit o' feeling between us for some time. I reckon it's got to be fought out, now."

"Then yer've really struck ore?"

"Yes."

"And the young woman? Hes she got enything ter do with it?"

"Not a thing, Timmons; but I want to keep her out of the hands of that bunch. Give me a lamp and I'll go up-stairs and think this game out."

CHAPTER IX
A NIGHT AND A MORNING

Stella Donovan never forgot the miseries of her first night in Haskell. When old man Timmons finally left her, after placing the flaring lamp on a chair, and went pattering back down the bare hall, she glanced shudderingly about at her unpleasant surroundings, none too pleased with the turn of events.

The room was scarcely large enough to contain the few articles of furniture absolutely required. Its walls were of unplaned plank occasionally failing to meet, and the only covering to the floor was a dingy strip of rag-carpet. The bed was a cot, shapeless, and propped up on one side by the iron leg of some veranda bench, while the open window looked out into the street. There was a bolt, not appearing particularly secure, with which Miss Donovan immediately locked the door before venturing across to take a glance without.

The view was hardly reassuring, as the single street was still the scene of pandemonium, the saloon and dance-hall almost directly opposite, operating in full blast. Oaths and ribald laughter assailed her ears, while directly beneath, although out of her view, a quarrel threatened to lead to serious consequences. She pulled down the window to shut out these sounds, but the room became so stuffy and hot without even this slight ventilation, as to oblige her opening it again. As a compromise she hauled down the curtain, a green paper affair, torn badly, and which occasionally flapped in the wind with a startling noise.

The bed-clothing, once turned back and inspected, was of a nature to prevent the girl from disrobing; but finally she lay down, seeking such rest as was possible, after turning the flickering flames of the lamp as low as she dared, and then finally blowing it out altogether. The glare from the street crept in through the cracks in the curtain, playing in fantastic light and shadow across ceiling and wall, while the infernal din never ceased.

Sleep was not to be attained, although she closed her eyes and muffled her ears. The misshapen bed brought no comfort to her tired body, for no matter how she adjusted herself, the result was practically the same. Not even her mind rested.

Miss Donovan was not naturally of a nervous disposition. She had been brought up very largely to rely upon herself, and life had never been sufficiently easy for her to find time in which to cultivate nerves. Her newspaper training had been somewhat strenuous, and had won her a reputation in New York for unusual fearlessness and devotion to duty. Yet this situation was so utterly different, and so entirely unexpected, that she confessed to herself she would be very glad to be safely out of it.

A revolver shot rang out sharply from one of the rooms below, followed by the sound of loud voices, and a noise of struggle. The startled girl sat upright on the cot, listening, but the disturbance ceased almost immediately, and she finally lay down again, her heart still beating wildly. Her thoughts, never still, wandered over the events of the evening—the arrival at Haskell station, the strange meeting with Westcott, and the sudden revelation that he was the partner of Frederick Cavendish.

The big, good-natured miner had interested her from the first as representing a perfect type of her preconceived ideal of the real Westerner. She had liked the firm character of his face, the quiet, thoughtful way in which he acted, the whole unobtrusive bearing of the man. Then, as they had walked that long mile together in the darkness, she had learned things about him—little glimpses of his past, and of dawning hopes—which only served to increase her confidence. Already he had awakened her trust; she felt convinced that if she needed friendship, advice, even actual assistance, here was one whom she could implicitly trust.

The racket outside died away slowly. She heard various guests return to their rooms, staggering along the hall and fumbling at their doors; voices echoed here and there, and one fellow, mistaking his domicile entirely, struggled with her latch in a vain endeavour to gain entrance. She was upon her feet, when companions arrived and led the invader elsewhere, their loud laughter dying away in the distance. It was long after this before nature finally conquered and the girl slept outstretched on the hard cot, the first faint grey of dawn already visible in the eastern sky.

She was young, though, and she awoke rested and refreshed, in spite of the fact that her body ached at first from the discomfort of the cot. The sunlight rested in a sheet of gold on her drawn curtain, and the silence of the morning, following so unexpectedly the dismal racket of the night, seemed to fairly shock her into consciousness. Could this be Haskell? Could this indeed be the inferno into which she had been precipitated from the train in the darkness of the evening before? She stared about at the bare, board walls, the bullet-scarred mirror, the cracked pitcher, before she could fully reassure herself; then stepped upon the disreputable rug, and crossed to the open window.

Haskell at nine in the morning bore but slight resemblance to that same environment during the hours of darkness—especially on a night immediately following pay-day at the mines. As Miss Donovan, now thoroughly awake, and obsessed by the memory of those past hours of horror, cautiously drew aside the corner of torn curtain, and gazed down upon the deserted street below, she could scarcely accept the evidence of her own eyes.

True, there were many proofs visible of the wild riot of the evening before—torn papers, emptied bottles, a shattered sign or two, an oil-lamp blown into bits by some well-directed shot, a bat lying in the middle of the road, and a dejected pony or two, still at the hitching-rack, waiting a delayed rider. But, except for these mute reminiscences of past frolic, the long street seemed utterly dead, the doors of saloons and dance-halls closed, the dust swirling back and forth to puffs of wind, the only moving object visible being a gaunt, yellow dog trotting soberly past.

However, it was not upon this view of desolation that Miss Donovan's eyes clung. They had taken all this in at a glance, startled, scarcely comprehending, but the next instant wandered to the marvellous scene revealed beyond that squalid street, and those miserable shacks, to the green beauty of the outspread valley, and the wondrous vista of mountain peaks beyond.

She straightened up, emitting a swift breath of delight, as her wide-open eyes surveyed the marvellous scene of mingled loveliness and grandeur. The stream, curving like a great snake, gleamed amid the acres of green grass, its swift waters sparkling in the sun. Here and there it would dip down between high banks, or disappear for a moment behind a clump of willows, only to reappear in broader volume. Beyond, seemingly at no distance at all, yet bordered by miles of turf and desert, the patches of vivid green interspersed with the darker colouring of spruce, and the outcropping of brown rocks, the towering peaks of a great mountain-chain swept up into the clear blue of the sky, black almost to their summits, which were dazzling with the white of unmelted snow. Marvellous, awe-inspiring as the picture was in itself alone, it was rendered even more wonderful when contrasted with the ugly squalidness of the town below, its tents and shacks sprawling across the flat, the sunlight revealing its dust and desolation.

The girl's first exclamation of delight died away as she observed these works of man projected against this screen of nature's building; yet her eyes dwelt lovingly for some time on the far-flung line of mountains, before she finally released the green shade, and shut out the scene. Her toilet was a matter of but a few minutes, although she took occasion to slip on a fresh waist, and to brighten up the shoes, somewhat soiled by the tramp through the thick dust the evening before. Indeed, it was a very charming young woman, her dress and appearance quite sufficiently Eastern, who finally ventured out into the rough hall, and down the single flight of stairs. The hotel was silent, except for the heavy breathing of a sleeper in one of the rooms she passed, and a melancholy-looking Chinaman, apparently engaged in chamber work at the further end of the hall. Timmons was alone in the office, playing with a shaggy dog, and the floor remained unswept, while a broken chair still bore evidence of the debauch of the previous night. The landlord greeted her rather sullenly, his eyes heavy and red from lack of sleep.

"Morning," he said, without attempting to rise. "Lie down thar, Towser; the lady don't likely want yer nosin' around. Yer a bit late fer breakfast; it's ginerally over with by eight o'clock."

"I am not at all hungry," she answered. "Is it far to the post-office?"

"'Bout two blocks, ter yer right. If yer intendin' ter stay yere, ye better have yer mail sent ter the hotel."

"Thank you; I'll see. I do not know yet the length of my stay."

"Are ye yere on business?"

"Partly; but it may require only a few days."

"Waal, if yer do stay over, maybe I kin fix yer up a bit more comfortable-like. Thar'll be some drummers a goin' out to-day, I reckon."

"Thank you very much; I'll let you know what I decide the moment I know myself. Is that a hunting-dog?"

"Bones mostly," he responded gloomily, but stroking the animal's head. "Leastwise, he ain't been trained none. I just naturally like a darg round fer company—they sorter seem homelike."

She passed out into the bright sunshine, and clear mountain air. The board-walk ended at the corner of the hotel, but a narrow cinder-patch continued down that side of the street for some distance. The houses were scattered, the vacant spaces between grown up to weeds, and more or less ornamented by tin cans, and as she advanced she encountered only two pedestrians—a cowboy, so drunk that he hung desperately to the upper board of a fence in order to let her pass, staring at her as if she was some vision, and a burly fellow in a checked suit, with some mail in his hand, who stopped after they had passed each other, and gazed back at her as though more than ordinarily interested. From the hotel stoop he watched until she vanished within the general store, which contained the post-office.

Through the rude window the clerk pushed a plain manila envelope into her outstretched hand. Evidently from the thinness of the letter, Farriss had but few instructions to give and, thrusting the unopened missive into her hand-bag, she retraced her steps to her room.

There she vented a startled gasp. The suitcase which she had left closed upon the floor was open—wide open—its contents disarranged. Some one had rummaged it thoroughly. And Miss Donovan knew that she was under suspicion.

CHAPTER X
AT A NEW ANGLE

The knowledge that she was thus being spied upon gave the girl a sudden thrill, but not of fear. Instead it served to strengthen her resolve. There had been nothing in her valise to show who she really was, or why she was in Haskell, and consequently, if any vague suspicion had been aroused as to her presence in that community, the searchers had discovered no proof by this rifling of her bag.

She examined the room thoroughly, and glanced out into the still, deserted hall before bolting the door. The cracks in the wall were scarcely wide enough to be dangerous, yet she took the precaution of shrinking back into the darkest corner before opening her hand-bag and extracting the letter. It bore a typewritten address, with no suspicious characteristics about the envelope, the return card (typewritten also) being the home address of Farriss.

Farriss's letter contained nothing of interest except the fact that Enright had also left for the West. He instructed her to be on the lookout for him in Haskell, added a line or two of suggestions, and ordered her to proceed with caution, as her quest might prove to be a dangerous one.

Miss Donovan tore the letter into small bits, wrapping the fragments in a handkerchief until she could throw them safely away. For some time she stood motionless at the window, looking out, but seeing nothing, her mind busy with the problem. She thought rapidly and clearly, more than ordinarily eager to solve this mystery. She was a newspaperwoman, and the strange story in which she was involved appealed to her imagination, yet its appeal was far more effective in a purely personal way. It was Frederick Cavendish who had formerly been the partner of Jim Westcott. This was why no answer had come to the telegrams and letters the latter had sent East. What had become of them? Had they fallen into the hands of these others? Was this the true reason for Beaton's presence in Haskell, and also why the La Rue woman had been hastily sent for? She was not quite ready to accept that theory; the occasion hardly seemed important enough by itself alone.

Westcott's discovery was not even proven yet; its value had not been definitely established; it was of comparatively small importance contrasted with the known wealth left by the murdered man in the East. No, there must be some other cause for this sudden visit to Colorado. But what? She gave little credence to the vague suspicions advanced by Valois; that was altogether too impossible, too melodramatic, this thought of the substitution of some other body. It might be done, of course; indeed, she had a dim remembrance of having read of such a case somewhere, but there could be no object attained in this affair. Frederick dead, apparently killed by a burglar in his own apartments, was quite understandable: but kidnapped and still alive, another body substituted for his, resembling him sufficiently to be unrecognised as a fraud, would be a perfectly senseless procedure. No doubt there had been a crime committed, its object the attainment of money, but without question the cost had been the life of Frederick Cavendish.

Yet why was the man Beaton out here? For what purpose had he wired the La Rue woman to join him? And why had some one already entered her room and examined the contents of Stella Donovan's bag? To these queries there seemed to be no satisfactory answers. She must consult with Westcott, and await an opportunity to make the acquaintance of Celeste La Rue.

She was still there, her elbows on the window-ledge, her face half concealed in the hollow of her hands, so lost in thought as to be oblivious to the flight of time, when the harsh clang of the dinner-bell from the porch below aroused her to a sense of hunger.

Ten minutes later Timmons, guiltless of any coat, but temporarily laying aside his pipe as a special act of courtesy, escorted her into the dining-room and seated her at a table between the two front windows. Evidently this was reserved for the more distinguished guests—travelling men and those paying regular day rates—for its only other occupant was the individual in the check suit whom she vaguely remembered passing on the street a few hours before.

The two long tables occupying the centre of the room were already well filled with hungry men indiscriminately attired, not a few coatless and with rolled-up sleeves, as though they had hurried in from work at the first sound of the gong. These paid little attention to her entrance, except to stare curiously as she crossed the floor in Timmons's wake, and immediately afterward again devoted themselves noisily to their food.

A waitress, a red-haired, slovenly girl, with an impediment in her speech, took her order and disappeared in the direction of the kitchen, and Miss Donovan discreetly lifted her eyes to observe the man sitting nearly opposite. He was not prepossessing, yet she instantly recognised his type, and the probability that he would address her if the slightest opportunity occurred. Beneath lowered lashes she studied the fellow—the prominent jaw and thick lips shadowed by a closely trimmed moustache; the small eyes beneath overhanging brows; the heavy hair brushed back from a rather low forehead, and the short, stubby fingers grasping knife and fork.

If he is a drummer, she thought, his line would be whisky; then, almost as suddenly, it occurred to her that perhaps he may prove to be Ned Beaton, and she drew in her breath sharply, determined to break the ice.

The waitress spread out the various dishes before her, and she glanced at them hopelessly. As she lifted her gaze she met that of her *vis-à-vis* fairly, and managed to smile.

"Some chuck," he said in an attempt at good-fellowship, "but not to remind you of the Waldorf-Astoria."

"I should say not," she answered, testing one of her dishes cautiously. "But why associate me with New York?"

"You can't hide those things in a joint like this. Besides, that's the way you registered."

"Oh, so you've looked me up."

"Well, naturally," he explained, as though with a dim idea that an explanation was required, "I took a squint at the register; then I became more interested, for I'm from little old New York myself."

"You are? Selling goods on the road away out here?"

"Not me; that ain't my line at all. I've got a considerable mining deal on up the cañon. I'll earn every dollar I'll make, though, eating this grub. Believe me, I'd like to be back by the Hudson right now."

"You've been here some time, then?"

"'Bout a month altogether, but not here in Haskell all that time. When did you leave New York?"

"Oh, more than a week ago," she lied gracefully.

He stroked his moustache.

"Then I suppose you haven't much late New York news? Nothing startling, I mean?"

"No; only what has been reported in the Western papers. I do not recall anything particularly interesting." She dropped her eyes to her plate and busied herself with a piece of tough beef. "The usual murders, of course, and things of that kind."

There was a moment's silence, then the man laughed as though slightly ill at ease.

"These fellows out here think they are a pretty tough lot," he said grimly, "but there are plenty of boys back on the East Side who could show them a few tricks. You know that part of the old town?"

"Not very well," she admitted with apparent regret, "but of course I read a good bit about it in the papers—the desperate characters, gunmen, and all those the police have so much trouble with. Are those stories really true?"

"There ain't a third of them ever told," and he leaned forward, quite at his ease again. "I have some business interests down that way, and so hear a good deal of what is going on at first hand. A New York gunman is so much worse than these amateurs out here there ain't no comparison. Why, I know a case——"

He stopped suddenly and took a sip of coffee.

"Tell me about it."

"'Tisn't anything to interest you, and, besides, it wouldn't sound well here at the table; some other time, maybe, when you and I get better acquainted. What ever brought a girl like you down in here?"

She smiled.

"I'm a feature writer; I'm doing a series on the West for *Scribbler's*," she told him. "I visit New Mexico next, but I'm after something else besides a description of mountains and men; I'm also going to hunt up an old friend interested in mining, who told me if I ever got out this way I must look him up.

"I haven't seen him for years. He was continually singing this valley's charms, and so here I am. And I'm planning a great surprise on him. And, of course, I'm literally drinking in atmosphere—to say nothing of local colour, which seems mostly to be men and revolvers."

The man opposite wet his lips with his tongue in an effort to speak, but the girl was busy eating and apparently paid no attention. Her calm indifference convinced him that her words were entirely innocent, and his audacity returned.

"Well," he ventured, "do you agree with this prospector friend?"

"The scenery, you mean?" glancing up brightly. "Why, it is wonderful, of course, and I am not at all sorry having made the journey, although it hardly compares with Tennessee Pass or Silver Plume. Still, you know, it will be pleasant to tell Mr. Cavendish when I go back that I was here."

He choked and his face seemed to whiten suddenly.

"Mr. Cavendish?" he gasped. "Of New York? Not the one that was killed?"

It was her turn to stare across the table, her eyes wide with horror, which she simulated excellently.

"Killed! Has a man by that name been killed lately in New York? It was Frederick Cavendish I referred to." Her pretence was admirable.

He was silent, realising lie had already said too much; the red had come back into his cheeks, but his hand shook as it rested clenched on the table.

"Tell me," she insisted, "has he been killed? How do you know?"

Her earnestness, her perfect acting, convinced him. It was a mere coincidence, he thought, that this name should have cropped up between them, but, now that it had, he must explain the whole affair so as not to arouse suspicion. He cleared his throat and compelled his eyes to meet those across the table.

"Well, I don't know much about it, only what I read," he began, feeling for words. "But that was the name; I remembered it as soon as you spoke, and that the papers said he had been mining in Colorado before he came into money. He was found dead in his apartments, apparently killed by a burglar who had rifled his safe."

"Is this true? Why have I never heard? When did it happen?"

"It must have been a month ago."

"But how did you learn these particulars? You have been West that length of time."

"I read about it in a New York paper," he answered a trifle sullenly. "It was sent to me."

She sat with her chin in the palm of one hand, watching him from beneath the shadow of lowered lashes, but his eyes were bent downward at his plate.

"Are you through?" he questioned suddenly.

"Yes; this—this awful news has robbed me of all appetite."

Neither had noticed Westcott as he entered the room, but his first glance about revealed their presence, and without an instant of hesitancy the big miner crossed the room and approached the table where the two were sitting.

Beaton, as though anticipating trouble, arose to his feet, but Westcott merely drew back a vacant chair and seated himself, his eyes ignoring the presence of the man and seeking the uplifted face of the girl questioningly.

"I hope I do not interrupt," he said pleasantly. "I had reason to suppose you were unacquainted with Mr. Beaton here."

"What reason?" her surprised tone slightly indignant.

"I believe the gentleman so informed me. It chanced that we had a slight controversy last night."

"Over me?"

"Over his curiosity regarding you—who you were; your presence here."

She pushed back her chair and stood up.

"A natural curiosity enough, surely. And you felt important enough to rebuke him on my behalf? Is that what I am to understand?"

"Why," he explained, startled by her strange manner, "I informed him that it was none of his business, and that if he mentioned your name in my presence again there was liable to be trouble. We scrapped it out."

"You—you scrapped it out? You mean there was a fight over me—a barroom squabble over me?"

"Not in the barroom; in the hotel office. Beaton drew a gun, and I had to slug him."

"But the affair originated over me—my name was brought into it?" she insisted. "You actually threatened him because he asked about me?"

"I reckon that was about how it started," he admitted slowly. "You see, I rather thought I was a sorter friend of yours, and that I ought to stand up for you."

"Did—did this man say anything against me?"

"No—not exactly; he—he just asked questions."

Her eyes were scornful, angry,

"Indeed! Well, permit me to say, Mr. Westcott, that I choose my own friends, and am perfectly competent to defend my own character. This closes our acquaintanceship." She moved about the end of the table, and touched Beaton's sleeve with her fingers. "Would you escort me to the foot of the stairs?" she asked, her voice softening. "We will leave this belligerent individual to his own company." Neither of them glanced back, the girl still speaking as they disappeared, but Westcott turned in his chair to watch them cross the room. He had no sense of anger, no desire to retaliate, but he felt dazed and as though the whole world was suddenly turned upside down. So she really belonged with that outfit, did she? Well, it was a good joke on him.

The waitress spoke to him twice before he was sufficiently aroused to give his order.

CHAPTER XI
DEAD OR ALIVE

Before Westcott finished his meal his mood had changed to tolerant amusement. That the girl had deliberately deceived him was plain, enough, revealed now in both her manner and words. What her true purpose might have been in apparently seeking his friendship at first could not now be conjectured—indeed, made little difference—but it was clear enough she really belonged to the Lacy crowd, and had no more use for him.

Westcott was sorry for the turn things had taken; he made no attempt to disguise this from his own mind. He was beginning to like Miss Donovan, to think about her, to feel a distinct interest in her. Some way she had impressed him deeply as a young woman of character and unusual charm—a breath out of the East to arouse his imagination and memory. He had begun to hope for a friendship which would endure, and now—the house of cards fell at a single touch.

He could scarcely comprehend the situation; how a girl of her apparent refinement and gentility could ever be attracted by a rough, brutal type such as Ned Beaton so evidently was. Why, the man's lack of taste in dress, the expression of his face, his ungrammatical language, stamped him as belonging to a distinctly lower order.

There surely must be some other cause drawing them together. Yet, whatever it was, there was no doubt but that he had been very properly snubbed. Her words stung; yet it was the manner in which she had looked at him and swept past at Beaton's side which hurt the most. Oh, well, an enemy more or less made small difference in his life; he would laugh at it and forget. She had made her choice of companionship, and it was just as well, probably, that the affair had gone no further before he discovered the sort of girl she really was.

Westcott reached this decision and the outer office at the same time, exchanged a careless word or two with Timmons, and finally purchased a cigar and retired to one corner to peruse an old newspaper. It was not so easy to read, however, for the news failed to interest or keep his mind from wandering widely. Soon he was staring out through the unwashed window, oblivious to everything but his own thoughts.

Who was this Beaton, and what connection could he have with Bill Lacy's gang? The row last night had revealed a mutual interest between the men, but what was its nature? To Westcott's judgment the burly New Yorker did not resemble an Eastern speculator in mining property; he was far more typical of a Bowery rough—a tool rather than an employer in the commission of crime.

Lacy's purpose he believed he understood to some extent—a claim that it was an extension of the La Rosita vein which Westcott had tapped in his recent discovery. There had been bad blood between them for some time—threats of violence, and rumours of lawsuits. No doubt Lacy would resort to any dirty trick to get him out of the way and gain control of the property. But he had no personal fear of Lacy: not, at least, if he could once get the backing of Cavendish's money. But these other people—Beaton, Miss Donovan, and still another expected to arrive soon from the East—how were they connected with the deal?

How were they involved in the controversy? Had Lacy organised a company and got hold of some money in New York? It might be possible, and yet neither the man nor the woman impressed him as financiers risking fortunes in the exploitation of mines. The problem was unsolvable; the only thing he could do was guard his property and wait until they showed their hand. If he could only hear from Fred Cavendish——

He was so deeply engrossed in these thoughts, the smoked-out cigar substituted by a pipe, that he remained unaware that Timmons had left the office, or that the Chinese man-of-all-work had silently tiptoed down the stairs and was cautiously peering in through the open doorway to make sure the coast was clear. Assured as to this, the wily Oriental sidled noiselessly across the floor and paused beside him.

"Zis Meester Vest-c-ott?" he asked softly.

The miner looked up at the implacable face in surprise, lowering his feet.

"That's my name, John; what is it?"

The messenger shook a folded paper out of his sleeve, thrust it into the other's hand hastily, and, with a hurried glance about, started to glide away as silently as he had come. Westcott stared at the note, which was unaddressed.

"Sure this is for me, John?"

"Ally same sure—for Meester Vest-c-ott."

He vanished into the dark hall, and there was the faint clatter of his shoes on the stairs.

Westcott, fully aroused, cast his glance about the deserted room, and unfolded the paper which had been left in his fingers. His eyes took in the few penciled words instantly.

Do not be angry. I had the best of reasons. Meet me near the lower bridge at three o'clock. Very important.

S. D.

He read the lines over again, his lips emitting a low whistle, his eyes darkening with sudden appreciation. Slowly he tore the paper into strips, crossed the room, and flung the remnants into the stove. It had been a trick, then, a bit of play-acting! But had it? Was not this rather the real fraud—this sudden change of heart? Perhaps something had occurred to cause the girl to realise that she had made a mistake; to awaken her to a knowledge that a pretence at friendship would serve her cause better than an open break.

This note might have a sinister purpose; be intended to deceive. No! He would not believe this. All his old lurking faith in her came back in a flash of revelation. He would continue to believe in her, trust her, feel that some worthy purpose had influenced her strange action. And, above all, he would be at the lower bridge on the hour set. He was at the desk when Timmons returned.

"What do I owe you, old man?"

He paid the bill jokingly and in the best of humour, careful to tell the proprietor that he was leaving for his mine and might not return for several days. He possessed confidence that Timmons would make no secret of this in Haskell after his departure. He was glad to notice that Beaton observed him as he passed the Good Luck Saloon and went tramping down the dusty road. He never glanced back until he turned into the north trail at the edge of town; there the path dropped suddenly toward the bed of the creek, and he was concealed from view. In the rock shadow he paused, chuckling grimly as he observed the New Yorker cross the street to the hotel, hastening, no doubt, to interview Timmons.

There was a crooked trail along the bank of the stream which joined the main road at the west end of the lower bridge. It led up the cañon amid rocks and cedars, causing it to assume a strangely tortuous course, and its lower end was shadowed by overhanging willows. Along this Westcott lingered at the hour set, watchful of the road leading toward Haskell.

The only carriage belonging to the town livery passed soon after his arrival, evidently bound for the station, and from his covert he recognised Beaton lolling carelessly in the back seat. This must mean that the man expected arrivals on the afternoon train, important arrivals whom he desired to honour. There was no sign, however, of Miss Donovan; the time was up, yet with no evidence of her approach.

Westcott waited patiently, arguing to himself that her delay might be caused by her wish to get Beaton well out of the way before she ventured to leave the hotel. At last he strode down the path to the bridge, and saw her leaning over the rail, staring at the ripples below.

"Why," he exclaimed in surprise, "how long have you been here?"

"Several minutes," and she turned to face him. "I waited until the carriage passed before coming onto the bridge. I took the foot-path from the hotel."

"Oh, I see—from the other way. I was waiting in the trail below. You saw who was in the carriage?"

"Beaton—yes," quietly. "He expects some friends, and wishes me to meet them—Eastern people, you know."

Her indifference ruffled his temper, aroused his suspicion of her purpose.

"You sent for me; there is some explanation, no doubt?"

The lady smiled, lifting her eyes to his face.

"There is," she answered. "A perfectly satisfactory one, I believe; but this place is too prominent, as I have a rather long story to tell. Beaton and his friends will be returning soon."

"There is a rock seat below, just beyond the clump of willows, quite out of sight from the road," he suggested. "Perhaps you would go with me there?"

"What trail is that?"

"It leads to mines up the cañon, my own included, but is not greatly travelled; the main trail is farther east."

She walked to the edge of the bridge, and permitted him to assist her down the steep bank. There was something of reserve about her manner, which prevented Westcott from feeling altogether at ease. In his own mind he began once more to question her purpose, to doubt the sincerity of her intentions. She appeared different from the frankly outspoken girl of the night before. Neither broke the silence between them until they reached the flat boulder and had found seats in the shelter of overhanging trees. She sat a moment, her eyes on the water, her cheeks shadowed by the wide brim of her hat, and Westcott noted the almost perfect contour of her face silhouetted against the green leaves. She turned toward him questioningly.

"I was very rude," she said, "but you will forgive me when I explain the cause. I had to act as I did or else lose my hold entirely on that man—you understand?"

"I do not need to understand," he answered gallantly. "It is enough that you say so."

"No, it is not enough. I value your friendship, Mr. Westcott, and I need your advice. I find myself confronting a very complicated case under unfamiliar conditions. I hardly know what to do."

"You may feel confidence in me."

"Oh, I do; indeed, you cannot realise how thoroughly I trust you," and impulsively she touched his hand with her own. "That is why I wrote you to meet me here—so I could tell you the whole story."

He waited, his eyes on her face.

"I received my letter this morning—the letter I told you I expected, containing my instructions. They—they relate to this man Ned Beaton and the woman he expects on this train."

"Your instructions?" he echoed doubtfully. "You mean you have been sent after these people on some criminal matter? You are a detective?"

There must have been a tone of distrust to his voice, for she turned and faced him defiantly.

"No; not that. Listen: I am a newspaperwoman, a special writer on the New York *Star*." She paused, her cheeks flushing with nervousness. "It—it was very strange that I met you first of all, for—for it seems that the case is of personal interest to you."

"To me! Why, that is hardly likely, if it originated in New York."

"It did"—she drew in a sharp breath—"for it originated in the murder of Frederick Cavendish."

"The murder of Cavendish! He has been killed?"

"Yes; at least that is what every one believes, except possibly one man—his former valet. His body was found lying dead on the floor of his private apartment, the door of his safe open, the money and papers missing. The coroner's jury brought in a verdict of murder on these facts."

"And the murderer?"

"Left no clue; it was believed to be the work of a burglar."

"But when was this?"

She gave the date, and he studied over it.

"The same day he should have received my telegram," he said gravely. "That's why the poor fellow never answered." He turned to her suddenly. "But what became of my others," he asked, "and of all the letters I wrote?"

"That is exactly what I want to learn. They must have been delivered to his cousin, John Cavendish. I'll tell you all I know, and then perhaps, between us, we may be able to figure it out."

Briefly and clearly, she set before him the facts she and Willis had been able to gather: the will, the connection between Enright and John Cavendish, the quarrel between John and Frederick, the visit of John to Enright's office, the suspicion of Valois that the murdered man was not Cavendish, and, finally, the conversation overheard in Steinway's, the torn telegram, and the meeting between Celeste La Rue and Enright.

When she had finished, Westcott sat, chin in hand, turning the evidence over in his mind. "Do you believe Frederick Cavendish is dead?" he asked suddenly.

"Yes."

Westcott struck his hand down on the rock, his eyes glowing dangerously.

"Well, I don't!" he exclaimed. "I believe he is alive! My theory is that this was all carefully arranged, but that circumstances compelled them to act quickly, and before they were entirely ready. Two unexpected occurrences hurried them into action."

She leaned forward, stirred by his earnestness.

"What?"

"The quarrel in the restaurant, leading to the making of the will," he answered gravely, "and my telegram. The two things fit together exactly. He must have received my first message that same night. In my judgment he was glad of some excuse to leave New York and determined to take the first train West. His quarrel with John, coupled with his disgust of the company he kept, caused him to draw up this will hurriedly. He left the club intending to pack up and take the first train."

"And was killed before he could do so?"

"Possibly; but if that dead man had no scar on his chest, he was not Frederick Cavendish; he was an impostor; some poor victim deliberately substituted because of his facial resemblance. Tell me, if it was Fred who was murdered, what became of the money he was known to have in his private safe? What became of the original copy of the will he had in his pocket when he left the club?"

She shook her head, convinced that his argument had force.

"I—I do not know."

"Yet these things are true, are they not? No money, no will was found. There is but one reason possible, unless others entered after the murder and stole these things. My belief is that Fred returned to his apartments, took what money he required, packed his valise, and departed without a word to any one. He often did things like that—hastily, on the spur of the moment."

"But what happened afterward?"

"The rest is all theory. I do not know, but I'll make a guess. In some way the conspirators learned what had occurred, but not in time to intercept his departure; yet they had everything ready for action, and realised this was the opportunity. Frederick had disappeared leaving no trace behind; they could attend to him later, intercept him, perhaps—— Wait! Keep still. There comes the carriage from the train."

He drew her back into the denser undergrowth and they looked out through the leaves to where the road circled in toward the bridge. The hoof-beats of horses alone broke the silence.

CHAPTER XII
VIEWED FROM BOTH SIDES

The team trotted on to the bridge, and then slowed down to a walk. Above the dull reverberation of hoofs the listeners below could hear the sound of voices, and an echo of rather forced laughter. Then the carriage emerged into full view. Beside the driver it contained three passengers—Beaton on the front seat, his face turned backward toward the two behind, a man and a woman. Westcott and Miss Donovan, peering through the screen of leaves, caught only a swift glimpse of their faces—the man middle-aged, inclined to stoutness, with an unusually red face, smoking viciously at a cigar, the woman young and decidedly blonde, with stray locks of hair blowing about her face, and a vivacious manner. The carriage rolled on to the smooth road, and the driver touched up the horses with his whip, the lowered back curtain shutting off the view.

The girl seized Westcott's arm while she directed his gaze with her free hand. "Look!" she cried. "The woman is La Rue. And the man—the man is Enright! He is the lawyer I told you of, the one whose hand is not clear in this affair. And he is here!"

"Good!" Westcott exclaimed. "I'm glad they're both here. It means that there will be more to observe, and it means that there will be action—and that, too, quick! They are out here for a definite purpose which must soon be disclosed. And, Miss Donovan, I may be a little rock-worn and a little bit out of style, but I think their presence here has something to do with the whereabouts of Fred Cavendish."

The girl looked straight into his honest, clear eyes. His remark opened a vast field for speculation. "You think he is alive then?" she said earnestly. "It is an interesting hypothesis. Perhaps—perhaps he may be in this neighbourhood, even. And that," she added, her Irish eyes alight, "would be more interesting still."

"I hadn't finished my argument when that carriage appeared," Westcott answered. "Do you remember? Well, that might be the answer. Beaton has been in this neighbourhood ever since about the time of that murder in New York. Nobody knows what his business is, but he is hand-in-glove with Bill Lacy and his gang. Lacy, besides running a saloon, pretends to be a mining speculator, but it is my opinion there is nothing he wouldn't do for money, if he considered the game safe. And now, with everything quiet in the East, and no thought that there is any suspicion remaining, Beaton sends for the woman to join him here. Why? Because there is some job to be done too big for him to tackle alone. He's merely a gunman; he can do the strong-arm stuff, all right, but lacks brains. There is a problem out here requiring a little intellect; and it is my guess it is how to dispose of Cavendish until they can get away safely with the swag."

"Exactly! That would be a stake worth playing for."

"It certainly would; and, as I figure it out, that is their game. John Cavendish is merely the catspaw. Right now there is nothing for them to do but wait until the boy gets full possession of the property; then they'll put the screws on him good and proper. Meantime Frederick must be kept out of sight—must remain dead."

"I wonder how this was ever planned out—if it be true?"

"It must have originated in some cunning, criminal brain," he admitted thoughtfully. "Not Beaton's, surely; and, while she is probably much brighter, I am inclined to think the girl is merely acting under orders. There is somebody connected with this scheme higher up—a master criminal."

Miss Donovan was no fool; newspaper work had taught her to suspect men of intellect, and that nothing, however wicked, low or depraved, was beyond them.

"Enright!" she said definitely. "Obviously now. I've thought so from the first. But always he worked so carefully, so guardedly, that sometimes I have doubted. But now I say without qualifications—Enright, smooth Mr. Enright, late of New York."

"That's my bet," Westcott agreed, his hand on her shoulder, forgetful of his intense earnestness, "Enright is the only one who could do it, and he has schemed so as to get John into a hole where he dare not emit a sound, no matter what they do to him. Do you see? If the boy breathes a suspicion he'll be indicted for murder. If they can only succeed in keeping Frederick safely out of sight until after the court awards the property to his heir, they can milk John at their leisure. It's a lawyer's graft, all right."

"Then Frederick may be confined not far away?"

"Likely enough; it's wild country. There are a hundred places within fifty miles where he might be hidden away for years. That is the job which was given to Beaton; he had the dirty work to perform, while the girl took care of John. I do not know how he did it—knockout drops, possibly, in a glass of beer; the blow of a fist on a train-platform at night; a ride into the desert to look at some thing of interest—there are plenty of ways in which it could be quietly done by a man of Mr. Beaton's expert experience."

"Yes, but he does not know this country—if it was only New York now."

"But Bill Lacy does, and these fellows are well acquainted—friends apparently. Lacy and I are at daggers-points over a mining claim, and he believes my only chance is through the use of money advanced by Fred Cavendish. He'd ride through hell to lick me. Why, look here, Miss Donovan, when Bill Lacy had me stuck up against the wall last night at the hotel with a gun at my head, he lost his temper and began to taunt me about not getting any reply from my telegrams and letters. How did he know about them? Beaton must have told him. There's the answer; those fellows are in cahoots, and if Fred is actually alive, Bill Lacy knows where he is, and all about it."

She did not answer. Westcott's theory of the situation, his quick decision that Frederick Cavendish still lived, completely overturned her earlier conviction. Yet his argument did not seem unfair or his conclusion impossible. Her newspaper experience had made her aware that there is nothing in this world so strange as truth, and nothing so unusual as to be beyond the domain of crime.

"What do you think?" he asked quietly.

"Oh, I do not know; it all grows less comprehensible every moment. But whatever is true I cannot see that anything remains for us to do, but wait and watch the actions of these people; they are certain to betray themselves. We have been here together now longer than we should, and I must return to the hotel."

"You expect Beaton to seek you?"

She smiled.

"He appeared very devoted, quite deeply interested; I hope it continues."

"So do I, now that I understand," earnestly. "Although I confess your intimacy was a shock to me this noon. Well, I am going to busy myself also and take a scouting trip to La Rosita."

"Is that Lacy's mine?"

"Yes; up the gulch here about two miles. I may pick up some information worth having. I am to see you again—alone?"

"We must have some means of communication; have you any suggestion?"

"Yes, but we'll take for our motto, 'Safety first.' We mustn't be seen together, or suspected in any way of being friends. The livery-stable keeper has a boy about twelve, who is quite devoted to me; a bright, trustworthy little fellow. He is about the hotel a good deal, and will bring me word from you any time. You need have no fear that I shall fail to respond to any message you send."

"I shall not doubt." She held out her hand frankly. "You believe in me now, Mr. Westcott?"

"Absolutely; indeed I think I always have. That other thing hurt, yet I kept saying to myself, 'She had some good reason.'"

"Always think so, please, no matter what happens. I was nearly wild until I got the note to you; I was so afraid you would leave the hotel. We must trust each other."

He stood before her, his hat in hand, a strong, robust figure, his bronzed face clearly revealed; the sunlight making manifest the grey hair about his temples. To Miss Donovan he seemed all man, instinct with character and purpose, a virile type of the out-of-doors.

"To the death," and his lips and eyes smiled. "I believe in you utterly."

"Thank you. Good-bye."

He watched her climb the bank and emerge upon the bridge. He still stood there, bare-headed, when she turned and smiled back at him, waving her hand. Then the slender figure vanished, and he was left alone. A moment later, Westcott was striding up the trail, intent upon a plan to entrap Lacy.

They would have felt less confident in the future could they have overheard a conversation being carried on in a room of the Timmons House. It was Miss La Rue's apartments, possessing two windows, but furnished in a style so primitive as to cause that fastidious young lady to burst into laughter when she first entered and gazed about. Both her companions followed her, laden with luggage, and Beaton, sensing instantly what had thus affected her humour, dropped his bag on the floor.

"It's the best there is here," he protested. "Timmons has held it for you three days."

"Oh, I think it is too funny, Ned," she exclaimed, staring around, and then flinging her wraps on the bed. "Look at that mirror, will you, and those cracks in the wall? Say, do I actually have to wash in that tin basin? Lord! I didn't suppose there was such a place in the world. Why, if this is the prize, what kind of a room have you got?"

"Tough enough," he muttered gloomily, "but you was so close with your money I had to sing low. What was the matter with you, anyhow?"

"Sweetie wouldn't produce, or couldn't, rather. He hasn't got his hands on much of the stuff yet. Enright coughed up the expense money, or most of it. I made John borrow some, but I needed that myself."

"Well, damn little got out here, and Lacy pumped the most of that out of me. However, if you feel like kicking about this room, you ought to see some of the others—mine, for instance, or the one Timmons put that other woman in."

"Oh, yes," she said, finding a seat and staring at him. "That reminds me. Did you say there was a girl here from New York? Never mind quarrelling about the room, I'll endure it all right; it makes me think of old times," and she laughed mirthlessly. "Sit down, Mr. Enright, and let's talk. How's the door, Ned?"

He opened it and glanced out into the hall, throwing the bolt as he came back.

"All right, Celeste, but I wouldn't talk quite so loud; the partitions are not very tight."

"No objections to a cigarette, I suppose," and she produced a case. "Thanks; now I feel better—certainly, light up. Well, Ned, the first thing I want to know is, who is this other New York skirt, and how did she happen to blow in here just at this time?"

Beaton completed the lighting of his cigar, flinging the match carelessly out of the window.

"Oh, she's all right," he said easily. "Just an innocent kid writer for *Scribbler's* who's trying to make good writing about the beautiful scenery around here. I was a bit suspicious of her at first myself, but picked her up this morning an' we had quite a talk. Mighty pretty little girl."

Miss La Rue elevated her eyebrows, watchfully regarding him through smoke wreaths.

"Oh, cut it, Ned," she exclaimed curtly. "We all know you are a perfect devil with the women. The poor thing is in love with you, no doubt, but that doesn't answer my question, who is she?"

"Her name is Donovan."

"That sounds promising; what do you make it, shanty Irish?"

"I should say not," warmly. "She's a lady, all right. Oh, I know 'em, if I don't meet many of that kind. We got chummy enough, so she told me all about herself—her father's a big contractor and has money to burn."

"Did you ever hear the beat of that, Enright? Neddy is about to feather his nest. Well, go on."

"That's about all, I guess, only she ain't nothin' you need be afraid of."

"Sure not, with a watch-dog like you on guard. But if you ask me, I don't like the idea of her happening in here just at this time. This is no place for an innocent child," and she looked about, her lip curling. "Lord, I should say not. Do you happen to remember any New York contractor by that name, Mr. Enright?"

The rotund lawyer, his feet elevated on the window-sill, a cigar between his lips, shook his head in emphatic dissent.

"Not lately; there was a Tim Donovan who had a pull in the subway excavation—he was a Tammany man—but he died, and was never married. There may have been others, of course, but I had tab on most of them. Did she mention his name, Beaton?"

"No; anyhow, I don't remember."

"What's the girl look like?"

"Rather slender, with brown hair, sorter coppery in the sun, and grey eyes that grow dark when she's interested. About twenty-three or four, I should say. She's a good-looker, all right; and not a bit stuck up."

"Did you get her full name?"

"Sure; it's on the register—Stella Donovan."

Enright lowered his feet to the floor, a puzzled look un his face, his teeth clinched on his cigar.

"Hold on a bit till I think." he muttered. "That sounds mighty familiar—Stella Donovan! My God, I've heard that name before somewhere; ah, I have it—she's on the New York *Star*. I've seen her name signed to articles in the Sunday edition." He wheeled and faced Miss La Rue. "Do you remember them?"

"No; I never see the *Star*."

"Well, I do, and sometimes she's damn clever. I'll bet she's the girl."

"A New York newspaperwoman; well, what do you suppose she is doing out here? After us?"

Enright had a grip on himself again and slowly relit his cigar, leaning back, and staring out the window. His mind gripped the situation coldly.

"Well, we'd best be careful," he said slowly. "Probably it's merely a coincidence, but I don't like her lying to Beaton. That don't look just right. Yet the *Star* can't have anything on us: the case is closed in New York; forgotten and buried nearly a month ago. Even my partner don't know where I am."

"I had to show John the telegram in order to get some money."

"You can gamble he won't say anything—there's no one else?"

"No; this game ain't the kind you talk about."

"You'd be a fool to trust anybody. So, if there's no leak we don't need to be afraid of her, only don't let anything slip. We'll lay quiet and try the young lady out. Beaton here can give her an introduction to Miss La Rue, and the rest is easy. What do you say, Celeste?"

"Oh, I'll get her goat; you boys trot on now while I tog up a little for dinner; when is it, six o'clock?"

"Yes," answered Beaton, still somewhat dazed by this revealment of Miss Donovan's actual identity. "But don't try to put on too much dog out here, Celeste; it ain't the style."

She laughed.

"The simple life, eh! What does your latest charmer wear—a skirt and a shirtwaist?"

"I don't know; she was all in black, but looked mighty neat."

"Well, I'll go her one better—a bit of Broadway for luck. So-long, both of you, and, Enright, you better come up for me; Ned, no doubt, has a previous engagement with Miss Donovan."

Mr. Enright paused at the door, his features exhibiting no signs of amusement.

"Better do as Beaton says, make it plain," he said shortly. "The less attention we attract the less talk there will be, and this is too damn serious an affair to be bungled. You hear?"

She crossed over and rested her hands on his arm.

"Sure; I was only guying Ned—it's a shirt-waist for me. I'll play the game, old man."

CHAPTER XIII
THE SHOT OF DEATH

Westcott's purpose in visiting the La Rosita mine was a rather vague one. His thought had naturally associated Bill Lacy with whatever form of deviltry had brought Beaton to the neighbourhood of Haskell, and he felt convinced firmly that this special brand of deviltry had some direct connection with the disappearance of Frederick Cavendish. Just what the connection between these people might prove to be was still a matter of doubt, but as Miss Donovan was seeking this information at the hotel, all that remained for him to do at present was an investigation of Lacy.

Yet it was not in the nature of the big miner to go at anything recklessly. He possessed a logical mind and needed to think out clearly a course of action before putting it into execution. This revelation had come to him suddenly, and the conclusion which he had arrived at, and expressed to the girl, was more of an inspiration than the result of calm mental judgment. After she had disappeared on her walk back to Haskell, Westcott lit his pipe and resumed his seat on the big rock again, to think it all out in detail, and decide on a course of action. He was surprised how swiftly and surely the facts of the case as already understood marshalled themselves into line in support of the theory he had advanced. The careful review of all Miss Donovan had told him only served to increase his confidence that his old partner still lived. No other conception seemed possible, or would account for the presence of Ned Beaton in Haskell, or the hurried call for Miss La Rue. Yet it was equally evident this was not caused by any miscarriage of their original plans. It was not fear that had led to this meeting—no escape of their prisoner, no suspicion that their conspiracy had been discovered, no alarm of exposure—but merely the careful completion of plans long before perfected. Apparently every detail of the crime, which meant the winning of Frederick Cavendish's fortune, had been thus far successfully carried out. The money was already practically in their possession, and not the slightest suspicion had been aroused. It had been a masterpiece of criminal ingenuity, so boldly carried out as to avoid danger of discovery.

Westcott believed he saw the purpose which had actuated the ruling spirit—a desire to attain these millions without bloodshed; without risking any charge of murder. This whole affair had been no vulgar, clumsy crime; it was more nearly a business proposition, cold-blooded, deliberately planned, cautiously executed. Every step had been taken exactly in accord with the original outlines, except possibly that they had been hurried by Cavendish's sudden determination to return West, and his will disinheriting

John. These had compelled earlier action, yet no radical change in plans, as the machinery was already prepared and in position. Luck had been with the conspirators when Frederick called in Enright to draw up the will. What followed was merely the pressure of his finger on the button.

Enright! Beyond doubt his were the brains dominating the affair. It was impossible to believe that either Celeste La Rue or Ned Beaton—chorus girl or gunman—could have ever figured out such a scheme. They were nothing but pawns, moved by the hand of the chief player. Aye! and John Cavendish was another!

The whole foul thing lay before Westcott's imagination in its diabolical ingenuity—Enright's legal mind had left no loophole. He intended to play the game absolutely safe, so far, at least, as he was personally concerned.

The money was to go legally to John without the shadow of a suspicion resting upon it; and then—well, he knew how to do the rest; already he had a firm grip on a large portion. Yes, all this was reasonably clear; what remained obscure was the fate of Frederick Cavendish.

Had they originally intended to take his life, and been compelled to change the plan? Had his sudden, unexpected departure from New York, on the very eve possibly of their contemplated action, driven them to the substitution of another body? It hardly seemed probable—for a man bearing so close a resemblance could not have been discovered in so short a time. The knowledge of the existence of such a person, however, might have been part of the original conspiracy—perhaps was the very basis of it; may have first put the conception into Enright's ready brain. Aye, that was doubtless the way of it. Frederick was to be spirited out of the city, accompanied, taken care of by Beaton or some other murderous crook, and this fellow, a corpse, substituted. If he resembled Frederick at all closely, there was scarcely a chance that his identity would be questioned. Why should it be—found in his apartments? There was nothing to arouse suspicion; while, if anything did occur, the conspirators were in no danger of discovery. They risked a possible failure of their plan, but that was all. But if this was true what had since become of Frederick?

Westcott came back from his musings to this one important question. The answer puzzled him. If the man was dead why should Beaton remain at Haskell and insist on Miss La Rue's joining him? And if the man was alive and concealed somewhere in the neighbourhood, what was their present object? Had they decided they were risking too much in permitting him to live? Had something occurred to make them feel it safer to have him out of the way permanently? What connection did Bill Lacy have with the gang?

Westcott rose to his feet and began following the trail up the cañon. He was not serving Cavendish nor Miss Donovan by sitting there. He would, at least, discover where Lacy was and learn what the fellow was engaged at. He walked rapidly, but the sun was nearly down by the time he reached the mouth of his own drift.

While waiting word from the East which would enable him to develop the claim, Westcott had thought it best to discontinue work, and hide, as best he could, from others the fact that he had again discovered the lost lead of rich ore. To that end, after taking out enough for his immediate requirements in the form of nuggets gathered from a single pocket, which he had later negotiated quietly at a town down the railroad, he had blocked up the new tunnel and discontinued operations. He had fondly believed his secret secure, until Lacy's careless words had aroused suspicion that the latter might have seen his telegrams to Cavendish. His only assistant, a Mexican, who had been with him for some time, remained on guard at the bunk-house, and, so far as he knew, no serious effort had been made to explore the drift by any of Lacy's satellites. Now, as he came up the darkening gulch, and crunched his way across the rock-pile before the tunnel entrance, he saw the cheerful blaze of a fire in the Mexican's quarters and stopped to question him.

"*Señor*—you!"

"Yes, José," and Westcott dropped on to a bench. "Anything wrong? You seem nervous."

"No, *señor*. I expected you not to-night; there was a man there by the big tree at sunset."

"You saw him?"

"Yes, but not his face, *señor*. He think me gone at first, but when I walk out on the edge of the cliff then he go—quick, like that. When the door creak I say maybe he come back."

"One of the La Rosita gang likely. Don't fight them, José. Let them poke around inside if they want to; they won't find anything but rock. There is no better way to fool that bunch than let them investigate to their heart's content. Got a bite there for me?"

"*Si, señor*, aplenty."

"All right then; I'm hungry and have a bit of work ahead. Put it on the table here, and sit down yourself, José."

The Mexican did as ordered, glancing across at the other between each mouthful of food, as though not exactly at ease. Westcott ate heartily, without pausing to talk.

"You hear yet Señor Cavendish?" José asked at last.

"No." Westcott hesitated an instant, but decided not to explain further. "He must be away, I think."

"What you do if you no hear at all?"

"We'll go on with the digging ourselves, José. It'll pay wages until I can interest capital somewhere to come in on shares."

"You no sell Lacy then?"

"Sell Lacy! Not in a thousand years. What put that in your head?"

The Mexican rubbed the back of his pate.

"You know Señor Moore—no hair so?" an expressive gesture.

"Sure; what about him?"

"He meet me at the spring; he come up the trail from Haskell on horseback with another man not belong 'round here."

"What did he look like—big, red-faced fellow, with checked suit and round hat?"

"*Si, señor*; he say to Moore, 'Why the hell you talk that damn greaser,' an' Moore laugh, an' say because I work for Señor Westcott."

"But what was it Moore said to you, José?"

"He cussed me first, an' when I wouldn't move, he swore that Lacy would own this whole hill before thirty days."

"Was that all? Didn't the other fellow say anything?"

"No, *señor*; but he swung his horse against me as they went by—he mighty poor rider."

"No doubt; that is not one of the amusements of the Bowery. Where did they go? Up to La Rosita?"

"*Si, señor*; I watched, they were there two hour."

Westcott stared into the fireplace; then the gravity of his face relaxed into a smile.

"Things are growing interesting, José," he said cheerfully. "If I only knew just which way the cat was about to jump I'd be somewhat happier. There seemed to be more light than usual across the gulch as I came up—what's going on?"

"They have put on more men, *señor*—a night shift. Last night I went in our drift clear to the end, and put my ear to the rock. It was far away, but I hear."

"No, no, José; that's impossible. Why, their tunnel as over a hundred yards away; not even the sound of dynamite would penetrate that distance through solid rock. You heard your heart beat."

"No, *señor*," and José was upon his feet gesticulating. "It was the pick—strike, strike, strike; then stop an' begin, strike, strike, strike again. I hear, I know."

"Then they must be running a lateral, hoping to cut across our vein somewhere within their lines."

"And will that give them the right, *señor*?"

Westcott sat, his head resting on one hand, staring thoughtfully into the dying fire; the yellow flame of the oil lamp between them on the table flickered in the draft from the open window. Here was a threatening combination of forces.

"I am not sure, Jose," he answered slowly. "The mining law is full of quirks, although, of course, the first discoverer of a lead is entitled to follow it—it's his. The trouble here is, that instead of giving notice of discovery, I have kept it a secret, and even blocked up the tunnel. If the La Rosita gang push their drift in, and strike that same vein, they will claim original discovery, and I reckon they'd make it stick. I didn't suppose Lacy had the slightest idea we had struck colour. Nobody knew it, but you and I, Jose."

"Never I say a word, *señor*."

"I am sure of that, for I know exactly where the news came from. Lacy spilled the beans in a bit of misunderstanding we had last night down in Haskell. My letters and telegrams East to Cavendish went wrong, and the news has come back here to those fellows. They know just what we've struck, and how our tunnel runs; I was fool enough to describe it all to Cavendish and send him a map of the vein. Now they are driving their tunnel to get in ahead of us."

He got to his feet, bringing his fist down with such a crash on the table as to set the lamp dancing.

"But, by God, it's not too late! We've got them yet. The very fact that Lacy is working a night shift is evidence he hasn't uncovered the vein. We'll tear open that tunnel the first thing in the morning, José, and I'll make proof of discovery before noon. Then we'll put a bunch of good men in here, and fight it out, if those lads get ugly. Come on, let's take a look in there tonight."

He picked up the lamp, and turned. At the same instant a sudden red glare flamed in the black of the open window, accompanied by a sharp report. The bullet whizzed past Westcott's head so closely as to sear the flesh, crashed into the lamp in his hand, extinguishing it, then struck something beyond. There was no cry, no sound except a slight movement in the dark. Westcott dropped to the floor, below the radius of dim light thrown by the few embers left in the fireplace, and revolver in hand, sought to distinguish the outlines of the window frame. Failing in this, he crept noiselessly across the floor, unlatched the closed door, and emerged into the open air.

It was a dark night, with scarcely a star visible, the only gleam of radiance coming from a light across the gulch, which he knew burned in the shaft-house of the La Rosita.

Everything about was still, with the intense silence of mountain solitude. Not a breath of air stirred the motionless cedars. Cautiously he circled the black cabin, every nerve taut for struggle, every sense alert. He found nothing to reward his search—whoever the coward had been, he had disappeared among the rocks, vanishing completely in the black night. The fellow had not even waited to learn the effect of his shot. He had fired pointblank into the lighted room, sighting at Westcott's head, and then ran, assured no doubt the speeding bullet had gone straight to the mark. It was not until he came back to the open door that the miner thought of his companion. What had become of José? Could it be that the Mexican was hit? He entered, shrinking from the task, yet resolute to learn the truth; felt his way along the wall as far as the fireplace, and stirred the embers into flame. They leaped up, casting a flickering glow over the interior. A black, shapeless figure, scarcely discernible as a man, lay huddled beneath the table. Westcott bent over it, feeling for the heart and turning the face upward. There was no visible mark of the bullet wound, but the body was limp, the face ghastly in the grotesque dance of the flames. The assassin had not wasted his shot—José Salvari would never see Mexico again.

CHAPTER XIV
LACY LEARNS THE TRUTH

Westcott straightened the body out, crossing the dead hands, and covered the face with a blanket stripped from a bunk. The brief burst of flame died down, leaving the room in semi-darkness. The miner was conscious only of a feeling of dull rage, a desire for revenge. The shot had been clearly intended for himself. The killing of José had been a mere accident. In all probability the murderer had crept away believing he had succeeded in his purpose. If he had lingered long enough to see any one emerge from the hut, he would naturally imagine the survivor to be the Mexican. Good! This very confidence would tend to throw the fellow off his guard; he would have no fear of José.

Westcott's heart rose in his throat as he stood hesitating. The dead man was only a Mexican, a servant, but he had been faithful, had proven himself an honest soul; and he had died in his service, as his substitute. All right, the affair was not going to end now; this was war, and, while he might not know who had fired the fatal shot, he already felt abundantly satisfied as to who had suggested its efficacy. There was only one outfit to be benefited by his being put out of the way—Bill Lacy's gang. If they already had Fred Cavendish killed, or held prisoner in their power, it would greatly simplify matters if he should meet death accidentally, or at the hands of parties unknown. Why not? Did he not stand alone between them and fortune? Once his lips were sealed, who else could combat their claims? No one; not a human being knew his secret—except the little he had confided that afternoon to Stella Donovan.

The thought of the girl served to break his reflections. This was all a part of that tragedy in New York. Both were in some way connected together, the assassination in the Waldron apartments, and the shooting of José here in this mountain shack. They seemed far apart, yet they were but steps in the same scheme.

He could not figure it all out, yet no doubt this was true—the struggle for the Cavendish millions had come to include the gold he had discovered here in the hills. Bill Lacy was merely the agent of those others, of Ned Beaton, of Celeste La Rue, of Patrick Enright. Aye, that was it—Enright! Instinctively, from the very first moment when he had listened to the girl's story, his mind had settled on Enright as the real leader. The lawyer's arrival in Haskell with the La Rue woman only served to strengthen that conviction. For certainly a man playing for potential stakes as big as those

Enright was gaming for, would intrust no cunning moves to a mere Broadway chorus-girl. No, Enright was on the ground in person because the matter in prospect needed a director, an excessively shrewd trickster, and the others were with him to do his bidding. If Cavendish really lived, all their plans depended on his being kept out of sight, disposed of, at least until they had the money safe in their grasp.

He reached beneath the blanket and drew forth the dead Mexican's revolver, slipped the weapon into his own belt, opened the door and went out, closing it tightly behind him. José could lie there until morning. While the darkness lasted he had work to do. His purpose settled, there was no hesitancy in his movements. His was the code of the West; his methods those of the desert and the mountains, the code and method of a fighting man.

A dim trail, rock strewn, led to the spring, where it connected with an ore road extending down the valley to Haskell. Another trail across the spur shortened the distance to the La Rosita shaft-house. But Westcott chose to follow none of these, lest he run into some ambuscade. The fellow who had fired into the shack was, unquestionably, hiding somewhere in the darkness, probably along one of these trails in the hope of completing his work.

To avoid encountering him the miner crept along the far side of the cabin through the dense shadow, and then struck directly across the hill crest, guided by the distant gleam of light. It was a rough climb, dangerous in places, but not unfamiliar. Slowly and silently, cautious to dislodge no rolling stone, and keeping well concealed among the rocks, he finally descended to the level of the shaft feeling confident that his presence was not discovered. He was near enough now to hear the noise of the hoisting-engine, and to mark the figure of the engineer in the dim light of a lantern.

Rock was being brought up the shaft, and cast onto the dump, but was evidently of small value, proof to the mind of the watcher that the gang below were merely engaged in tunnel work, and had not yet struck ore in any paying quantity.

He lay there watching operations for several minutes, carefully studying out the situation. He had no clearly defined plan, only a desire to learn exactly what was being done. The office beyond the shaft was lighted, although the faint gleam was only dimly revealed along the edge of lowered curtains concealing the interior. However, this evidence that some one was within served to attract Westcott's attention, and he crept around, under the shadow of the dump, and approached the farther corner. He could perceive now two men on the hoisting platform, and hear the growl of their voices, but without being able to distinguish speech. Every few moments there sounded the crash of falling rock as the buckets were emptied. Revolver in hand he made the round of the building to assure himself that no guard had been posted there, then chose the window farthest away from the shaft, and endeavoured to look in.

The heavy green curtain extended to the sill, but was slit in one corner. With his eye close to this slight opening he gained a partial glimpse of the interior. It was that of a rough office with a cot in one corner as though occasionally utilised for a sleeping room, the other furniture consisting of a small desk with roll-top, an unpainted table, and a few chairs. In one corner stood a rusty-looking safe, the door open, and a fat-bellied wood-stove occupied the centre of the floor.

There were three men in the room, and Westcott drew a quick breath of surprise as he recognised the two faces fronting him—Bill Lacy at the desk, a pipe in his mouth, his feet elevated on a convenient chair, and Beaton, leaning back against the wall, apparently half asleep with his eyes closed. The third man was facing Lacy, but concealed by the stove; he seemed to be doing the talking, and held a paper in his hand resembling a map. Suddenly he arose to his feet, and bent over the edge of the desk, and Westcott knew him—Enright!

The man spoke earnestly, evidently arguing a point with emphasis, but the sound of his voice failed to penetrate to the ears of the listener without. Desperately determined to learn what was being said, the miner thrust the heavy blade of his jack-knife beneath the ill-fitting window sash, and succeeded in noiselessly lifting it a scant half inch. He bent lower, the speaker's voice clearly audible through the narrow opening.

"That isn't the point, Lacy," the tone smooth enough, yet containing a trace of anger. "You are paid to do these things the way I plan. This mining proposition is all right, but our important job just now is at the other end. A false move at this time will not only cost us a fortune, but would send some of us to the pen. Don't you know that?"

"Sure I do; but I thought this was my end of it."

"So it is; but it can wait until later, until we have the money in hand, and have decided about Cavendish. You say your tunnel is within twenty feet of the lead, which it must be according to this map, and you propose breaking through and holding on until the courts decide. Now don't you know that will kick up a hell of a row? It will bring us all in the limelight, and just at present we are better off underground. That's why I came out here. I am no expert in mining law, and am not prepared to say that your claim is not legal. It may be, and it may not be—we'll waive that discussion. The point is this—from all I can learn of Westcott, he is the kind who will fight to the last ditch. Perhaps he hasn't any chance, but if he ever does learn how we got hold of his letters and discovered the location of that vein of ore, he's going to turn this whole affair inside out, and catch us red-handed. You made a fool play to-night."

"That wasn't my fault," Lacy protested sullenly. "The fellow misunderstood; however, there won't be no fuss made over a Mexican."

"I'm not so sure of that; Westcott will know it was meant for him and be on his guard. Anyhow it was a fool's trick."

"Well, we do things different out here from what you do in New York. It's my way to take no chances, and when a man's dead he can't talk."

"I'm not so sure of that; there's been many a lad hung on the testimony of a dead man. Now see here, Lacy, this is my game, and I propose playing it in my own way. You came in under those conditions, didn't you?"

"I reckon so, still there wasn't much to it when I came in. This mining stunt developed later out of those letters Westcott sent East. This man Beaton here offered me so much to do a small job for him, and I named my price without caring a whoop in hell what it was all about. I don't now, but I've learned a few things since, and am beginning to think my price was damn low. You never came way out here just to stop me from tunnelling into Westcott's mine."

The other hesitated.

"No," he admitted at last, "I did not even learn what was being done until after I got here."

"Beaton sent for you?"

"Not exactly. I never had any personal connection with him in the case. I am not sure he ever heard of me, unless the woman told him. He was working under her orders, and wired her when Cavendish got away to come out at once. He didn't know what to do."

Lacy laughed, and began to refill his pipe.

"That was when I first began to smell a mouse," he said, more at ease. "The fellow was so scared I caught on that this was no common kidnapping outfit, like I had thought before. He wasn't easy pumped, but I pumped him. I told him we'd have the guy safe enough inside of twenty-four hours—hell! there wasn't no chance for him to get away, for the blame fool headed East on foot straight across the desert—but he sent off the wire just the same. That's what I thought brought you along." He leaned over, and lowered his voice. "There was a dead man back East, wasn't there?"

"What difference does that make?"

"None, particularly, except to naturally increase the worth of my services. I'm not squeamish about stiffs, but I like to know what I am doing. What are you holding on to this other fellow for?"

Enright walked nervously across the room, chewing at his cigar, only to come back and face his questioner.

"Well, I suppose I might as well tell you," he said almost savagely. "You know so damn much now, you better know it all. You're in too deep already to wiggle out. We made rather a mess of it in New York, and only a bit of luck helped us through. We had the plans ready for three months, but nothing occurred to give us a chance. Then all at once Cavendish got his first telegram from Westcott, and decided to pull out, not telling any one where he was going. That would have been all right, for we had a man shadowing him, but at the last moment he quarrelled with the boy we had the woman slated up with."

"Hold on; what boy? Let me get this straight."

"His nephew, and only relative—John Cavendish."

"Oh, I see; he was his heir; and you had him fixed?"

"We had him where he couldn't squeal, and have yet. That was Miss La Rue's part of the game. But, as I was saying, there was a quarrel and the uncle suddenly decided to draw up a will, practically cutting John out entirely."

"Hell! Some joke that!"

"There was where luck came to our help. He employed me to draw the will, and told me he planned to leave the city for some time. As soon as I could I told the others over the phone, and we got busy."

Lacy struck his knee with his hand, and burst into a laugh.

"So, he simply disappeared! Your idea was that an accident might happen, and our friend Beaton here took the same train to render any necessary assistance."

"No," said Enright frankly, "murder wasn't part of our plan; it's too risky. We had other means for getting this money—legally."

Lacy stared incredulous.

"And there hasn't been no killin'?"

Enright shook his head.

"Not by any of us."

"Then how about that dead man in New York—the one that was buried for Cavendish? Oh, I read about that. Beaton showed it to me in the paper."

"That's the whole trouble," Enright answered gravely. "I do not know who he was, or how he came there. All I know is, he was not Frederick Cavendish. But his being found there dead in Cavendish's apartments, and identified, puts us in an awful hole, if the rest of this affair should ever become known. Do you see? The charge would be murder, and how are we going to hold the real Cavendish alive, and not have it come out?"

"The other one—the stiff—wasn't Cavendish?"

"Certainly not; you know where Cavendish is."

"I never saw Fred Cavendish; I wouldn't know him from Adam's off-ox. I've got the fellow Beaton turned over to me."

"Well, he's the man; the dead one isn't."

"How do you know?"

"Because Frederick Cavendish bought and signed a round-trip ticket to Los Angeles, and boarded the midnight train. My man reported that to me, and Beaton just had time to catch the same train before it pulled out. Isn't that true, Ned?"

"Yes, it is, and I never left him."

"But," insisted Lacy stubbornly, "did you see the dead one?"

"Yes. I kept away from the inquest, but attended the funeral to get a glance at his face. It seemed too strange to be true. The fellow wasn't Cavendish; I'd swear to that, but he did look enough like him to fool anybody who had no suspicions aroused. You see no one so much as questioned his identity—Cavendish had disappeared without a word even to his valet; this fellow, despite the wounds on his face, looking enough like him to be a twin, dressed like him, is found dead in his apartments. Dammit, it's spooky, the very thought of it."

"But you saw a difference?"

"Because I looked for it; I never would have otherwise. Of course what I looked at was a dead face in the coffin, a dead face that was seared and burned. But anyway, I was already convinced that he was not the man. I am not sure what I should have thought if I had met him alive upon the street."

Lacy appeared amused, crossing the room, and expectorating into the open stove.

"You fellows make me laugh," he said grimly. "I am hardly idiot enough to be taken in by that sort of old wives' tale. However, if that is your story stick to it—but if you were to ever tell it in court, it would take a jury about five minutes to bring in their verdict. Still I see what you're up against—the death of this fellow means that you are afraid now to leave Cavendish alive. If he ever appears again in the flesh this New York murder will have to be accounted for. Is that it?"

"It leaves us in an awkward position."

"All right. We understand each other then. Let's get to business. You want me to help out in a sort of accident, I presume—a fall over a cliff, or the premature discharge of blasting powder; these things are quite common out here."

Neither Enright nor Beaton answered, but Lacy was in no way embarrassed by their silence. He knew now he had the whip-hand.

"And to prevent any stir at this end, before you fellows get hold of the stuff, you want me to call off my working gang and let Westcott alone. Come, now, speak up."

"Yes," acknowledged Enright. "I don't care so much for Westcott, but I want things kept quiet. There's a newspaperwoman down at the hotel. I haven't been able to discover yet what she is doing out here, but she's one of the big writers on the New York *Star*. If she got an inkling of this affair——"

"Who is she? Not the girl you had that row over, Beaton?"

The gunman nodded.

"She's the one."

"Do you suppose Jim Westcott knew her before? He brought her to the hotel and was mighty touchy about her."

"Hell, no; she told me all about that—why she cut that fellow dead in the dining-room when he tried to speak to her the next day."

Lacy whistled a few bars, his hands thrust deep into his trouser-pockets. Then, after a few minutes' cogitation, he resumed:

"All right then; we'll take it as it lies. The only question unsettled, Enright, is—what is all this worth to me?"

CHAPTER XV
MISS LA RUE PAYS A CALL

Some slight noise caused Westcott to straighten up, and turn partially around. He had barely time to fling up one arm in the warding off of a blow. The next instant was one of mad, desperate struggle, in which he realised only that he dare not relax his grip on the wrist of his unknown antagonist. It was a fierce, intense grapple, every muscle strained to the utmost, silent except for the stamping of feet, deadly in purpose.

The knife fell from the cramped fingers, but the fellow struggled like a demon, clutching at the miner's throat, but unable to confine his arms. Twice Westcott drove his clenched right into the shadowed face, smashing it the last time so hard the man's grip relaxed, and he went staggering back. With a leap forward, the battle-fury on him, Westcott closed before the other could regain position. Again the clenched fist struck and the fellow went down in the darkness, whirling backward to the earth—and lay there, motionless.

An instant, panting, breathless, scarcely yet comprehending what had occurred, the victor stared at the huddled figure, his arm drawn back. Then he became aware of excitement within, the sound of voices, the tramp of feet on the floor, the sudden opening of a door. A gleam of light shot out, revealing the figures of men. With one spring he was across the shapeless form on the ground, and had vanished into the darkness beyond.

Lacy was first to reach the unconscious body, stumbling over it in the black shadow, as he rushed forward, revolver in hand. He cursed, rising to his knees, and staring about in the silent darkness.

"There's a man lying here—dead likely. Bring a light. No, the fellow is alive. Dammit, it's Moore, and completely knocked out. Here you—what happened?"

The fellow groaned, opened his eyes, and looked about dazedly.

"Speak up, man!" and Lacy dragged him to a sitting position in no gentle fashion. "Who hit you?"

"There—there was a fellow at that window there. I—I saw him from below, and crept up behind but he turned around just as I struck."

"Who was he?"

"I never saw his face. He hit me first."

"He was at that window, you say?"

"Yes; kneelin' down like he was lookin' into the room. Oh, Lord!"

Lacy crunched over to the side of the shack, and bent down to get a better view. His fingers came in contact with the knife which upheld the sash, and he plucked it out, holding it up into the beam of light passing through the rent in the torn curtain. He stared at the curiously carved handle intently.

"This is certainly hell," he said soberly. "That's Jim Westcott's jack-knife. He's been listening to all we said. Now we are up against it."

"What's that?" The question came from Enright, still at the corner of the house, unable to tell what had happened.

"Westcott has been here listening to our talk. He pried up the window with this knife, so he could hear. Moore caught him, and got knocked out."

"He—he heard our talk in—in there," repeated the dazed lawyer, his lips trembling. "And—has got away? Good God! man, where has he gone? After the sheriff?"

Lacy stared at him through the darkness, and burst into a roar of unrestrained laughter.

"Who? Jim Westcott? The sheriff? Well, hardly at this stage of the game. That's your way down East, no doubt, but out in this country the style is different. No, sir; Westcott isn't after any sheriff. In the first place he hasn't any evidence. He knows a thing or two, but he can't prove it; and if we move faster than he does we'll block his game—see?"

"What do you mean?"

Lacy leaned forward, and hissed his answer into Enright's ear.

"Put Cavendish where he can't get at him. There's no other chance. If Jim Westcott ever finds that fellow alive our goose is cooked. And we've got the advantage—we know where the man is."

"And Westcott doesn't?"

"Exactly, but he will know. He'll comb these hills until he finds the trail—that's Jim Westcott. Come on back inside, both of you, and I'll tell you my plan. No, there is no use trying to run him down to-night—a hundred men couldn't do it. What's that, Moore? Go on to the shaft-house, and let Dan fix you up. No, we won't need any guard. That fellow will never come back here again to-night. Come on, boys."

The door closed behind them, shutting out the yellow glow, and leaving the hillside black and lonely. A bucket of rock rattled onto the dump, and

Moore, limping painfully, swearing with every step, clambered up the dark trail toward the shaft-house.

Miss Donovan did not go down to supper. Beaton waited some time in the office, his eyes on the stairs, but she failed to appear, and he lacked the necessary courage to seek her in her own room. Then Enright called him and compelled his attendance. The absence of the girl was not caused from any lack of appetite as she subsidised the Chinaman to smuggle her a supply of food by way of the back stairs, which she ate with decided relish, but she had no desire to show any anxiety regarding a meeting with the newcomers.

Her newspaper experience had given her some knowledge of human nature and she felt convinced that her task of extracting information would be greatly simplified if these people sought her company first. To hold aloof would have a tendency to increase their interest, for Beaton would certainly tell of her presence in the hotel, and, if their purpose there had any criminal intent, suspicion would be aroused.

This theory, however, became somewhat strained as the time passed quietly, and seemed to break entirely when from her window she saw Beaton and the heavy-set man ride out of town on a pair of livery horses. She watched them move down the long street, and turn into the trail leading out across the purple hills. The lowering darkness finally hid them from view. She was still at the window beginning to regret her choice when some one rapped at the door. She arose to her feet, and took a step or two forward, her heart beating swifter.

"Come in."

The door opened, and the light from the windows revealed Miss La Rue, rather tastefully attired in green silk, her blond hair fluffed artfully, and a dainty patch of black court-plaster adorning one cheek. She stood hesitating on the threshold, her eyes searching the other's face.

"Pardon me, please," the voice somewhat high-pitched, "but they told me down-stairs you were from New York."

"Yes, that is my home; won't you come in?"

"Sure I will. Why I was so lonesome in this hole I simply couldn't stand it any longer. Have you only one chair?" She glanced about, her eyes widening. "Heavens, what a funny room! Why, I thought mine was the limit, but it's a palace beside this. You been here long?"

"Since yesterday; take the chair, please; I am used to the bed—no, really, I don't mind in the least. It is rather funny, but then I haven't always lived at the Ritz-Carlton, so I don't mind."

"Huh! for the matter of that no more have I, but believe me, there would be some howl if they ever gave me a room like this—even in Haskell. I know your name; it's Stella Donovan—well, mine is Celeste La Rue."

"A very pretty name; rather unusual. Are you French?"

The other laughed, crossing her feet carelessly, and extracting a cigarette case from a hand-bag.

"French? Well, I guess not. You don't mind if I smoke, do you? Thanks. Have one yourself—they're imported. No? All right. I suppose it is a beastly habit, but most of the girls I know have picked it up. Seems sociable, somehow. No, I'm not French. My dad's name was Capley, and I annexed this other when I went on the stage. It tickles the Johnnies, and sounds better than Sadie Capley. You liked it yourself."

"It is better adapted to that purpose—you are an actress then?"

"Well, nobody ever said so. I can dance and sing a bit, and know how to wear clothes. It's an easier job than some others I've had, and gets me into a swell set. Tell me, when were you in New York?"

"About a month ago."

"Well, didn't you see the Revue?"

"The last one? Certainly."

"That's where I shone—second girl on the right in the chorus, and I was in the eccentric dance with Joe Steams; some hit—what?"

"Yes, I remember now; they called you the Red Fairy—because of your ruby ring. What in the world ever brought you out here?"

Celeste laughed, a cloud of smoke curling gracefully above her blonde hair.

"Some joke, isn't it? Well, it's no engagement at the Good Luck Dance Hall yonder, you can bet on that. The fact is I've quit the business, and am going to take a flier in mining."

"Mining? That sounds like money in these days. They tell me there is no placer-mining any longer, and that it requires a fortune to develop. I wouldn't suppose a chorus girl——"

"Oh, pshaw!" and Miss La Rue leaned forward, a bright glow on each cheek. "There are more ways of making money in New York than drawing a salary. Still, that wasn't so bad. I pulled down fifty a week, but of course that was only a drop in the bucket. I don't mind telling you, but all a good-looking girl needs is a chance before the public—there's plenty of rich fools in the world yet. I've caught on to a few things in the last five years. It pays better to be Celeste La Rue than it ever did to be Sadie Capley. Do you get me?"

Miss Donovan nodded. Her acquaintance with New York fast life supplied all necessary details, and it was quite evident this girl had no sense of shame. Instead she was rather proud of the success she had achieved.

"I imagine you are right," she admitted pleasantly. "So you found a backer? A mining man?"

"Not on your life. None of your wild west for me. As soon as some business is straightened out here, it's back to Broadway."

"Who is it?" ventured the other cautiously. "Mr. Beaton?"

"Ned Beaton!" Miss La Rue's voice rose to a shriek. "Oh, Lord! I should say not! Why that fellow never had fifty dollars of his own at one time in his life. You know Beaton, don't you?"

"Well, hardly that. We have conversed at the table down-stairs."

"I suppose any sort of a man in a decent suit of clothes looks good enough to talk to out here. But don't let Beaton fool you. He's only a tin-horn sport."

"Then it is the other?"

"Sure; he's the real thing. Not much to look at, maybe, but he fairly oozes the long green. He's a lawyer."

"Oh, indeed," and Miss Donovan's eyes darkened. She was interested, now feeling herself on the verge of discovery. "From New York?"

"Sure, maybe you've heard of him? He knew you as soon as Beaton mentioned your name; he's Patrick Enright of Enright and Dougherty."

Miss Donovan's fingers gripped hard on the footboard of the bed, and her teeth clinched to keep back a sudden exclamation of surprise. This was more than she had bargained for, yet the other woman, coolly watching, in spite of her apparent flippancy, observed no change in the girl's manner. Apparently the disclosure meant little.

"Enright, you say? No, I think not. He claimed to know me? That is rather strange. Who did he think I was?"

Miss La Rue bit her lip. She had found her match evidently, but would strike harder.

"A reporter on the *Star*. Naturally we couldn't help wondering what you was doing out here. You are in the newspaper business, ain't you?"

"Yes," realising further concealment was useless, "but on my vacation. I thought I explained all that to Mr. Beaton. I am not exactly a reporter. I am what they call a special writer—sometimes write for magazines like *Scribbler's*, other times for newspapers. I do feature-stuff."

"Whatever that is."

"Human-interest stories; anything unusual; strange happenings in every-day life, you know."

"Murders, and—and robberies."

"Occasionally, if they are out of the ordinary." She took a swift breath, and made the plunge. "Like the Frederick Cavendish case—do you remember that?"

Miss La Rue stared at her across the darkening room, but if she changed colour the gloom concealed it, and her voice was steady enough.

"No," she said shortly, "I never read those things. What happened?"

"Oh, nothing much. It occurred to my mind because it was about the last thing I worked on before leaving home. He was very rich, and was found dead in his apartments at the Waldron—evidently killed by a burglar."

"Did they get the fellow?"

"No, there was no clue; the case is probably forgotten by this time. Let's speak about something else—I hate to talk shop."

Miss La Rue stood up, and shook out her skirt.

"That's what I say; and it seems to me it would be more social if we had something to drink. You ain't too nice to partake of a cocktail, are you? Good! Then we'll have one. What's the hotelkeeper's name?"

"Timmons."

"Do you suppose he'd come up if I pounded on the floor?"

Miss Donovan slipped off the bed.

"I don't believe he is in the office. He went up the street just before dark. You light the lamp while I'll see if I can find the Chinaman out in the hall."

She closed the door behind her, strode noisily down the hall, then silently and swiftly retraced her steps and stooped silently down to where a crack yawned in the lower panel. That same instant a match flared within the room and was applied to the wick of the lamp. The narrow opening gave only a glimpse of half the room—the wash-stand, the chair, and lower part of the bed. She saw Miss La Rue drop the match, then open her valise and go through it, swiftly. She found nothing, and turned to the wash-stand drawer. The latter was empty, and was instantly closed again, the girl staring about the room, as though at her wit's end. Suddenly she disappeared along the edge of the bed, beyond the radius of the crack in the door. What was it she was doing? Searching the bed, no doubt; seeking something hidden beneath the pillow, or mattress.

Whatever her purpose, she was gone scarcely a moment, gliding silently back to the chair beside the window, with watchful eyes again fixed on the closed door. Miss Donovan smiled, and straightened up, well satisfied with her ruse. It had served to demonstrate that the ex-chorus-girl was far from being as calmly indifferent as she had assumed and it had made equally evident the fact that her visit had an object—the discovery of why Miss Donovan was in Haskell. Doubtless she had made the call at Enright's suggestion. Very well, the lady was quite welcome to all the information obtained. Stella opened the door, and the eyes of the two met.

"The Chinaman seems to have gone home," the mistress of the room said quietly. "At least he is not on this floor or in the office, and I could see nothing of Timmons anywhere."

"Then I suppose we don't drink," complained Miss La Rue. "Well, I might as well go to bed. There ain't much else to do in this jay town."

She got up, and moved toward the door.

"If you're only here viewing the scenery, I guess you won't remain long."

"Not more than a day or so. I am planning a ride into the mountains before leaving," pleasantly. "I hope I shall see you again."

"You're quite liable to," an ugly curl to the lip, "maybe more than you'll want. Good night."

Miss Donovan stood there motionless after the door closed behind her guest. She was conscious of the sting in those final words, the half-expressed threat, but the smile did not desert her lips. Her only thought was that the other was angry, irritated over her failure, her inability to make a report to her masters. She looked at the valise on the floor, and laughed outright, but as her eyes lifted once more, she beheld her travelling suit draped over the head-board of the bed, and instantly the expression of her face changed. She had forgotten hanging it there. That must have been where the woman went when she disappeared. It was not to rummage the bed at all, but to hastily run through the pockets of her jacket. The girl swiftly crossed the room, and flung coat and skirt onto the bed. She remembered now thrusting the telegram from Farriss into a pocket on the morning of its receipt. It was gone!

CHAPTER XVI
CAPTURED

Her first thought was to search elsewhere, although she immediately realised the uselessness of any such attempt. The message had been in her pocket as she recalled distinctly; she had fully intended destroying it at the same time she had torn up the letter of instruction, but failed to do so. Now it was in the hands of the La Rue woman, and would be shown to the others. Stella blew out the light and sat down by the open window endeavouring to figure out what all this would mean. It was some time before she could recall to memory the exact wording of the telegram, but finally it came to her bit by bit:

If any clues, advise immediately. Willis digging hard. Letter of instruction follows.

FARRISS.

There was no mention of names, yet these people could scarcely fail to recognise that this had reference to the Cavendish case. Their fears would lead to this conclusion, and they could safely argue that nothing else would require the presence in Haskell of a New York newspaper writer. Besides, if the man Enright had recognised her and knew of her connection with the *Star*, it was scarcely probable that he would be wholly unfamiliar with the name of Farriss, the city editor. No, they would be on guard now, and she could hope to win no confidence. The thought of personal danger never once entered her mind. Timidity was not part of her nature and she gave this phase of the matter no thought. All that seriously troubled her was the knowledge that she was handicapped in the case, unable to carry out the plans previously outlined.

From now on she would be watched, guarded against, deceived. That these people—Enright particularly—were playing a desperate game for big stakes, was already evident. They had not hesitated at murder to achieve their ends, and yet the girl somehow failed to comprehend that this discovery by them, that she was on their trail, placed her in personal peril.

There were two reasons causing indifference—a carelessness engendered by long newspaper experience, and a feeling that the telegram told so little they would never realise how far the investigation had progressed. All she could do then, would be to remain quiet, watch closely for results, and, if necessary, have some one else sent out from the home office to take up the work. But meanwhile she must communicate with Westcott, tell him all that had occurred. She would send him a note the first thing in the morning.

Somewhat reassured by this reasoning, she was still seated there, staring out into the night, when Enright and Beaton returned. It must have been late, for the street was practically deserted, the saloons even being closed. The hotel was silent, although a lamp yet burned in the office, the dull glow falling across the roadway in front of the door. Stella heard the tread of horses' feet, before her eyes distinguished the party approaching, and she drew back cautiously. In the glow of the light she could perceive four men in saddle halted in front of the hotel, three of whom dismounted, and entered the building, the fourth grasping the reins of the riderless animals, and leading them up the street. No word was spoken, except an order to the departing horseman, and the girl could not be certain of the identity of those below, although convinced the first two to disappear within were Enright and Beaton. She heard the murmur of voices below and the heavy steps of the men as they came slowly up the stairs. Then a door opened creakingly and she caught the sound of a woman's voice.

"Is that you, Ned?"

"Sure; what are you doing up at this hour?"

"Never mind that. Who have you got with you?"

"Enright and Lacy—why?"

"I want you all to come in here a minute; don't make so much noise."

A voice or two grumbled, but feet shuffled along the bare floor, and the door creaked again as it was carefully closed behind them. Stella opened her own door a crack and listened; the hall, lighted only by a single oil-lamp at the head of the stairs, was deserted and silent. She stole cautiously forward, but the voices in Miss La Rue's room were muffled and indistinct, not an audible word reaching her ears. The key was in the lock, shutting out all view of the interior. Well, what was the difference? She knew what was occurring within—the stolen telegram was being displayed, and discussed. That would not delay them long, and it would never do for her to be discovered in the hall.

Convinced of the uselessness of remaining, she returned to her own room, closing and bolting the door.

This time she removed some of her clothing, and lay down on the bed, conscious of being exceedingly tired, yet in no degree sleepy. She rested there, with wide-open eyes, listening until the distant door creaked again, and she heard the footsteps of the men in the hall. They had not remained in the chorus girl's room long, nor was anything said outside to arouse her suspicions. Reassured, Miss Donovan snuggled down into her pillow, unable to distinguish where the men went, but satisfied they had sought their rooms. They would attempt nothing more that night, and she had better gain what rest she could. It was not easy falling asleep, in spite of the silence, but at last she dropped off into a doze.

Suddenly some unusual noise aroused her, and she sat upright, unable for the moment to comprehend what had occurred. All was still, oppressively still; she could hear the pounding of her own heart. Then something tingled at the glass of her window, sharply distinct, as though a pebble had been tossed upward. Instantly she was upon her feet, and had crossed the room, her head thrust out. The light in the office had been extinguished, and the night was black, yet she could make out dimly the figure of a man close in against the side of the house, a mere hulking shadow. At the same instant he seemed to move slightly, and some missile grazed her face, and fell upon the floor, striking the rug with a dull thud. She drew back in alarm, yet immediately grasped the thought that this must be some secret message, some communication from Westcott.

Drawing down the torn curtain, she touched a match to the lamp and sought the intruding missile. It had rolled beneath the bed—a small stone with a bit of paper securely attached. The girl tore this open eagerly, her eyes searching the few lines:

Must see you to-night. Have learned things, and am going away. Go down back stairs, and meet me at big cottonwood behind hotel; don't fail.

J. W.

Her breath came fast as she read, and crunched the paper into the palm of her hand. She understood, and felt no hesitancy. Westcott had made discoveries so important he must communicate them at once and there was no other way. He dare not come to her openly at that hour. Well, she was not afraid—not of Jim Westcott. Even in her hurry she was dimly conscious of the utter, complete confidence she felt in the man; even of the strange interest he had inspired. She paused in her hasty dressing, wondering at herself, dimly aware that a new feeling partly actuated her desire to meet the man again—a feeling thoroughly alien to the Cavendish mystery. She glanced into the cracked mirror and laughed, half ashamed at her eagerness, yet utterly unable to suppress the quickened beat of her pulse.

She was ready almost in a minute, and had blown out the lamp. Again she ventured a glance out into the street below, but the skulking figure had disappeared, no one lurked anywhere in the gloom. There was not a sound to disturb the night. She almost held her breath as she opened the door silently and crept out into the hall. Stella possessed no knowledge of any back stairway, but the dim light enabled her to advance in comparative quiet.

Once a board creaked slightly, even under her light tread, and she paused, listening intently. She could distinguish the sound of heavy sleepers, but no movement to cause alarm, and, assured of this, crept forward. The hall turned sharply to the right, narrowing and becoming dark as the rays of light failed to negotiate the corner. Twenty feet down this passage ended in a door. This was unlocked, and yielded easily to the grasp of her hand. It opened upon a narrow platform, and she ventured forth. Gripping the hand-rail she descended slowly into the darkness below, the excitement of the adventure causing her heart to beat like a trip-hammer.

At the bottom she was in a gloom almost impenetrable, but her feet felt a cinder path and against the slightly lighter sky her eyes managed to distinguish the gaunt limbs of a tree not far distant, the only one visible and doubtless the cottonwood referred to in the note.

Shrinking there in the black shadow of the building she realised suddenly the terror of her position—the intense loneliness; the silence seemed to smite her. There occurred to her mind the wild, rough nature of the camp, the drunkenness of the night before; the wide contrast between that other scene of debauchery and this solitude of silence leaving her almost unnerved. She endeavoured to recall her surroundings, how the land lay here at the rear of the hotel. She could see only a few shapeless outlines of scattered buildings, not enough to determine what they were like. She had passed along that way toward the bridge that afternoon, yet now she could remember little, except piles of discarded tin cans, a few scattered tents, and a cattle corral on the summit of the ridge.

Still it was not far to the tree, and surely there could be no danger at this hour. If there had been Westcott would never have asked her to come. The very recurrence of his name gave her strength and courage. Her hands clenched with determination and she drew in a long breath, her body straightening. Why, actually, she had been frightened of the dark; like a child she had been peopling the void with the demons of fancy. It struck her as so ridiculous that she actually laughed to herself as she started straight toward the tree, which now seemed to beckon her.

It was a rough path, sandy, interspersed with small rocks, and led down into a gully. The tree stood on the opposite bank, which was so steep she had to grasp its outcropping roots in order to pull herself up. Even after gaining footing she saw nothing of Westcott, heard no sound indicating his presence.

A coyote howled mournfully in the distance, and a stray breath of air stirred one of the great leaves above into a startled rustling. She crept about the gnarled trunk, every nerve aquiver, shaded her eyes with one hand, and peered anxiously around into the gloom. Suddenly something moved to her right, and she shrank back against the tree, uncertain if the shapeless thing approaching was man or beast. He was almost upon her before she was sure; then her lips gave utterance to a little sob of relief.

"Oh! You frightened me so!"

The man stopped, scarcely a yard away, a burly figure, but with face indistinguishable.

"Sorry to do that," he said, "but no noise, please."

She shrank back to the edge of the bank, conscious of the grip of a great fear.

"You—you are not Mr. Westcott?" she choked. "Who are you? What is it you want?"

The man laughed, but made no move.

"Hard luck to come out here to meet Jim, an' run up against a totally different proposition—hey, miss?" he said grimly. "However, this ain't goin' ter be no love affair—not yit, at least. If I wuz you I wouldn't try makin' no run fer it; an' if yer let out a screech, I'll hav' ter be a bit rough."

"You—you are after me?"

"Sure; you've been playin' in a game what's none o' your business. Now I reckon it's the other party's turn to throw some cards. Thought yer was comin' out yere ter meet up with Jim Westcott, didn't yer?"

She made no answer, desperately seeking some means of escape, the full significance of her position clear before her.

"Got a nice little note from Jim," the fellow went on, "an' lost no time a gittin' yere. Well, Westcott is not liable to be sendin' fer yer again very soon. What ther hell——"

She had dashed forward, seeking to place the trunk of the tree between them, the unexpected movement so sudden, she avoided his grasp. But success was only for an instant. Another hand gripped her, hurling her back helplessly.

"You are some sweet little lady's man, Moore," snarled a new voice raspingly. "Now let me handle this business my own way. Go get that team turned around. I'll bring the girl. Come on now, miss, and the less you have to say the better."

She grasped at the bark, but the fellow wrenched her loose, forcing her forward. Her resistance evidently angered him, for he suddenly snatched her up into the iron grip of his arms and held her there, despite her struggles.

"Keep still, you damn tiger-cat," he hissed, "or I'll quiet you for good. Don't take this for any play acting, or you'll soon be sorry. There now, try it again on your own feet."

"Take your hands off me then."

"Very well—I will; but I've got something here to keep you quiet," and he touched his belt threateningly.

"What is it you want of me? Who are you?"

"We'll discuss that later. Just now, move on—yes, straight ahead. You see that wagon over there? Well, that is where you are bound at present. Move on pronto."

She realised the completeness of the trap into which she had fallen, the futility of resistance. If the man who seemed in control exhibited any consideration, it was not from the slightest desire to show mercy, but rather to render the work as easy as possible. She was as helplessly in his power as though bound and gagged. Before them appeared the dim outline of a canvas covered wagon silhouetted against the sky, to which was hitched a team of horses.

As they approached the shapeless figures of two men appeared in the gloom, one at the head of the team and the other holding back the canvas top. Her guard gripped her arm, and peered about through the darkness.

"Isn't Ned here yet?"

"Yes, all right," answered a muffled voice to the left. "I just came out; here are the grips and other things."

"Sure you cleaned up everything?"

"Never left a pin; here, Moore, pass them up inside."

"And about the note?"

"She wrote that, and pinned it on the pillow."

"Good, that will leave things in fine shape," he laughed. "I'd like to see Jim's face when he reads that, and the madder he gets the less he will know what to do."

"And you want us to stay?" asked the other doubtfully.

"Stay—of course; I am going to stay myself. It is the only way to divert suspicion. Good Lord, man, if we all disappeared at once they would know easy enough what had happened. Don't you ever believe Westcott is that kind of a fool. More than that—there will be no safety for us now until we get him out of the way; he knows too much. Whereas your fat friend—old money-bags?"

"He thought it best to keep out of it; he's back inside."

"I imagined so; this sort of thing is not in his line. All ready, Joe?"

The man at the wagon muttered some response.

"Then up you go, miss; here, put your foot on the wheel; give her a lift, will you?"

Anxious to escape further indignities, and comprehending the uselessness of any further struggle, with a man on either side of her, Miss Donovan silently clambered into the wagon, and seated herself on a wide board, evidently arranged for that purpose. The fellow who had held back the top followed, and snuggled into the seat beside her. She noticed now he held a gun in his hand, which he deposited between his knees. The leader drew back the flap of canvas endeavouring to peer into the dark interior.

"All set?"

"Sure."

"Well, keep awake, Joe, and mind what I told yer. Now, Moore, up with you, and drive like hell; you must be in the bad lands before daylight."

A fellow clambered to the seat in front, his figure outlined against the sky, and picked up the reins. Those within could hear the shuffling of the horses' feet as though they were eager to be off. The driver leaned forward.

"Whoa, there, now; quiet, Jerry. Did you say I was to take the ridge road?"

"You bet; it's all rock and will leave no trail. Take it easy and quiet until you are beyond Hennessey's ranch, and then give them the whip."

The next moment they were under way, slowly advancing through the darkness.

CHAPTER XVII
IN THE SHOSHONE DESERT

Her guard spoke no word as the wagon rolled slowly onward, but she judged that he leaned back against the bow supporting the canvas in an effort to make himself as comfortable as possible. She could see nothing of the fellow in the darkness, but had formed an impression that he was of medium size, his face covered with a scraggly beard. The driver sat bundled up in formless perspective against the line of sky, but she knew from his voice that he was the man who had first accosted her. In small measure this knowledge afforded some degree of courage, for he had then appeared less brutal, more approachable than the others. Perhaps she might lead him to talk, once they were alone together, and thus learn the purpose of this outrage.

Yet deep down in her mind she felt little doubt of the object in view, or who were involved. Excited as she was, and frightened, the girl was still composed enough to grasp the nature of her surroundings, and she had time now, as the wagon rumbled forward, to think over all that had been said, and fit it into the circumstances.

Moreover she had recognised another voice—although the speaker had kept out of sight, and spoken only in disguised, rumbling tones—that of Ned Beaton. The fact of his presence alone served to make the affair reasonably clear. The telegram stolen from her room by Miss La Rue had led to this action. They had suspected her before, but that had served to confirm their suspicions, and as soon as it had been shown to Enright, he had determined to place her where she would be helpless to interfere with their plans.

But what did they propose doing with her? The question caused her blood to run cold. That these people were desperate she had every reason to believe; they were battling for big stakes: not even murder had hitherto stood in their way? Why then, should they hesitate to take her life, if they actually deemed it necessary to the final success of their plans? She remembered what Beaton had said about her room—the condition in which it had been left. It was not all clear, yet it was clear enough, that they had taken every precaution to make her sudden disappearance appear natural. They had removed all her things, and left a note behind in womanly handwriting to explain her hurried departure. There was a master criminal mind, watchful of every detail, behind this conspiracy. He was guarding against every possibility of rescue.

The driver began to use his whip and urge the team forward, the wagon pounding along over the rough road at a rate which compelled the girl to hang on closely to keep her seat. The man beside her bounced about, and swore, but made no effort to touch her, or open conversation. The uncertainty, the fear engendered by her thought, the drear silence almost caused her to scream. She conquered this, yet could remain speechless no longer.

"Where are you taking me?" she asked suddenly.

There was no reply, and she stared toward her silent companion, unable to even perceive his outlines. His silence sent a thrill of anger through her, and she lost control. Her hand gripped the coarse shirt-sleeve in determination to compel him to speak.

"Answer me or I'll scream!"

He chuckled grimly, not in the least alarmed.

"Little good that'll do yer now, young woman," he said gruffly, and the driver turned his head at the sound, "unless yer voice will carry five miles or so; where are we now, Matt?"

"Comin' down ter the Big Slough," answered the other, expectorating over the wheel, and flickering a horse with his whip-lash. "'Twouldn't do no harm now ter fasten back the canvas, Joe; maybe she'd feel a bit more ter home that away."

There was a good-natured drawl to the voice which had a tendency to hearten the girl. The driver seemed human, sympathetic: perhaps he would respond to questioning. The other merely grunted, and began to unloosen the cover. She leaned forward, and addressed the rounded back of the fellow in front.

"Are you Mr. Moore?"

He wheeled partly about, surprised into acknowledgment.

"Well, I ain't heered the mister part fer some time, but my name's Matt Moore, though, how the hell did you know it?"

"The other man called you by name—don't you remember? Besides I had heard about you before."

"Well, I'll be damned. Do yer hear that, Joe? Who told yer 'bout me?"

"Mr. Westcott; he mentioned you as being one of the men who attacked him in the hotel office yesterday. He said you were one of Lacy's men. So when I heard your name mentioned to-night I knew in whose hands I had fallen. Was the brute who ordered you about Bill Lacy?"

"I reckon it was, miss," doubtfully. "It don't make no difference, does it, Joe?"

"Not as I kin see," growled the other. "Leastwise, her knowin' thet much. 'Tain't likely to do her no good, whichever way the cat jumps. I reckon I'll have a smoke, Matt; I'm dry as a fish."

"Same here; 'bout an hour till daylight, I reckon, Joe; pass the terbacco after yer light up."

The glow of the match gave her swift view of the man's face; it was strange and by no means reassuring, showing hard, repulsive, the complexion as dark as an Indian's, the eyes bold and a bit bloodshot from drink. Meeting her glance, he grinned unpleasantly.

"I don't pose fer no lady's man, like Matt," he said sneeringly, the match flaring between his fingers. "That's what Bill sent me 'long fer, 'cause he know'd I'd 'tend ter business, an' not talk too much."

"Your name is Joe?"

"Out yere—yes; Joe Sikes, if it pleases yer eny ter know. Yer might call me Mr. Sikes, if yer want ter be real polite."

He passed the tobacco-bag up to Moore, who thrust the reins under him while deliberately filling his pipe, the team trotting quietly along what seemed to be a hard road. The wagon lurched occasionally, as the wheels struck a stone, but the night was still so dark, the girl could perceive little of their surroundings in spite of the looped-up curtains. There seemed to be a high ridge of earth to their right, crowned by a fringe of low trees, but everything appeared indistinct and desolate. Outside the rumble of their own progress the silence was profound.

"And you will not tell me where we are going?" she insisted, "or what you propose doing with me?"

The pipe-glow revealed Sikes's evil countenance; Moore resumed his reins, and there was the sharp swish of a whip lash.

"'Twouldn't mean nuthin' ter yer if I did," said the former finally, after apparently turning the matter over slowly in his mind. "Yer don't know nuthin' 'bout this country. 'Tain't no place a tenderfoot like you kin find yer way back frum; so, as fer as I see, thar ain't nuthin' fer yer to do but just naturally wait till we takes yer back."

"I am to be held a prisoner—indefinitely?"

"I reckon so; not that I knows enything 'bout the programme, miss; but that's 'bout the understandin' that Matt an' I has—ain't it, Matt?"

The driver turned his head, and nodded.

"Sure; we're just ter take keer of yer till he comes."

"Lacy?"

"Er—some word from him, miss. It might not be safe for him to come himself. Yer see," apologetically, "I don't just know what the game is, and Bill might want to skip out before you was turned loose. I knowed wunst when he was gone eight months, an' nobody knowed where he was—do yer mind thet time, Joe, after he shot up Medicine Lodge? Well, I reckon thar must be some big money in this job, an' he won't take no chance of gettin' pinched. That seems to be the trouble, miss—you've sorter stuck yerself in whar it warn't none o' yer business. Thet's what got Lacy down on yer."

"Yes; but what is it to you, and—and Mr. Sikes, here?"

Matt grinned.

"Nuthin' much ter me, or ter—ter Mr. Sikes—how's it sound, Joe?—'cept maybe a slice o' coin. Still there's reason fer us both ter jump when Bill Lacy whistles. Enyhow thar ain't no use a talkin' 'bout it, fer we've got ter do what we're told. So let's shut up."

"You say you do not know what this all means?"

"No, an' what's more, we don't give a damn."

"But if I told you it was robbery and murder——that you were aiding in the commission of crime!"

"It wouldn't make a plum bit o' difference, ma'm," said Sikes deliberately, "we never reckoned it wus enything else—so yer might just as well stop hollerin', fer yer goin' whar we take yer, an' ye'll stay thar till Bill Lacy says yer ter go. Hit 'em up, Matt; I'm plum' tired of talkin'."

The grey dawn came at last, spectral and ghastly, gradually yielding glimpse of the surroundings. They were travelling steadily south, the horses beginning to exhibit traces of weariness, yet still keeping up a dogged trot. All about extended a wild, desolate scene of rock and sand, bounded on every horizon by barren ridges. The only vegetation was sage brush, while the trail, scarcely visible to the eye, would circle here and there among grotesque formations, and occasionally seemed to disappear altogether. Nowhere was there slightest sign of life—no bird, no beast, no snake even, crossed their path. All was dead, silent, stricken with desolation. The spires and chimneys of rock, ugly and distorted in form, assumed strange shapes in the grey dusk. It was all grey wherever the eyes turned; grey of all shades, grey sand, grey rocks, grey over-arching sky, relieved only by the soft purple of the sage—a picture of utter loneliness, of intense desolation, which was a horror. The eye found nothing to rest upon—no landmark, no distant tree, no gleam of water, no flash of colour—only that dull monotony of drab, motionless, and with no apparent end.

Stella stared about at it, and closed her eyes, unable to bear the sight; her head drooped wearily, every nerve giving away before the depressing scene outspread in every direction. Sikes, watching her slightest movement, seemed to sense the meaning of the action.

"Hell, ain't it?" he said expressively. "You know whar we are?"

"No; but I never before dreamed any spot could be so terrible."

"This is the Shoshone desert; thar ain't nobody ever comes in yere 'cept wunst in a while a prospector, maybe, er a band o' cattle rustlers. Even the Injuns keep out."

She lifted her eyes again, shuddering as they swept about over the dismal waste.

"But there is a trail; you could not become lost?"

"Well, yer might call it a trail, tho' thar ain't much left of it after a sand storm. I reckon thar ain't so many as could follow it any time o' year, but Matt knows the way all right—you don't need to worry none about that. He's drove many a load along yere—hey, Matt?"

"You bet; I've got it all marked out, the same as a pilot on the Missouri. Ye see that sway-back ridge yonder?" pointing with his whip into the distance ahead. "That's what I'm headin' for now an' when I git thar a round rock will show up down a sorter gully. Furst time I came over yere long with Lacy, I wrote all these yere things down."

Conversation ceased, the drear depression of the scene resting heavily on the minds of all three. Moore sat humped shapelessly in his seat, permitting the horses to toil on wearily, the wagon rumbling along across the hard packed sand, the wheels leaving scarcely a mark behind. Sikes stared gloomily out on his side, the rifle still between his knees, his jaws working vigorously on a fresh chew of tobacco. Stella looked at the two men, their faces now clearly revealed in the brightening dawn, but the survey brought little comfort. Sikes was evidently of wild blood—a half-breed, if his swarthy skin and high cheek bones meant any characteristics of race— scarcely more than a savage by nature, and rendered even more decadent by the ravages of drink. He was sober enough now, but this only left him the more morose and sullen, his bloodshot eyes ugly and malignant. The girl shrank from him as a full realisation of what the man truly was came to her with this first distinct view.

Moore was a much younger man, his face roughened, and tanned, to almost the colour of mahogany, yet somehow retaining a youthful look. He was not unprepossessing in a bold, daring way; a fellow who would seek adventure, and meet danger with a laugh. He turned as she looked at him, and grinned back at her, pointing humorously to a badly discoloured eye.

"Friend o' yours gave me that," he admitted, quite as a matter of course. "Did a good job, too."

"A friend of mine?" in surprise.

"Sure; you're a friend o' Jim Westcott, ain't yer? Lacy said so, and Jim's the laddy-buck who whaled me."

"Mr. Westcott! When?"

"Last night. You see it was this way. I caught him hanging round the office at La Rosita, an' we had a fight. I don't just know what I did to him, but that's part o' what he did to me. I never knowed much about him afore, but he's sure some scrapper; an' I had a knife in my fist, too."

"Then—then," her breath choking her, "he got away?"

Moore laughed, no evidence of animosity in his actions.

"I reckon so, miss. I ain't seen nuthin' of him since, an' the way Bill Lacy wus cussing when I got breathin' straight agin would 'a' shocked a coyote. He'll git him, though."

"Get him?"

"Sure—Bill will. He always gets his man. I've seen more'n one fellow try to put something over on Lacy, but it never worked in the end. He's hell on the trigger, an' the next time he and Bill come together, Westcott's bound to get his. Ain't that the truth, Joe?"

Sikes nodded his head, a gleam of appreciation in his eyes.

"I'd like fer to see the scrap," he said slowly. "They tell me Westcott ain't so slow on the draw—but Bill will get him!"

The sun rose a red ball of fire, colouring the ridges of sand, and painting the grotesque rocks with crimson streamers. As it ascended higher into the pale blue of the sky the heat-waves began to sweep across the sandy waste. In the shadow of a bald cliff the wagon was halted briefly, and the two men brought forth materials from within, making a hasty fire, and preparing breakfast. Water was given the team also, before the journey was resumed; while during the brief halt the girl was left to do as she pleased. Then they moved on again, surrounded by the same drear landscape, the very depression of it keeping them silent. Sikes nodded sleepily, his head against a wagon bow. Once Moore roused up, pointing into the distance with one hand.

"What do yer make o' that out thar?" he asked sharply. "'Tain't a human, is it?"

Sikes straightened up with a start, and stared blankly in the direction indicated. Apparently he could perceive nothing clearly, for he reached back into the wagon-box, and drew forth a battered field-glass, quickly adjusting it to his eyes. Stella's keener vision made out a black, indistinct figure moving against the yellow background of a far away sand-ridge, and she stood up, clinging to Moore's seat, to gain a better view. Sikes got the object in focus.

"Nothin' doing," he announced. "It's travellin' on four legs—a b'ar, likely, although I never afore heard of a b'ar being in yere."

They settled down to the same monotony, mile after mile. The way became rockier with less sand, but with no more evidence of life. A high cliff rose menacingly to their right, bare of the slightest trace of vegetation, while in the opposite direction the plain assumed a dead level, mirages appearing occasionally in the far distance. Far away ahead a strange buttress of rock rose into the sky resembling the turret of a huge castle. The sun was directly overhead when Moore turned his team suddenly to the left, and drove down a sharp declivity leading into a ravine.

"Drop the canvas, Joe," he said shortly, "there's only 'bout a mile more."

CHAPTER XVIII
IN MEXICAN POWER

The passage was so narrow, and so diversified by sharp turns, that Miss Donovan, shut in behind the closed cover, could perceive little of its nature. Apparently the ravine was a mere gash in the surface of the desert plain, to be originally discovered purely through accident. One might pass a hundred yards to either side, and never realise its existence, the hard rock, covered by a thin layer of sand, retaining no trace of wheel-marks in guidance. How Moore had ever driven so unerringly to the spot was a mystery. Yet he had done so, and now the team was slowly creeping down the narrow ledge utilised as a road, the slipping wheels securely locked, as they drifted here and there about the sharp corners, ever descending into the unknown depths.

The cliffs arose precipitously on either side, absolutely bare. To the left nothing could be seen but black rock, but on the other side an open space yawned, perhaps twenty feet across, its bottom imperceptible. The horses stumbled over the rough stones, held only by Moore's firm grip on the reins, and the light began to fade as they descended. At last nothing appeared above but a narrow strip of sky, and the glimmer of sun had totally vanished. Almost at the same moment the driver released the creaking brake, and at a trot the wagon swept forward between two pinnacles of rock, and came out into an open valley.

The transition was so sudden and startling as to cause the girl to give utterance to a cry of surprise. She had been clinging desperately to the seat in front, expecting every instant to be hurled headlong. Intense fear gripped her and it seemed as if every drop of blood in her veins stood still. The change was like a leap into fairy land; as though they had emerged from the mouth of hell into the beauty of paradise. They were in a green, watered valley, a clear stream wandering here and there through its centre, shadowed by groves of trees. All about, as far as eye could reach, stood great precipices, their bold, rugged fronts rising hundreds of feet, unbroken, and unscalable; the sun directly above bathed these with showers of gold, and cast a blanket of colour across the sheltered valley.

This valley itself was nearly square, possibly extending not over a mile in either direction, merely a great hole rimmed by desert, a strange, hidden oasis, rendered fertile and green by some outburst of fresh water from the rocks. Emerging upon it in midst of the barren desolation through which they had been toiling for hours, blinded by alkali dust, jolted down that dangerous decline, it seemed like some beautiful dream, a fantasy of imagination.

Miss Donovan doubted the evidence of her own eyes, half convinced that she slept. It was Moore's voice which aroused her.

"Mendez must have got back, Joe," he said eagerly. "There are horses and cattle over yonder."

The other pushed up the canvas and looked out.

"That's right. Must just got here, or there'd 'a' been a guard up above. The fellow is comin' now—see?"

He was loping along carelessly, Mexican from high hat to jingling spurs, sitting the saddle as though moulded there, a young fellow, dark faced, but with a livid scar along one cheek.

"Juan Cateras, the little devil," muttered Sikes, as the rider drew nearer. "There's some pot brewing if he is in it."

The rider drew up his horse, and lifted his hat, his smiling lips revealing a row of white teeth.

"A pleasant day, *señor*," he said graciously, his dark eyes searching the faces of the two men, and then dwelling with interest on the woman. "Ah, your pardon, *señorita*; your presence is more than welcome here." He rested one hand on the wagon box, the expression of his face hardening. "Yet an explanation might not be out of place—the Señor Mendez may not be pleased."

"We came under orders from Lacy," replied Moore confidently. "You have seen us both before."

"True, but not the lady; you will tell me about her?"

Sikes climbed down over the wheel.

"It is like this, *señor*," he began. "Lacy did not know your party was here; he thought you were all south for another month yet. He would keep this girl quiet, out of the way for a time. She is from New York, and knows too much."

"From New York?" The quick eyes of the Mexican again sought her face. "She is to be held prisoner?"

"Yes, *señor*."

"Again the case of that man Cavendish?"

"We were not told, only ordered to bring her here and guard her until we heard otherwise. It was not known you were back."

"We came three hours ago; you see what we brought," with a wave of the hand. "All was clear above?"

"Not a sign; I searched with field-glasses."

"Then I will ride with you to Mendez; 'tis well to have the matter promptly over with."

The wagon, rumbled on, Moore urging the wearied team with whip and voice to little result. Sikes remained on foot, glad of the change, striding along in front, while the Mexican rode beside the wheel, his equipment jingling, the sunlight flashing over his bright attire. He made a rather gallant figure, of which he was fully conscious, glancing frequently aside into the shadow beneath the canvas top to gain glimpse of its occupant. At last their eyes met, and he could no longer forbear speech, his English expression a bit precise.

"Pardon, *señorita*, I would be held your friend," he murmured, leaning closer, "for it is ever a misfortune to incur the enmity of Señor Lacy. You will trust me?"

"But," she ventured timidly, "I do not know you, *señor*; who you may be."

"You know Señor Mendez?"

She shook her head negatively.

"'Tis strange! Yet I forget you come from New York. They know him here on this border. If you ask these men they will tell you. Even Señor Lacy takes his orders from Pascual Mendez. He care not who he kill, who he fight—some day it come his turn, and then he liberate Mexico—see? The day is not yet, but it will come."

"You mean he is a revolutionist?"

"He hate; he live to hate; to revenge the wrong. Twice already he lead the people, but they fail him—the cowards. He return here where it is safe: yet the right time will come."

"But you, *señor*?"

"I am his lieutenant—Juan Cateras," and he bowed low, "and I ride now to tell him of his guest."

She watched him as he spurred forward, proud of his horsemanship, and making every effort to attract her attention. Moore turned in his seat, and grinned.

"Some tin soldier," he said sneeringly, "that's a feller I always wanted ter kick, an' some day I'm a goin' ter do it."

"You heard what he said?"

"Sure; he was tellin' yer 'bout old Mendez being a Mexican revolutionary leader down in Mex, wa'n't he? Hell of a leader he is! I reckon he's been mixed up in scrapes enough down thar, but they had mighty little to do with revolutin'. He's just plain bad man, miss—cattle thief, an' all round outlaw. There's a price on his head in three States, but nobody dares go after it, because of the dangerous gang he controls."

Her eyes sought the distant figure doubtfully.

"And this man—this Juan Cateras—what of him?"

"One of the devil's own imps; I'd a heap rather play with a rattlesnake than him." He paused, to assure him self that Sikes was safely out of hearing. "I thought maybe I better tell yer while I had a chance. That fellar is plumb pisen, miss."

She reached out her hand, and touched him.

"Thank you," she said gratefully, "I—I am glad you did. Am—am I to be left here with these—these men?"

"No, not exactly. I suppose they'll naturally sorter expect to run things while they're here, fer this yere valley is their camp, Mendez has been hidin' out yere fer some time. But Joe and I are goin' to stay, and even old Mendez ain't liable to make no enemy outer Bill Lacy. They had a row wunst, an' I reckon they don't neither of 'em want another. I ain't greatly afeerd o' Mendez, but I wouldn't put nuthin' past this Cateras lad, if he got some hell idea in his head. He's Injun-Mex, an' that's the worst kind."

The wagon lurched down a steep bank, splashed its way across the narrow stream, and up the other side, the horses straining in their harness to the sharp snap of the driver's whip. A towering precipice of rock confronted them, and at its very foot stood two cabins of log construction, so closely resembling their stone background as to be almost imperceptible, at the distance of a few yards. Sikes leaned on his rifle waiting, and as Moore halted the panting team, and leaped over the wheel to the ground, Cateras came forth from one of the open doors and crossed the intervening space on foot. He was smoking a cigarette, the blue wreath of smoke circling above his head in the still air.

"The lady is to be placed in my care," he said almost insolently. "Your hand, *señorita*."

Miss Donovan hesitated, the memory of Moore's words of warning yet ringing in her ears. The handsome face, with its smiling lips and eyes, suddenly appeared to her a mask assumed to conceal the unclean soul behind. Moore broke the silence with a protest.

"In your care, *señor*? The girl is here as prisoner to Bill Lacy."

"So I told Mendez," he said indifferently. "But he is in ill humour this morning, and took small interest in the affair. It was only when I promised to take full charge that he consented to your remaining at all. 'Tis my advice that you let well enough alone. You know who rules here."

"If there is evil done, the debt will be paid."

Cateras laughed, one hand at his incipient moustache.

"Billy Lacy, you mean, no doubt. That is a matter for him to settle with Mendez. It is not my affair, for I only obey my chief. However, *señors*, 'tis no evil that is contemplated, only we prefer guarding the secrets of this valley ourselves. That is what angers Mendez, the fact that Lacy uses this rendezvous as a prison during our absence. We found one here when we returned—guarded by an American. Now you come with another. *Caramba!* You think we stand this quietly? How do we know what may result from such acts? What sheriff's posse may be on your trail? Bill Lacy! *Dios!* if Bill Lacy would make prisoners, let him keep them somewhere else than here. Mendez takes no prisoners—he knows a better way than doing things like that."

"But, *señor*, this is a woman."

"Of which I am well aware," bowing gallantly. "Otherwise I should not have interfered, and offered my services. But we have talked enough. You have had the word, and you know the law of our compact. Do you obey me, or shall I call the chief—God be merciful to your soul, if I do."

Moore stood silent, realising the full meaning of the threat; he glanced aside at Sikes, but that individual only shook his head.

"All right then," went on the Mexican sharply. "'Tis well you show sense. You know what to do with your team; then the both of you report to Casas at the upper camp—you know him?"

"Yes, *señor*."

"Tell him I sent you. He will have his orders; they are that you be shot if you attempt to leave before Mendez gives the word. 'Tis not long now till we learn who is chief here—Bill Lacy or Pascual Mendez. Come, *señorita*, you are safe with me."

Concealing a dread that was almost overpowering, yet realising the impossibility of resistance, Stella permitted him to touch her hand, and assist her to clamber over the wheel. The baffled, helpless rage in Moore's face was sufficient proof of the true power possessed by Cateras, that his was no idle boast. Under some conditions the change in captors might have been welcomed—certainly she felt no desire to remain in the hands of the two who had brought her there, for Sikes, plainly enough, was a mere drunken brute, and Moore, while of somewhat finer fibre, lacked the courage and manhood to ever develop into a true friend.

Yet she would have infinitely preferred such as these—men, at least, of her own race—to this smirking Mexican, hiding his devilish instincts behind a pretence at gallantry. She knew him, now, understood him, felt convinced, indeed, that this was all some cunning scheme originating within his own brain. He had hastened ahead to Mendez; told a tale in his own way, rendering the chief's suspicions of Lacy more acute, and thus gaining permission to assume full charge. Her only hope was to go herself into the presence of the leader, and make a plea to him face to face. Moore was already at the horses' heads, and was turning them about in the trail. Cateras, smiling, pressed her arm with his fingers.

"This way, *señorita*."

"Wait," and her eyes met his, showing no sign of fear. "You take me, I presume, to Señor Mendez?"

"Of what need?" in surprise. "He has already placed me in charge."

"Yet without hearing a word as to why I am here," indignantly. "I am an American woman, and you will yet pay dearly for this outrage. I demand an interview with the chief, and refuse to go with you until it is granted."

"You refuse! Ha!" and he burst into laughter. "Why, what power have you got, you little fool? Do you know where you are? What fear do we have of your damn Americanos. None!" and he snapped his fingers derisively. "We spit on the dogs. I will show you—come!"

He gripped her shoulder in his lean hand, his eyes glaring into her face savagely. The grasp hurt, and a sudden anger spurred her to action. With a quick twist she freed herself, and, scarcely knowing how it was done, snatched the heavy driver's whip from Moore's hand. The next instant, before the astounded Mexican could even throw up an arm in defence, the infuriated girl struck, the stinging lash raising a red welt across the swarthy cheek. Cateras staggered back, his lips giving utterance to a curse.

Again she struck, but this time his fingers gripped the leather, and tore it from her hands, with sufficient force to send her to her knees. With a spring forward the man had her in his grasp, all tiger now, the pretence at gentleness forgotten. He jerked her to her feet, with fingers clutching her neck mercilessly.

"Here, Silva, Merodez," he cried, "come take this spitfire. *Caramba*! we'll teach her."

Two men ran from between the huts and Cateras flung her, helpless from her choking, into their grasp.

"Take her within—no, there; the second door, you fools."

Breathless from effort, a mere child in their grip, Miss Donovan struggled vainly. They forced her through the door, and Cateras, still cursing furiously followed, the whip in his hands.

CHAPTER XIX
WESTCOTT FINDS HIMSELF ALONE

It never occurred to Westcott on his escape through the darkness that his night's adventure would in any way endanger Miss Donovan. He was on the property of La Rosita Mining Company upon his own account, and not in reference to the Cavendish Case at all—or, at least, this last was merely incidental.

To be sure he had listened to a confession from Enright bearing directly upon the affair in New York, a confession so strange he could scarcely grasp its true meaning. But this never brought to his mind the thought that suspicion already rested upon the girl's presence in Haskell. His whole interest centred for the moment on Lacy's daring attempt to break through the wall of rock below and lay claim to his lead of ore. Not until this effort had been abandoned would he dare to desert his mine—and even then safety could be assured only by the establishment of an armed guard in the tunnel prepared to repel any invasion.

While undoubtedly the mining law of the State would eventually sustain his claim, yet the fact that he had for so long kept his discovery secret would seriously operate against him; while, if Lacy's gang once acquired actual possession of the property, the only way of proving prior ownership would be through an official survey and long protracted proceedings in court.

Here he would be at great disadvantage because of lack of money and influence. In this respect Westcott realised, fully what he was up against, for while it was quietly known that Lacy was a questionable character, his name associated with the leadership of a desperate gang, yet his wealth and power rendered him a decidedly dangerous opponent. As proprietor of the biggest saloon, dance-hall, and gambling den in Haskell, he wielded an influence not to be ignored—especially as the sheriff of the county was directly indebted to him for his office. A dangerous man himself, with the reputation of a killer, he had about him others capable of any crime to carry out his orders, confident that his wealth and influence would assure their safety. To such as he the stealing of a mine was a mere incident.

This was the situation confronting Westcott as he crouched behind a rock on the black hillside, endeavouring to decide upon a course of action. The events of the last few hours had almost entirely forced aside memory of the girl at the hotel—and her mission. He was fighting now for his own life, his own future—and fighting alone. The blade of Moore's knife had slashed his forearm, in the early moments of their fierce struggle, and blood was trickling down his wrist, yet not in sufficient quantity to give him any great concern. Once beyond the probability of pursuit, he turned up his sleeve and made some effort to minister to the gash, satisfying himself quickly that it was of trivial nature.

From where he lay he could see across the bare, rock-strewn hillside to the distant hut, outlined by the gleam of light within, and perceive the black silhouette of the shaft-house. The sound of clanking machinery reached his ears, but the voices of the men failed to carry so far. He could dimly distinguish their figures as they passed in and out of the glare of light, and was aware that Moore had been found and carried within the hut, but remained ignorant of the fact that the leaving of a knife in the window had revealed his identity. There was no attempt at pursuit, which gave him confidence that Lacy failed to comprehend the importance of what had been overheard, yet he clung closely to his hiding-place until all the men had re-entered the office.

However, he was too wary to approach the window again, fearing some trap, but crept cautiously along the slope of the hill through the black shadows until he attained safe shelter close in against the dump. His hope was that Enright's arguments would induce Lacy to discontinue operations for the present and thus give him time in which to prepare for resistance. In this he was not disappointed. What took place within the office could only be guessed at, but in less than half an hour a man emerged from the open door and hailed the fellows at work in the shaft-house. The messenger stood in the full glare of light, revealing to the silent watcher the face and figure of Moore, convincing evidence that this worthy had not been seriously injured during the late encounter.

"Hey, Tom!" he shouted.

The lantern above was waved out over the edge of the timbered platform and a deep voice responded.

"Well, what'che want?"

"Send word down to the boys to come up. They're laid off fer a while, an' their pay's ready for 'em."

"Lay 'em off! Who says so?"

"Lacy, of course; hustle them out now—them's the orders."

"Well, that beats hell!" But the lantern vanished as he went grumbling back to his engine.

They came up, talking excitedly among themselves, stumbled down the rough path, and filed into the open door of the lighted office. There were twenty of them, according to Westcott's count, and the interview within must have been satisfactory as they departed quietly enough, disappearing down the trail toward Haskell. Moore remained outside, apparently checking the fellows off as they passed, and when the last one vanished again hailed the shaft-house:

"What's the matter with you, Tom? Why don't you close down and come and get your stuff?"

"You want me too?"

"Sure—we're here waitin' fer yer."

Westcott clung to his hiding-place, but greatly relieved in mind. This unexpected action had postponed his struggle and left him free to plan for defence. For the first time almost his brain grasped the full significance of this movement, its direct connection with the disappearance of Frederick Cavendish, and the presence of Stella Donovan. Enright had suggested and urged the closing down of the mine temporarily to avoid unnecessary publicity—to throw Westcott off the trail. His argument must have been a powerful one to thus influence Lacy—nothing less than a pledge of money could cause the latter to forego immediate profit.

Undoubtedly the lawyer had convinced the man of the certainty of their gaining possession of the Cavendish fortune, and had offered him a goodly share for his assistance. Then the plan was at a head—if Cavendish was not dead he was safely in their hands, where his death could be easily accomplished, if other means failed.

This was to be Lacy's part of the bargain, and he was already too deeply involved in the hellish conspiracy to withdraw. Enright, with his lawyer-astuteness, had seen to that—had even got this Western gambler securely into his grip and put on the screws. The miner, realising now the full situation, or, at least, imagining that he did, smiled grimly and waited in his covert on the hillside for the conspirators to make their next move. He dare not approach the cabin any closer, or permit his presence to become known, for Moore was kept outside the door on guard. However, the delay was not a long one, horses being brought up from the near-by corral, and the entire party mounting rode down the trail toward Haskell. The cabin was left dark and deserted, the mine silent. Westcott made no effort to follow, feeling assured that no important movement would be attempted that night.

It was late the next morning before he rode into Haskell and, stabling his horse, which bore all the marks of hard riding, proceeded toward the Timmons House. He had utilised, as best he could, the hours since that cavalcade had departed from La Rosita to put his own affairs in order so that he might feel free to camp on the conspirators' trail and risk all in an effort to rescue Cavendish. The night had been a hard one, but Westcott was still totally unconscious of fatigue—his whole thought centred on his purpose.

Alone he had explored the tunnels in Lacy's mine, creeping about in the darkness, guided only by the flash of an electric torch, until he thoroughly understood the nature of the work being accomplished. As soon as dawn came he sought two reliable men in the valley below, and posted them as guards over his own property; but, before he finally rode away, the three brought forth the body of the murdered Mexican and reverently buried it on a secluded spot of the bleak hillside.

Then, convinced that every precaution had been taken, Westcott turned his horse's head toward Haskell. As he rode slowly up the street in the bright sunlight his mind reverted to Stella Donovan. The stern adventures of the night had temporarily driven the girl from his thoughts, but now the memory returned, and her bright, womanly face arose before him, full of allurement. He seemed to look once more into the wonderful depths of her eyes and to feel the fascination of her smile. Eager for the greeting, which he felt assured awaited him, he strode through the open door into the office. The room was vacant, but as he crossed the floor toward the desk the proprietor entered through the opening leading into the barroom beyond. Timmons had quite evidently been drinking more than usual—the effect being largely disclosed by loquacity of speech.

"Hello, Jim!" he cried at sight of the other. "Thought you'd be back, but, damn it, yer too late—she's—she's gone; almighty pretty girl, too. I told the boys it was a blame shame fer her ter run off thataway."

"Who has run off?" And Westcott's hand crushed down on the man's shoulder with a force that half-sobered him. "What are you talking about?"

"Me! Let up, will yer? Yer was here hopin' ter see that New York girl, wasn't yer?"

"Miss Donovan? Yes."

"I'd forgot her name. Well, she ain't yere—she's left."

"Left—gone from town?"

"Sure; skipped out sudden in the night; took the late train East, I reckon. Never sed no word to nobody—just naturally packed up her duds an' hiked."

Westcott drew a deep breath.

"Surely you do not mean she left without any explanation? She must have paid her bill."

"Oh, she was square enough—sure. She left money an' a note pinned to her pillow; sed she'd just got a message callin' her back home—want ter see whut she wrote?"

"You bet I do, Timmons! Have you got the note here?"

Timmons waddled around behind the desk and ran his hand into a drawer. Evidently he considered the matter a huge joke, but Westcott snatched the paper from his fingers impatiently and eagerly read the few hastily penciled lines:

Have received a message calling me East at once. Shall take the night train, and enclose sufficient money to pay for my entertainment.

S. D.

He stared at the words, a deep crease between his eyes. It was a woman's handwriting, and at first glance there was nothing impossible in such an action on her part. Yet it was strange, if she had departed so suddenly, without leaving any message for him. After that meeting at the bridge, and the understanding between them, it didn't seem to Westcott at all probable that she would thus desert without some plausible explanation. His eyes narrowed with aroused suspicion as he looked up from the slip of paper and confronted the amused Timmons across the desk.

"I'll keep this," he said soberly, folding it and thrusting it into his pocket.

"All right"—and Timmons smiled blandly—"I got the money."

"And that was all, was it—just this note and the cash? There was nothing addressed to me?"

The hotel-keeper shook his head.

"When did you see her last?"

"'Bout nine o'clock, I reckon; she come down inter the dinin'-room fer a drink o' water."

"She said nothing then about going away?"

"She didn't speak to nobody—just got a swig an' went up-stairs agin."

"How much longer were you up?"

"Oh, maybe an hour; there was some boys playing poker here an' I waited round till they quit."

"No message for Miss Donovan up to that time?"

"No."

"You left the door unlocked?"

"Sure; them New York fellers was both out. I oughter waited till they come in, maybe, but I was plum' tired out."

"When did they come back?"

"Oh, 'bout midnight, I reckon. Bill Lacy an' Matt Moore was along with 'em. They didn't disturb me none; just went inter the sample-room, an' slept on the floor. I found 'em thar in the mornin', and Bill told me how they come to be thar—leastwise 'bout himself, fer Moore had got up an' gone afore I got down."

"I see! And these New York people—they are still here?"

"They wus all three down ter breakfast; ain't seen nuthin' of 'em since; I reckon they're up-stairs somewhar."

"What became of Lacy?"

"He's down in his saloon; he sed if you showed up, an' asked fer him, ter tell yer that's whar he'd be."

"He told you that? He expected me to show up then?"

"I reckon as how he did," and Timmons grinned in drunken good humour. "He's pretty blame smart, Bill Lacy is; he most allars knows whut's goin' ter happen." He leaned over the desk and lowered his voice. "If yer do hunt him up, Jim," he said confidentially, "you better go heeled."

Westcott laughed. The first shock of the discovery of Miss Donovan's disappearance had passed, and he was himself again. He must have time to think and arrange some plan and, above all, must retain a clear mind and proceed coolly.

"All right, old man," he said easily. "I'll try and look out for myself. I haven't eaten yet to-day. What can you find for me in the larder?"

CHAPTER XX
TO COMPEL AN ANSWER

Although feeling the need of food, Westcott entered the dining-room of the Timmons' House more desirous of being alone than for any other purpose. He realised that he was suddenly brought face to face with a most serious condition, and one which must be solved unaided. He dare not venture upon a single step forward until he had first thought out carefully the entire course to be followed. Two lives, and perhaps three, including his own, were now in imminent peril, and any mistake on his part would prove most disastrous. First of all he must keep his own counsel. Not even the half-drunken Timmons could be allowed to suspect the real depth of his interest in this affair.

Fortunately, it was so late in the morning he was left undisturbed at a side table, screened from the open door leading into the office. Sadie, the waitress, took his order and immediately disappeared, leaving him to his own thoughts. These were far from happy ones, as his mind rapidly reviewed the situation and endeavoured to concentrate upon some practical plan of action.

So Bill Lacy expected him? Had left word where he was to be found? What was the probable meaning of this? Westcott did not connect this message directly with the strange disappearance of Miss Donovan. Whether or not Lacy was concerned in that outrage had nothing to do with this, for the man could scarcely be aware of his deep interest in the girl. No, this must be his own personal affair, complicated by the case of Cavendish. Moore must have recognised him during their fight, and reported to his master who it was that had been discovered listening at the window. Realising the nature of that conversation, Lacy naturally anticipated being sought the very moment Westcott came to town. That was what this meant. All right, he would hunt Lacy as soon as he was ready to do so; and, as Timmons suggested, would go "heeled."

But the girl? What had really become of the girl? There was no way of proving she had not gone East, for there was no agent at the station at that hour, and the night train could be halted by any one waving a signal light. Westcott drew the brief note from his pocket, smoothed out its creases and read the few words over again. The writing was unquestionably feminine, and he could recall seeing nothing Miss Donovan had ever indited, with which it could be compared. But would she have departed, however hurriedly, without leaving him some message? To be sure there had been little enough between them of intimacy or understanding; nothing he could really construe into a promise—yet he had given her complete trust, and had felt a friendly response. He could not compel himself to believe she would prove unfaithful. Unconsciously he still held the letter in his hand when the waitress came in with his breakfast. She glanced about to make certain they were alone and leaned over, her lips close to his ear.

"Is that the note they say that New York young lady left?"

"Yes, Sadie," in surprise. "Why?"

"Well, she never wrote it, Mr. Westcott," hurriedly placing the dishes before him, "that's all. Now don't yer say a word to anybody that I told yer; but she didn't go East at all; she wus took in a wagon down the desert road. I saw 'em take her."

"You saw them? Who?"

"Well, I don't just know that, 'cept it was Matt Moore's team, an' he wus drivin' it. I didn't see the others so es to be sure. Yer see us help sleep over the kitchen, an' 'bout one o'clock I woke up—here comes Timmons; he mustn't see me talkin' ter yer."

She flicked her napkin over the table, picked up an emptied dish and vanished through the swinging-doors. Timmons, however, merely came in searching for the Chinaman, and not finding the latter immediately, retired again to the office, without even addressing his guest, who was busily eating. Sadie peered in once more and, seeing all was clear, crossed over beside Westcott.

"Well, as I was sayin'," she resumed, "I thought I heard a noise outside, an' got up an' went to the winder. I couldn't see much, not 'nough so I could swear to nuthin'; but there was three or four men out there just across that little gully, you know, an' they had a woman with 'em. She didn't scream none, but she was tryin' ter git away; wunst she run, but they caught her. I didn't see no wagon then, it was behind the ridge, I reckon. After a while it drove off down the south trail, an' a little later three men come up them outside stairs back into the hotel. They was mighty still 'bout it, too."

"You couldn't tell who they were?"

"They wa'n't like nuthin' but shadders; it was a purty dark night."

"So it was, Sadie. Do you imagine Timmons had anything to do with the affair?"

"Timmons? Not him. There wa'n't no figure like his in that bunch; I'd know him in the dark."

"But the woman might not have been Miss Donovan; isn't there another young lady here from the East?"

Sadie tossed her head, but with her eyes cautiously fixed on the office door.

"Humph; you mean the peroxid blonde! She ain't no *lady*. Well, it wa'n't her, that's a cinch; she was down yere to breakfast, a laughin' an' gigglin' with them two men 'bout an hour ago. They seemed ter feel mighty good over something but I couldn't quite make out just what the joke was. Say, did yer ever hear tell of a Mexican named Mendez?"

"Well, rather; he's a cattle thief, or worse. Arizona has a big reward out for him, dead or alive."

"That's the gink, I bet yer; has he got a hang-out anywhar 'round this country?"

"Not so far as I know; in fact, I haven't heard the fellow's name mentioned for six months, or more. What makes you suspect this?"

Sadie leaned even closer, her voice trembling with excitement, evidently convinced that her information was of the utmost importance.

"For God's sake, Mr. Westcott," she whispered, "don't never tell anybody I told yer, but she was awful good ter me, an' that pasty-faced blonde makes me sick just ter look at her. You know the feller they call Enright, I reckon he's a lawyer."

Westcott nodded.

"Well, he was doin' most of the talkin', an' I was foolin' round the sideboard yonder, pretendin' ter clean it up. Nobody thought I was in ear distance, but I got hold ov a word now an' then. He kept tellin' 'em, 'specially the blonde, 'bout this Mexican, who's a friend of Bill Lacy, an' I judge has a place whar he hangs out with his gang somewhar in the big desert."

"Was anything said about Miss Donovan?"

"Not by name; they was too smart for that; but that was the direction Matt Moore drove off last night—there's Enright comin' down-stairs now; won't yer hav' some more cakes, sir?"

Westcott pushed back his chair and rose to his feet. He had extracted all the information the girl possessed, and had no wish to expose her to suspicion. There was no longer a doubt in his mind as to the fate of Miss Donovan. She had been forcibly abducted by this gang of thieves, and put where her knowledge could do them no harm. But where? The clue had been given him, but before it could be of any value he must learn more of this Mexican, Mendez. The name itself was familiar enough, for it was one often spoken along the border in connection with crime, but beyond this meant nothing to him. The fellow had always appeared a rather mythical character, but now became suddenly real. The marshal might know; if not, then he must choke the truth out of Lacy. Determined to make the effort, he muttered a swift word of thanks to Sadie and left the room.

Enright was not in the office, but had evidently merely passed through and gone out. Timmons was sound asleep in a chair by the window, oblivious to any ordinary noise. From the open doorway Westcott took careful survey Of the street, adjusting his belt so that the butt of his revolver was more convenient to the hand. He had no conception that his coming interview with Lacy was to be altogether a pleasant one, and realised fully the danger confronting him.

Very few of the citizens of Haskell were abroad, although a small group were ornamenting the platform in front of Healey's saloon opposite. At that moment the little marshal, his broad-brimmed hat cocked over one eye, emerged from the narrow alleyway between the Red Dog and the adjacent dance-hall, and stood there doubtfully, his gaze wandering up and down the deserted street. As Westcott descended the hotel-steps, the marshal saw him, and came forward. His manner was prompt and businesslike.

"Hello, Jim," he said rather briskly, "I was sorter lookin' 'round fer yer; somebody said yer hoss was up at the stable. Had a little trouble up your way last night, I hear."

"Nothing to bother you, Dan; my Mexican watchman was shot up through a window of the shack."

"Kill him?"

"Instantly; I told the coroner all about it. Whoever the fellow was I reckon he meant the shot for me, but poor José got it."

"Yer didn't glimpse the critter?"

"No, it was long after dark. I've got my suspicions, but they'll keep. Seen Bill Lacy this morning?"

The marshal's thin lips smiled grimly as his eyes lifted to Westcott's face.

"He's back there in his office. That's what I stopped yer for. He said he rather expected ye'd be along after awhile. What's up between yer, Jim? Not this Mexican shootin' scrape?"

"Not unless he mentions it, Dan, although I reckon he might be able to guess how it happened. Just now I've got some other things to talk about—he's cutting into my vein."

"The hell he is!"

"Sure; I got proof of it last night. He's running a cross channel. I was down his shaft."

"I heard he's knocked off work; discharged his men."

"Yes, but only to give him time in which to pull off some other deviltry. That gave me opportunity to learn just what was being done. I slipped into the workings after the gang had left, and now I've blocked his game. Say, Dan, what do you know about that Mexican, Mendez?"

"Nuthin' good. I never put eyes on the fellow. Some claim he's got a place where he hides, out thar in the Shoshone desert, but I never got hold of anybody yet as really knew."

"There is such a man, then?"

"Sure. Why he an' his gang had a pitched battle down on Rattlesnake 'bout six months ago; killed three of the sheriff's posse, an' got away. Seemed like the whole outfit naturally dropped inter the earth. Never saw hide ner hair of 'em afterward."

"I've heard that he and Bill Lacy were in cahoots."

"Likely enough; ain't much Lacy ain't into. He's been sellin' a pile of cattle over at Taylorsville lately, an' likely most of 'em was stole. But hell! What can I do? Besides, that's the sheriff's job, ain't it? What yer goin' in to see him about, Jim?"

"Only to ask a few questions."

"There ain't goin' ter be no fight er nuthin'?" anxiously.

Westcott laughed.

"I don't see any cause for any," he answered. "But Bill might be a bit touchy. Maybe, Dan, it might be worth while for you to hang around. Do as you please about that."

He turned away and went up the wooden steps to the door of the Red Dog. The marshal's eyes followed him solicitously until he disappeared within; then he slipped back into the alleyway, skirting the side of the building, until he reached a window near the rear.

Westcott closed the door behind him and took a swift view of the barroom. There were not many present at that hour—only a few habitual loafers, mostly playing cards; a porter was sweeping up sawdust and a single bartender was industriously swabbing the bar with a towel. Westcott recognised most of the faces with a slight feeling of relief. Neither Enright nor Beaton were present, and it was his desire to meet Lacy alone, away from the influence of these others. He crossed over to the bar.

"Where's Bill?" he asked.

"Back there," and the dispenser of drinks inclined his head toward a door at the rear. "Go on in."

The fellow's manner was civil enough, yet Westcott's teeth set with a feeling that he was about to face an emergency. Yet there was no other way; he must make Lacy talk. He walked straight to the door, opened it, stepped into the room beyond, and turned the key in the lock, dropping it into his pocket. Then he faced about. He was not alone with Lacy; Enright sat beside the desk of the other and was staring at him in startled surprise. Westcott also had a hazy impression that there was or had been another person. The saloon-keeper rose to his feet, angry, and thrown completely off his guard by Westcott's unexpected action.

"What the hell does that mean?" he demanded hotly. "Why did you lock the door?"

"Naturally, to keep you in here until I am through with you," returned the miner coldly. "Sit down, Lacy; we've got a few things to talk over. You left word for me at the hotel, and, being a polite man, I accepted your invitation. I supposed I would find you alone."

Lacy sank back into his chair, endeavouring to smile.

"This gentleman is a friend of mine," he explained. "Whatever you care to say can be said before him."

"I am quite well aware of that and also that he is now present so that you may use him as a witness in case anything goes wrong. This is once you have got in bad, Mr. Patrick Enright, of New York."

The lawyer's face whitened, and his hands gripped the arms of his chair.

"You—you know me?"

"By reputation only," and Westcott bowed, "but that is scarcely to your credit. I know this, however, that for various reasons you possess no desire to advertise your presence in Haskell. It would be rather a difficult matter to explain back in the city just what you were doing out here in such intimate association with a chorus girl and a Bowery gunman, let alone our immaculate friend, Lacy, yonder. The courts, I believe, have not yet distributed the Cavendish money."

Enright's mouth was open, but no sound came from his lips; he seemed to be gasping for breath.

"I merely mention this," went on Westcott slowly, "to help you grasp the situation. We have a rough, rude way of handling such matters out here. Now Lacy and I have got a little affair to settle between us and, being a fair-minded man, he sent for me to talk it over. However, he realises that an argument of that nature might easily become personal and that if anything unpleasant occurred he would require a witness. So he arranges to have you present. Do you see the point, Mr. Enright?"

The lawyer's eyes sought Lacy, and then returned to the stern face confronting him. His lips sputtered:

"As—as a witness?"

"Sure; there may be honour among thieves, but not Lacy's kind." He strode forward and with one hand crunched Enright back into his chair. "Now, listen to me," he said fiercely. "I've got only one word of advice for you: don't take any hand in this affair, except as a peacemaker, for if you do, you are going to get hurt. Now, Bill Lacy, I'm ready to talk with you. I was down in your shaft last night."

The saloonman lit a cigar and leaned back in his chair.

"I ought to have thought of that, Westcott," he admitted. "Still, I don't know that I give a damn."

"The work hadn't been left in very good shape, and I found the cross tunnel and measured it. You are within a few feet of my vein. The county surveyor ought to have been out there two hours ago."

Lacy straightened up, all semblance of indifference gone, an oath on his lips.

"You cur! You filed complaint? When?"

"At seven o'clock this morning. We'll fight that out in the courts. However, that isn't what I came here for at all. I came to ask you a question and one of you two are going to answer before I leave—keep your hand up, and in sight, Lacy; make another move like that and it's liable to be your last. I am not here in any playful mood, and I know your style. Lay that gun on the desk where I can see it—that's right. Now move your chair back."

Lacy did this with no good grace, his face purple with passion. Westcott had been too quick, too thoroughly prepared for him, but he would watch his opportunity. He could afford to wait, knowing the cards he had up his sleeve. "Some considerable gun-play just to ask a question," he said tauntingly, "must be mighty important. All right, what is it?"

"Where did your man Moore take Miss Donovan last night?"

CHAPTER XXI
THE MARSHAL PLAYS A HAND

Neither man had anticipated this; neither had the slightest conception that any suspicion of this kind pointed at them. The direct question was like the sudden explosion of a bomb. What did Westcott know? How had he discovered their participation in the affair? The fact that Westcott unhesitatingly connected Matt Moore with the abduction was in itself alone sufficient evidence that he based his inquiry on actual knowledge. Enright had totally lost power of speech, positive terror plainly depicted in his eyes, but Lacy belonged to another class of the *genus homo*. He was a Western type, prepared to bluff to the end. His first start of surprise ended in a sarcastic smile.

"You have rather got the better of me, Westcott," he said, shrugging his shoulders, as though dismissing the subject. "You refer to the New York newspaper woman?"

"I do—Miss Stella Donovan."

"I have not the pleasure of that lady's acquaintance, but Timmons informed me this morning that she had taken the late train last night for the East—isn't that true, Enright?"

The lawyer managed to nod, but without venturing to remove his gaze from Westcott's face. The latter never moved, but his eyes seemed to harden.

"I have had quite enough of that, Lacy," he said sternly, and the watchful saloon-keeper noted his fingers close more tightly on the butt of his revolver. "This is no case for an alibi. I know exactly what I am talking about, and—I am going to have a direct answer, either from you or Enright.

"This is the situation: I was the man listening at the window of your shack last night. Moore may, or may not have recognised me, but, nevertheless, I was the man. I was there long enough to overhear a large part of your conversation. I know why you consented to close down La Rosita for the present; I know your connection with this gang of crooks from New York; I know that Fred Cavendish was not murdered, but is being held a prisoner somewhere, until Enright, here, can steal his money under some legal form. I know you have claimed, and been promised, your share of the swag—isn't that true?"

"It's very damn interesting anyway—but not so easy to prove. What next?"

"This: Enright told you who Stella Donovan was, and what he suspected her object might be. Force is the only method you know anything about, and no other means occurred to you whereby the girl could be quickly put out of the way. This was resorted to last night after you returned to Haskell. I do not pretend to know how it was accomplished, nor do I greatly care. Through some lie, no doubt. But, anyway, she was inveigled into leaving the hotel, seized by you and some of your gang, forced into a wagon, and driven off by Matt Moore."

"You are a good dreamer. Why not ask Timmons to show you the letter she left?"

"I have already seen it. You thought you had the trail well covered. That note was written not by Miss Donovan, but by the blonde in your outfit. The whole trouble is that your abduction of Stella Donovan was witnessed from a back window of the hotel."

Lacy leaped to his feet, but Westcott's gun rose steadily, and the man stood with clenched hands, helpless in his tracks.

"Who says that?" he demanded.

"I am mentioning no names at present, but the very fact that I know these things ought to be sufficient. You better sit down, Lacy, before you forget yourself and get hurt. If you imagine this gun isn't loaded, a single step forward will test it. Sit down! I am not through yet."

There was a quiet, earnest threat in the voice which Lacy understood, the sort of threat which meant strict attention to business, and he relaxed into his chair.

"I'll get you for this, Westcott," he muttered savagely, hate burning in his eyes. "I haven't played my last cards—yet."

The miner smiled grimly, but with no relaxation of vigilance. He was into it now, and proposed seeing it through.

"I have a few left myself," he returned soberly. "Your man Moore drove south, taking the road leading into the Shoshone desert, and he had another one of your gang with him. Then you, and two others, went back into the hotel, using the outside stairs. I take it the two others were Enright, here, and Ned Beaton."

He leaned forward, his face set like flint.

"Now see here, Lacy. I know these things. I can prove them by a perfectly competent witness. It is up to you to answer my questions, and answer them straight. I've got you two fellows dead to rights anyway you look at it. If you dare lay hands on me I'll kill you; if you refuse to tell me what I want to know, I'll swear out warrants inside of thirty minutes. Now what do you choose?"

For the first time Lacy's eyes wavered, their defiance gone, as he glanced aside at Enright, who had collapsed in his chair, a mere heavily breathing, shapeless thing. The sight of the coward seemed to stiffen him to a species of resistance.

"If I answer—what then?" he growled desperately.

"What is offered me?"

Westcott moistened his lips. He had not before faced the situation from this standpoint, yet, with only one thought in his mind, he answered promptly.

"I am not the law," he said, "and all I am interested in now is the release of Fred Cavendish and Stella Donovan. I'll accomplish that if it has to be over your dead bodies. Beyond this, I wash my hands of the whole affair. What I want to know is—where are these two?"

"Would you believe me if I said I did not know?"

"No, Lacy. It has come down to the truth, or your life. Where is Pasqual Mendez?"

He heard no warning, no sound of movement, yet some change in the expression of the man's eyes confronting him caused him to slightly turn his head so as to vaguely perceive a shadow behind. It was all so quickly, silently done, he barely had time to throw up one hand in defence, when his arms were gripped as though in a vise, and he was thrown backward to the floor, the chair crushed beneath his weight. Lacy fairly leaped on his prostrate body, forgetting his gun lying on the desk in the violence of hate, his hands clutching at the exposed throat. For an instant Westcott was so dazed and stunned by this sudden attack from behind as to lie there prone and helpless, fairly crushed beneath the bodies of his two antagonists.

It was this that gave him his chance, for, convinced that he was unconscious, both men slightly relaxed their grip, thus giving him opportunity to regain breath, and stiffen his muscles for a supreme effort. With one lashing out of a foot that sent Enright hurtling against the farther wall, he cracked Lacy's head against a corner of the desk, and closed in deadly struggle with the third man, whom he now recognised as Beaton.

Before the latter could comprehend what had happened the miner was on top, and a clenched fist was driven into his face with all the force of a sledge-hammer. But barroom fighting was no novelty to the gunman, nor had he any scruples as to the methods employed. With teeth sunk in his opponent's arm, and fingers gouging at his eyes, the fellow struggled like a mad dog; yet, in spite of every effort to restrain him, Westcott, now filled with the fierce rage of battle, broke free, fairly tearing himself from Beaton's desperate clutch, and pinning him helplessly against the wall.

At the same instant Lacy, who had regained his feet, leaped upon him from behind, striking with all his force, the violence of the blow, even though a grazing one, driving the miner's head into the face of the gunman.

Both went down together, but Westcott was on his feet again before Lacy could act, closing with the latter. It was hand-to-hand, the silent struggle for mastery between two men not unevenly matched, men asking and receiving no mercy. The revolver of one lay on the floor, the other still reposed on the open desk, and neither could be reached. It was a battle to be fought out with bare hands. Twice Westcott struck, his clenched fist bringing blood, but Lacy clung to him, one hand twisted in his neck-band, the other viciously forcing back his head. Unable to release the grip, Westcott gave back, bending until his adversary was beyond balance; then, suddenly straightening, hurled the fellow sidewise. But by now Beaton, dazed and confused, was upon his feet. With the bellow of a wild bull he flung himself on the struggling men, forcing Lacy aside, and smashing into Westcott with all the strength of his body. The impetus sent all three crashing to the floor.

Excited voices sounded without; then blows resounded against the wood of the locked door, but the three men were oblivious to all but their own struggle. Like so many wild beasts they clutched and struck, unable to disentangle themselves. Enright, his face like chalk, got to his knees and crept across the floor until his hand closed on Westcott's revolver. Lifting himself by a grip on the desk, he swung the weapon forward at the very instant the miner rose staggering, dragging Beaton with him. There was a flash of flame, a sharp report, and Westcott sprang aside, gripping the back of a chair. The gunman sank into shapelessness on the floor as the chair hurtled through the air straight at Enright's head.

With a crash the door fell, and a black mass of men surged in through the opening, the big bartender leading them, an axe in his hand. Beaton lay motionless just as he had dropped; Enright was in one corner, dazed, unnerved, a red gash across his forehead, from which blood dripped, the revolver, struck from his fingers, yet smoking on the floor; Westcott, his clothes torn, his face bruised by blows, breathing heavily, went slowly backward, step by step, to the farther wall, conscious of nothing now but the savagely hostile faces of these new enemies. Lacy, staggering as though drunk, managed to attain his feet, hate, the desire for revenge, yielding him strength. This was his crowd, and his mind was quick to grasp the opportunity.

"There's the man who did it," he shouted, his arm flung out toward Westcott. "I saw him shoot. See, that's his gun lying on the floor. Don't let the murderer get away!"

He started forward, an oath on his lips, and the excited crowd surged after, growling anger. Then the mass of them seemed suddenly rent asunder, and the marshal ploughed his way through heedlessly, his hat gone, and a blue-barrelled gun in either hand. He swept the muzzle of one of these into the bartender's face menacingly, his eyes searching the maddened crowd.

"Wait a minute, you," he commanded sharply. "I reckon I've got something to say 'bout this. Put down that axe, Mike, or ye'll never draw another glass o' beer in this camp. You know me, lads, an' I never draw except fer business. Shut your mouth, Lacy; don't touch that gun, you fool! I am in charge here—this is my job; and if there is going to be any lynching done, it will be after you get me. Stand back now; all of you—yes, get out into that barroom. I mean you, Mike! This man is my prisoner, and, by God, I'll defend him. Ay! I'll do more, I'll let him defend himself. Here, Westcott, pick up your gun on the floor. Now stand here with me! We're going out through that bunch, and if one of those coyotes puts a paw on you, let him have it."

The crowd made way, reluctantly enough, growling curses, but with no man among them sufficiently reckless to attempt resistance. They lacked leadership, for the little marshal never once took his eye off Lacy. At the door he turned, walking backward, trusting in Westcott to keep their path clear, both levelled revolvers ready for any movement. He knew Haskell, and he knew the character of these hangers-on at the "Red Dog." He realised fully the influence of Bill Lacy, and comprehended that the affair was far from being ended; but just now he had but one object before him—to get his prisoner safely outside into the open. Beyond that he would trust to luck, and a fair chance. His grey eyes were almost black as they gleamed over the levelled revolver barrels, and his clipped moustache fairly bristled.

"Not a step, you!" he muttered. "What's the matter, Lacy? Do you want to die in your tracks? Mike, all I desire is an excuse to make you the deadest bung-starter in Colorado. Put down that gun, Carter! If just one of you lads come through that door, I'll plug these twelve shots, and you know how I shoot—Lacy will get the first one, and Mike the second. Stand there now! Go on out, Jim; I'm right along with you."

They were far from free even outside the swinging doors and in the sunshine. Already a rumour of what had occurred had spread like wildfire, and men were on the street, eager enough to take some hand in the affray. A few were already about the steps, while others were running rapidly toward them, excited but uncertain.

It was this uncertainty which gave the little marshal his one slender chance. His eyes swept the crowd, but there was no face visible on whom he could rely in this emergency. They were the roughs of the camp, the idlers, largely parasites of Lacy; those fellows would only hoot him if he asked for help. No, there was no way but to fight it out themselves, and the only possibility of escape came to him in a flash. Suddenly as this emergency had arisen the marshal was prepared; he knew the lawless nature of the camp, and had anticipated that some time just such a situation as this might arise. Now that it had come, he was ready. There was scarcely an instant of hesitancy, his quick searching eyes surveying the scene, and then seeking the face of his prisoner.

"Willing to fight this out, Jim?" he asked shortly.

"You bet, Dan; what's the plan?"

"The big rock in Bear Creek. We can hold out there until dark. Perhaps there'll be some men come to help us by that time; if not we might crawl away in the night. Take the alley and turn at the hotel. Don't let anybody stop you; here comes those hell-hounds from inside. Christopher Columbus, I hate to run from such cattle, but it's our only chance."

There was no time to waste. They were not yet at the mouth of the alley when the infuriated pursuers burst through the saloon doors, cursing and shouting. Lacy led them, animated by the one desire to kill Westcott, fully aware that this alone would prevent the exposure of his own crime.

"There they go!" he yelled madly, and fired. "Get that dirty murderer, boys—get him!"

There were a dozen shots, but the two runners plunged about the corner of the building, and disappeared, apparently untouched. Lacy leaped from the platform to the ground, shouting his orders, and the crowd surged after him in pursuit, some choosing the alley, others the street. Revolvers cracked sharply, little spits of smoke showing in the sunlight; men shouted excitedly, and two mounted cowboys lashed their ponies up the dusty road in an effort to head off the fugitives. Twice the two turned and fired, yet at that, hardly paused in their race. Westcott held back, retarded by the shorter legs of his companion, nevertheless they were fully a hundred feet in advance of their nearest pursuers when they reached the hotel. In spite of Lacy's urging the cowardly crew exhibited small desire to close in. The marshal, glancing back over his shoulder, grinned cheerfully.

"We've got 'em beat, Jim," he panted, "less thar's others headin' us off; run like a white-head; don't mind me."

The road ahead was clear, except for the speeding cowboys, and the marshal made extremely quick work of them. There was a fusillade of shots, and when these ended, one rider was down in the dust, the other galloping madly away, lying flat on his pony, with no purpose but to get out of range. The two fugitives plunged into the bushes opposite, taking the roughest but most direct course to where the rather precipitous banks dropped off to the stream below. There was a dam a half mile down, and even at this point the water was wide and deep enough to make any attempt at crossing dangerous. But half-way over an upheaval of rock parted the current, forcing the swirling waters to either side, and presenting a stern grey face to the shore. The marshal, pausing for nothing, flung himself bodily down the steep bank, unclasping his belt, as he half ran, half rolled to the bottom.

"Here, take these cartridges," he said, "and hold 'em up. Save yer own, too, fer we're going to need 'em. That water out thar is plumb up to my neck. Come on now; keep them things dry, an' don't bother 'bout me."

He plunged in, and Westcott followed, both cartridge belts held above his head. There was a crackling of bushes on the bank behind them, showing their pursuers had crossed the road and were already beating up the brush. Neither man glanced back, assured that those fellows would hunt them first in the chaparral, cautiously beating the coverts, before venturing beyond.

The water deepened rapidly, and Westcott was soon to his waist, leaning to his right to keep his feet; he heard the marshal splashing along behind, convinced by his ceaseless profanity that he also made progress in spite of his shortness of limbs. Indeed they attained the rock shelter almost together, creeping up through a narrow crevasse, leaving a wet trail along the grey stone. This was accomplished none too soon, a yell from the bank telling of their discovery, followed by the crack of a gun. The marshal, who was still exposed, hastily crept under cover, wiping a drop of blood from his cheek where a splinter of rock dislodged by the bullet had slashed the flesh. He was, nevertheless, in excellent humour, his keen grey eyes laughing, as he peered out over the rock rampart.

"If they keep up shootin' like that, Jim, I reckon our insurance won't be high," he said, "I'm plumb ashamed of the camp, the way them boys waste lead. Must 'a' took twenty shots at us so far an' only skinned me with a rock. Hell! 'tain't even interestin'. Hand over them cartridges; let's see what sorter stock we got."

CHAPTER XXII
THE ROCK IN THE STREAM

Westcott was sensible now of a feeling of intense exhaustion. The fierce fighting in the room behind the saloon; the excitement of the attempt to escape; the chase, ending with the plunge through the stream had left him pitifully weak. He could perceive his hand tremble as he handed over the cartridge belt. The marshal noticed it also, and cast a swift glance into the other's face.

"About all in, Jim?" he inquired understandingly. "Little out of your usual line, I reckon. Take a bit o' rest thar, an' ye'll be all right. It's safe 'nough fer the present whar we are, fer as thet bunch o' chicken thieves is concerned. Yer wa'n't hurt, or nuthin', durin' the scrap?"

"No more than a few bruises, but it an happened so quickly I haven't any breath left. I'll be all right in a minute. How are we fixed for ammunition?"

"Blame pore, if yer ask me; not more'n twenty cartridges atween us. I wa'n't a lookin' fer no such scrap just now; but we'll get along, I reckon, fer thar ain't any o' that bunch anxious ter get hurt none, less maybe it might be Lacy. What gets my goat is this yere plug tobacco," and he gazed mournfully at the small fragment in his hand. "That ain't hardly 'nough ov it left fer a good chaw; how are you fixed, Jim?"

"Never use it, Dan, but here's a badly smashed cigar."

"That'll help some—say, ain't that one o' them shirky birds yonder? Sure; it's Bill himself. I don't know whether ter take a snap-shot at the cuss, er wait an' hear what he's got ter say—Hello, there!"

The fellow who stood partially revealed above the bank stared in the direction of the voice, and then ventured to expose himself further.

"Hello yourself," he answered. "Is that you, Brennan?"

The marshal hoisted himself to the top of the rock, the revolver in his hand clearly revealed in the bright sunlight.

"It's me all right, Lacy," he replied deliberately. "You ought ter organise a sharpshooters' club among that gang o' yours; I was plumb disgusted the way they handle fire-arms."

"Well, we've got yer now, Dan, so yer might as well quit yer crowin'. We don't have ter do no more shootin'; we'll just naturally sit down yere, an' starve yer out. Maybe yer ready to talk now?"

"Sure; what's the idea?"

"Well, yer an officer ov the law, ain't yer? Yer was chose marshal ter keep the peace, an' take care o' them that raised hell in Haskell. Ain't that yer job?"

"I reckon it is."

"And didn't I do more'n anybody else ter get yer appointed? Then what are yer goin' back on me for, and the rest ov the boys, an' takin' sides along with a murderer? We want Jim Westcott, an' you bet we're a-goin' ter get him."

The little marshal spat into the water below, his face expressionless. To all appearances he felt slight interest in the controversy.

"Nice of yer ter declare yer intentions, Lacy," he admitted soberly, "only it sorter looks as if yer didn't consider me as bein' much in the way. I reckon yer outlined my duty all right; that's exactly my way o' looking at it—ter keep the peace, an' take care o' them that raised hell in Haskell. I couldn't 'a' told it no better myself."

"Then what are yer fightin' fer Westcott fer?"

"'Cause he's my prisoner, an' is goin' ter get a fair trial. If he was the orneriest Mexican that ever come 'cross the line I'd stay with him—that's the law."

"An' yer won't give him up?"

"Not in a thousand years, an' yer might as well save yer breath, Bill, an' get out. I've told you straight, and I reckon you and your gang know me. Nobody never told you that Dan Brennan was a quitter, did they?"

"But you blame fool," and Lacy's voice plainly indicated his anger. "You can't fight this whole camp; we'll get yer, dead or alive."

"Yer welcome ter try; I ain't askin' no sorter favour; only yer better be blame keerful about it, fer my trigger finger appears ter be almighty nervous ter-day—drop that!"

His hand shot out like lightning, the blue steel of his revolver flashing. Lacy flung up his arms, and backed down out of view, but just beyond where he had stood, a gun barked from out the chaparral and a bullet crashed against the rock scarcely a foot from Brennan's head. The latter answered it so promptly the two reports sounded almost as one, and then rolled back into shelter, laughing as though the whole affair was a joke.

"One ov Mike's little tricks," he chuckled, peering back at the shore, "I know the bark of that old girl. Hope I pricked him. That guy used to be a good shot, too, afore he got to drinkin' so much. I reckon we're in fer a siege, Jim."

Westcott extended his hand.

"It's mighty white of you, Dan, to stay by me," he said gravely. "It's liable to cost you your job."

"Ter hell with the job. I kin earn more in the mines eny day. I'm not doin' eny more for you than I would fer eny other galoot in bad. I wouldn't let 'em lynch a hoss-thief without givin' 'em a fight first. Don't be givin' any sympathy ter me."

"But we haven't any chance."

"Well, I don't know about that now," and the marshal looked up and down the stream thoughtfully. "It might be worse. Look a here, Jim. I said I'd 'a' stayed with yer no matter what yer was guilty of, so long as yer was my prisoner, an' that's the gospel truth. There ain't a goin' ter be no lynchin' in Haskell while I'm marshal, unless them rats get me first. But this yere case ain't even that kind. It's a put-up job frum the beginnin' an' Bill Lacy ain't a goin' ter get away with it, as long as I kin either fight er bluff. This yere fuss ain't your fault, an' yer never shot the man either."

"No. I didn't, Dan. I never fired a gun."

"I know it; that's why all hell can't pry me loose. I saw most ov the row, an' I reckon I ain't so dumb that I can't catch onto the game what Lacy is tryin' ter play. I didn't hear what you an' him was talkin' about, so I don't know just the cause o' the rumpus, but the way he played his hand didn't make no hit with me."

"You saw what happened?"

"Sure; it didn't look good ter me, his gittin' yer ter come ter his place, specially when I knew he wasn't there alone; so, after ye'd gone in through the saloon, I sasshayed down the alley an' took a peek in through that rear window. The tarnation thing is barred up with sheet iron, an' I couldn't see much, nor hear a blame word, but I caught on that there was liable ter be a row a fore it was over with. Through that peep-hole I got sight o' you, Lacy, an' that fat feller—what's his name?"

"Enright, a New York lawyer."

"That's it; well I could make out the three of yer, but I never got sight of the other buck—his name was Beaton, wasn't it?—till he came out from behind the curtain and gripped yer. It was a put-up job all right, an' maybe I ought to have hustled round to the door an' took a hand. But I don't aim to mix up in no scrimmage as long as both sides has got a fair show. Course thar was three ag'in' one, but arter you kicked the wind out o' the lawyer, the odds wasn't so bad, an' I sorter hated to lose out seeing how the scrap came out. Holy smoke! but you sure put up some dandy fight, Jim. I ain't seen nuthin' better since I struck this yere camp. You had them two guys licked to a frazzle, when that Enright come back to life agin, an' crawled out on the floor an' picked up your gun. The fust thing I knew he had it, an' the next thing I knew he'd pulled the trigger. He meant it fer you, but Beaton got it."

"It was Enright then who fired the shot?"

"Sure it was Enright; I saw him, but that didn't cut any ice after I got inside. Do you see? The whole crowd was Lacy's gang; they'd do whatever he said. It was your gun that had the discharged cartridge; Bill was yellin' that you fired it, and Enright, o' course, would have backed him up to save his own neck. You was in a fight with the feller what was shot. See! It was a mighty ugly fix, an' nobody in that outfit would 'a' listened to me. It struck me, son, that Lacy was all-fired anxious to get rid of you—he saw a chance, and jumped for it. What was the row about—your mine?"

"Partly, but mostly another affair. The best thing I can do is tell you about it. What's going on up there?"

He pointed up the stream, and Brennan shaded his eyes to look, although careful to keep well under cover, confident that any movement would be observed from the shore. He gazed for some time before he seemed entirely satisfied.

"A bunch of the boys crossin' the old ford," he said quietly. "Goin' to picket the other bank, I reckon. There's likely to be some more comin' down the opposite way from the bridge. That's Lacy's idea—to starve us out."

"They seem quiet enough."

"There won't be any more fightin' unless we try to get away, I reckon. They know we are armed and can shoot. You better keep down, though, Jim, for they're sure a watchin' us all right, an' all Lacy cares about is to put you out o' the way. He'd just as soon do it with a bullet as a rope. Go on with your story."

Westcott told it simply, but in full detail, beginning with the discovery of ore in his mine, and including his telegram to Fred Cavendish; the discovery of what was supposed to be the dead body of the latter in the Waldron Apartments, New York; the investigations into the mystery of his death by Willis and Miss Donovan, and the despatching of Miss Donovan to Haskell to intercept Enright's party; the arrival of the latter and the events, so far as he understood them, leading up to the forcible abduction of the girl.

The marshal listened quietly to the narrative, the quick action of his jaws alone evidencing his interest, although he occasionally interposed a question. Except for Westcott's voice there was no sound, beyond the lapping of water against the rock, and no figures of men became visible along either bank. The party above had crossed the stream, and disappeared up a ravine, and nothing remained to indicate that these two were fugitives, hiding for their lives, and facing a desperate expedient in an effort to escape their pursuers. As the speaker finally concluded the silence was almost oppressive.

"How do yer suppose Bill Lacy got into the affair?" asked Brennan, at last thoughtfully. "I don't put no sorter deviltry beyond him, yer understand, but I don't quite see how he ever come to get mixed up in this yere New York mess. Seems like he had enough hell brewing here at home."

"I'm just as much in the dark as you are, as to that," admitted Westcott doubtfully. "I am convinced, however, that Cavendish is still alive, and that another body strangely resembling his was found in the New York apartments. According to Enright this was not part of their scheme, but merely an accident of which they took advantage. How true this is will never be known unless we discover Cavendish, and learn his story. Now, if he is alive, where has he been concealed, and for what purpose? Another thing begins to loom up. The mere hiding of the man was all right so long as the conspirators were not suspected. But now when they are aware that they are being followed, what is likely to happen? Will they become desperate enough to kill their victim, hoping thus to destroy absolutely the evidence of their crime? Will their vengeance also include Miss Donovan?"

"Not unless they can get you out of the way first," decided the marshal grimly. "That is Lacy's most important job—you are more dangerous to them now than the girl. That meeting to-day was prearranged, and Beaton was expected to land you. That was why he hid behind the curtain, but something caused him to make a false move; they never expected you to put up that sort o' fight, Jim, for nobody knew yer in this camp fer a fightin' man. But what's yer theory 'bout Cavendish? Let's leave the dead man in New York go, an' get down ter cases."

"I figure it out like this, Dan. I believe Fred got my telegram, and decided to come out here at once without telling anybody what his plans were. All he did was to make a will, so as to dispose of his property in case anything happened. His employing Enright for that job unfortunately put the whole thing in the hands of this crowd. They were ready to act, and they acted. Beaton must have taken the same train, and the two men got friendly;

probably they never knew each other in New York, but, being from the same place, it was easy enough to strike up an acquaintance. What occurred on board is all guesswork, but a sudden blow at night, on an observation platform, at some desert station, is not impossible; or it might be sickness, and the two men left behind to seek a physician. Here was where Lacy must have come in. He goes East occasionally, doesn't he?"

"Sure; come to think of it he was in New York 'bout three months ago on some cattle deal, an' I heard he had an agent there sellin' wildcat minin' stock. There ain't no doubt in my mind but he knew some o' these fellers. They wouldn't 'a' planned this unless they had some cache fixed out yere in this country—that's plain as a wart on the nose. But whar is it? I'll bet yer that if we ever find Cavendish, we'll find the girl along with him; an' what's more, that spot ain't liable ter be more'n fifty miles from Haskell."

"What makes you think that?"

"'Cause this is Lacy's bailiwick, an' thar ain't no man knows this country better'n he does; he's rode it night and day for ten years, an' most o' the hangers-on in this camp get money out o' him one way er another—mostly another. Then, why should Enright an' his crowd come yere, unless that was a fact? They must have come for something; that lawyer ain't yere on no minin' deal; an' no more has Beaton been layin' round town fer a month doin' nuthin' but drinkin' whisky. The whole blame outfit is right here in Haskell, and they wouldn't be if this wasn't headquarters. That's good common sense, ain't it?" He stopped suddenly, patting his hand on the rock, and then lifting his head to scan the line of shore. "They're there all right, Jim," he announced. "I just got a glimpse o' two back in the brush yonder. What made yer ask me 'bout Pasqual Mendez this mornin'? You don't hook the Mexican up with this affair, do yer?"

"Sadie told me she heard Enright speak of him at breakfast; that was all she heard, just the name."

"Sadie? Oh, the red-headed waitress at Timmons's, you mean? Big Tim's girl?"

"Yes; she was the one who saw Miss Donovan forced into the wagon, and driven off."

"And they took the old Shoshone trail; out past Hennessey's ranch?"

"So she described it. Does that mean anything?"

Brennan did not answer at once, sitting silent, his brows wrinkled, staring through a crevasse of the rock up the stream. Finally he grinned into the anxious face of the other.

"Danged if I know," he said drawlingly. "Maybe it does, and maybe again it don't. I was sorter puttin' this an' that tergether. There's a Mex who used to hang about here a couple of years ago they allers said belonged to Mendez's gang. His name is Cateras, a young feller, an' a hell ov a gambler. It just comes ter me that he was in the Red Dog three er four nights ago playin' monte. I didn't see him myself, but Joe Mapes said he was there, an' that makes it likely 'nough that Mendez isn't so blame far away."

"And he and Lacy have interests in common?"

"That is the rumour. I never got hold ov any proof, but Lacy has shipped a pile o' cattle out o' Villa Real, although why he should ever drive his cows there across the desert instead o' shippin' them here in Haskell or Taylorville, I never could understand. That's the principal reason I've got for thinkin' he an' Mendez are in cahoots, an' if they be, then the Mexican must have some kind o' a camp out there in the sand whar he hides between raids; though, damn if I know whar it can be." He paused reflectively. "It'll be like hunting a needle in the haystack, Jim, but I reckon you an' I'll have to get out that way, an' we might have luck enough to stumble onto the old devil."

Westcott changed his position, inadvertently bringing his head above the protection of the rock. Instantly there was a sharp report, and a speeding bullet grazed his hair, flattening out against the stone. The rapidity with which he ducked caused the marshal to laugh.

"Not hurt, are you? No. That was a rifle; Mike isn't such a bad shot with that weapon. He's over there behind that tree—see the smoke? If the cuss pokes his head out, I'll try the virtue of this .45; it ought to carry that far. Hah! there he is; I made the bark fly anyway."

CHAPTER XXIII
THE ESCAPE

The afternoon wore away slowly, the two men realising more and more clearly the nature of the siege. Their only safety lay in the protection of the rocks, as they were now entirely surrounded, and fired upon from either bank the moment either raised a head. No attempt was made, however, to assault their position, nor did they often return the fire, desiring to preserve for future use their small supply of ammunition. Brennan remained watchful, but silent, brooding over his plans for the night, but Westcott became overpowered by fatigue and slept quietly for several hours.

The sun was already sinking behind the range of mountains when he finally aroused himself, and sat up. There was no apparent change in the situation; the running water murmured musically against the rocks, the distant banks, already in shadow, exhibited no sign of human presence. Below in the distance was the deserted street of the town, and farther away a few of the shacks were visible. The scene was peaceable enough, and the awakened sleeper could scarcely comprehend that he was in truth a fugitive being hunted for his life, that all about him were men eager to kill, watchful of the slightest movement. It was rather the sight of Brennan which restored his faculties, and yielded clear memory. The latter greeted him with a good-humoured grin.

"Well, do you feel better, Jim?" he asked pleasantly. "Thought I'd let you sleep as long as I could, for we've got some job ahead of us. Sorry thar ain't no breakfast waitin', fer I wouldn't object ter a bit o' ham bone myself. I reckon if Lacy coops me up yere much longer, he's liable ter win his bet; I'm plumb near starved out already."

"I'm afraid they've got us, Dan."

"Oh, I don't know; leastwise I ain't put up no white flag yet. You're game fer a try at gettin' out o' yere, ain't yer, old man? I've sorter been reckonin' on yer."

"I'll take any chance there is," returned Westcott heartily, staring into the other's face. "Have you some plan?"

"Maybe 'tain't that exactly, but I've been doin' a powerful lot o' thinkin' since you was asleep, Jim, an' I reckon we might beat these fellers with a fair show o' luck. This is how I figure it out. Thar won't be no attack; that's a cinch. Lacy knows we can shoot, an' he also knows we're marooned yere without food. The easiest thing is ter starve us out."

"But there are good men in this camp, law abiding men," interrupted the miner. "What about them? Won't they take a hand?"

"Maybe they might if I was free ter get 'em together; but I ain't. Most o' 'em are out in the mines anyway; they don't know which party is right in this rumpus, an' they ain't got no leader. Lacy runs the town, an' he's got a big gang o' toughs behind him. There ain't nobody wants to buck up against his game. Of course the boys might get mad after a while, but I reckon we'd be starved plumb ter death long afore that happened. An' that ain't the worst ov it, Jim—the sheriff is Lacy's man. I wouldn't never dare turn you over ter him—not by a jugful."

"Then we are blocked at every turn."

"We sure are, unless we can dig out ourselves," gravely. "My notion is to get a fair start, drift out into Shoshone, whar we'll leave no trail, an' then hit for over the line. Sam Watts is sheriff of Coconino, an' he'd give us a square deal."

"On foot?"

"Hell, no! I ain't no such walker as all that. Come over yere; keep yer head down; now look out between these two rocks. Do yer see them cow-ponies hitched ter the rack alongside o' the Red Dog? Well, they've been thar fer a matter o' three hours, I reckon, an' their riders ain't liable ter leave as long as thar's any excitement in town. They're XL men, and mostly drunk by this time. It's my aim ter get a leg over one o' them animals. How does that notion strike you?"

Westcott shook his head doubtfully, his eyes still on those distant specks. The prospect looked practically hopeless.

"You don't think it can be done? Well now listen. Here's my scheme, an' I reckon it'll work. Naturally Lacy will think we'll try to get away—make a break for it in the dark. He'll have both them banks guarded, an' ther fellers will have orders ter shoot. He'd rather have us dead than alive. But, to my notion, he won't expect us ter try any getaway before midnight. Anyhow, that's how I'd figure if I was in his place. But my idea is to pull one off on him, an' start the minute it gets dark enough, so them lads can't see what's goin' on out yere."

"We'll fight our way through?"

"Not a fight, my son; we'll make it so softly that not a son-of-a-gun will ever know how it happened. When they wake up we'll be twenty miles out in the desert, an' still a goin'. Thar's a big log clinging ter the upper end o' the rock. I saw it when I fust come over; an' 'bout an hour ago I crept back through that gully an' took a good look. A shove will send it floatin'. An' with a good pair o' legs to steer with, thar ain't nuthin' to stop it this side the curve, an' I don't calculate any o' the rifle brigade will be down as fur as that—do you?"

"Not likely," and Westcott measured the distance with eyes that had lost their despondency. "Your idea is that we drift past under cover of the log?"

"Sure. We'll tie our guns an' cartridges on top, where they'll be out o' water, an' keep down below ourselves. Them fellers may glimpse the log an' blaze away, but 'tain't likely they'll have luck enough to hit either one o' us, an' the flare will show 'em it's only a log, an' they'll likely quit an' pass the word along. It sounds blame good ter me, Jim; what d'ye say?"

Westcott's hand went out, and the fingers of the two men clasped silently. There was no need for more speech; they understood each other.

The night closed down swiftly, as it does in the West, the purple of the hills becoming black as though by some magic. There was a heavy cloud hanging in the Western sky, constantly sweeping higher in pledge of a dark night. The banks of the stream became obscured, and finally vanished altogether; while the water ceased to glimmer and turned to an inky blackness. Lights twinkled in the distant shacks, and the front of the Red Dog burst into illumination. The saloon was too far away for the watchers to pick out the moving figures of men, but Brennan chuckled, and pointed his finger at the glare.

"Lacy ain't fergettin' the profit in all this," he whispered hoarsely. "The boys are goin' ter be dry, an' he'll sell 'em all they want—wouldn't mind if I had some myself. Is it dark enough, mate?"

"The sooner the better!"

"That's my ticket. Come on then, but don't make a sound; them lads are more liable to hear than they are to see us. Let me go first."

The log was at the other end of the little island, but there was a considerable rift in the rock surface, not deep, but of sufficient width to permit the passage of a body. The jagged stone made the way rough in the dark, and Westcott found himself at the upper extremity, gashed and bruised by the contact.

Brennan had already lowered himself into the water, assisted in the downward climb by some low, tough bushes whose tendrils clung tenaciously to the smooth rock. Westcott followed silently, and found footing in about three feet of water, where it swirled around the base of the island. From this low point, their eyes close to the surface of the stream, the men could dimly discern the shore lines silhouetted against the slightly lighter sky. They crouched there in deep shadow, but discovered no evidence that their effort at escape had been observed. A dog was barking somewhere not far away, and once there was a rustle along the nearer bank, as though a man wormed his way cautiously through the thick chaparral. But this sound also ceased after a moment, and all was still. Brennan put his lips close to his companion's ear.

"Got yer cartridges tied up? That's all right; hand 'em over. Now give me your belt. No; pass the end under the log an' buckle it; not too tight. You hang on to the outside, an' I'll push off. If yer have ter paddle ter keep in the current don't let yer hands er feet come to the surface—understand?"

"Certainly."

"All right then; are you all set? Holy smoke, this is going to be some yacht ride."

The log did not even grate as it loosened its slight hold on the rock, and began the voyage down-stream. The current was swift enough to bear it and its burden free from the island, although it moved slowly and noiselessly on its way. The two men deeply emerged on either side, with heads held rigid against the wet bark, were indistinguishable. Out from the deeper shadow of the rock they drifted into the wider stream below, Brennan gently controlling the unwieldy affair, and keeping it as nearly as possible to the centre, by the noiseless movement of a hand under water. The men scarcely ventured to breathe and it seemed as though they were ages slowly sidling along, barely able to perceive that they really moved. They must have gone a hundred yards or more before there was any alarm. Then a voice spoke from the bank to the right, followed almost instantly by the flash of a gun and a sharp report. The flare lit up the stream, and the bullet thudded into the log, without damage.

"What was it, Jack?" the voice unmistakably Lacy's. "Did you see something?"

"Nothin' but a floatin' log," was the disgusted reply, "but I made a bull's-eye."

"That's better than you did any time before to-day. Where is it? Oh, yes, I see the blame thing now. You don't need ter be any quail-hunter ter hit that. It's goin' 'bout a mile an hour. However, there is no harm done; the shot will show those fellows that we are awake out here."

Slowly the log floated on, vanishing in the darkness. No other alarm greeted its progress, and at last, confident that they were already safely below the extent of the guard lines, the two men, clinging to its wet sides, ventured to kick out quietly, and thus hasten its progress. It came ashore at the extreme end of the curve, and, after a moment of intent listening, the voyagers crept up the sand, and in whispers discussed the next effort of their escape. The belts were unstrapped from about the log, reloaded with cartridges, and buckled around dripping waists before they clambered cautiously up the low bank. The road was just beyond, but between them and it arose the almost shapeless form of a small house, a mere darker shadow in the gloom of the night.

"Where are we?" questioned Westcott.

"Just back of old Beecher's shack. He's trucking down Benson way, but is liable to have some grub stored inside. I was countin' on this for our commissary department. Come on, Jim; time is money just now."

The door was unlocked, and they trusted wholly to the sense of touch to locate the object of their search. However, as there were but two rooms, not overly stocked with furniture, the gloom was not a serious obstacle, so that in less than ten minutes they emerged once more into the open bearing their spoils—Westcott, a slab of bacon and a small frying-pan; Brennan, a paper sack of corn meal, with a couple of specimens of canned goods. He had also resurrected a gunny sack somewhere, in which their things were carefully wrapped, and made secure for transportation.

"Didn't feel no terbacco, did yer, Jim?" the marshal questioned solicitously. "I reckon not though; ol' Beecher never would leave nuthin' like that lyin' round. Well, Lord! we ought ter be thankful fer what we've got. Now if we can only get away with them hosses."

They wormed their way forward to the edge of the road through a fringe of bushes, Westcott laden with the bundle. Except for the sound of distant voices and an occasional loud laugh, the night was still. They could almost hear their own breathing, and the crackle of a dry twig underfoot sounded to strained nerves like the report of a gun. Crouching at the edge of the road they could see fairly well what was before them, as revealed by the lights shining forth through the dingy windows of the saloon. The Red Dog was not more than a hundred yards away, and seemingly well patronised in spite of the fact that its owner and many of his parasites were busily engaged elsewhere. The wide-open front gave view of much of the barroom including even a section of the bar. Numerous figures moving about were easily discernible, while up above in the gambling rooms, the outlines of men were reflected upon the windows.

A hum of voices echoed out into the night, but the platform in front of the door was deserted. Occasionally some wanderer either entered or departed, merging into the crowd within or disappearing through the darkness without. To the left of the building, largely within its shadow, stretched the hitch rail to which were fastened fully a dozen cow-ponies, most of them revealed only by their restless movements, although the few nearest the door were plainly enough visible in the reflection of light. A fellow, ungainly in "chaps," reeled drunkenly down the steps, mounted one of these and spurred up the road, yelling as he disappeared. The noise he made was re-echoed by the restless crowd within. The two men, crouched in the bushes, surveyed the scene anxiously, marking its every detail. Brennan's hand closed heavily on the arm of the other.

"We better pick out the two critters farthest from the light," he muttered, "an' trust ter luck. We'll have to lead 'em a ways afore we mount. They're XL outfit mostly, an' that means fair stock. Shall we try it, now?"

"The sooner the better."

"That's me. Blamed if ever I thought I'd be a hoss thief, but when a feller associates with Bill Lacy there's no knowin' what he will come to. Howsumever, the foreman an' I are good friends, an' I don't reckon he'd ever let me be hung fer this job. We better try the other side o' the road, Jim."

They were in the flicker of light for scarcely an instant, merely two darting shadows, vanishing once more swiftly and silently into the gloom. Nor were they much longer in releasing the two cow-ponies. Westcott tied his bundle to the cantle of the saddle and then, bridle reins in hand, the docile animals following their new masters without resistance, the men led them over the smooth turf well back from the range of light. They were a quarter of a mile from the Red Dog before Brennan, slightly in advance, ventured to enter the road.

"It's safe enough now, Jim, an' we don't wanter lose no time. Got the grub, haven't yer?"

"Tied it on the saddle; which way do we go?"

"Straight south at the bridge; that will bring us to the old trail in about five miles, an' after that the devil himself couldn't find us. Ever crossed Shoshone?"

"No."

"Well, it's a little bit o' hell after sunup, an' we'll have a twenty mile ride before we strike water. We'll start slow."

They swung into saddle, the road before them a mere black ribbon revealed only by the gleam of a few far-off stars peering through rifts in the clouds. Brennan rode slightly in advance, trusting his mount largely to pick out the way, yet leaning forward eagerly scanning every shadow and listening for the slightest warning sound. They were upon the grade leading to the bridge when his vigilance was rewarded. There was some movement to the left, where the hotel trail led down the bank, and instantly both men drew up their ponies and remained intent and rigid. Brennan's hand rested on the butt of his revolver, but for the moment neither could determine what was moving in the intense blackness of the hillside. Then something spectral advanced into the starlight of the road and confronted them.

"Is this you, Mr. Cassady?" asked a woman's voice softly.

CHAPTER XXIV
THE CAVE IN THE CLIFF

Dazed, helpless, yet continuing to struggle futilely, Stella realised little except giving a glance at the hated faces of her captors. She heard Cateras's voice ordering the men forward, vibrant with Spanish oaths, and trembling yet with the fury which possessed him—but all else was a dim haze, out of which few remembrances ever came. They were in a large room, opening into another behind, a heavy door between. She was dragged forward, and thrust through this with no knowledge of what it was like. She could not think; she was only conscious of a deadly, paralysing horror. Cateras slammed the intervening door, and strode past.

What occurred was not clear to her mind; but suddenly what appeared to be an open fireplace seemed to swing aside, leaving revealed a great black opening in the rock. To the lieutenant's snarl of command, one of the men released his grip of her arm, and lit a lantern which he took from a near-by shelf. The dim flicker of light penetrated a few feet into the dark hole, only serving to render the opening more grim and sinister. The girl shrank back, but the fellow still holding her tightened his grip. Cateras seemed to have regained his good humour, although the red welt across his face stood forth ugly in the flare. His thin lips smiled, and he bowed hat in hand, hatefully polite.

"Go ahead with the light, Silva; not too fast, my man; the room beyond the *señor's*. Now, Merodez, release the girl."

"Ah, so you can stand alone, *señorita*; that is well. Step in here, ahead of me, and follow the lantern—there is nothing to fear."

She hesitated, and the smile on the Mexican's lips changed into a cruel grin.

"Shall I make you again?"

"No, *señor*."

"Then you will do as I bid."

"Yes, *señor*; I cannot resist."

The passage was clean and dry, and seemed to lead directly back into the cliff. The faint light revealed the side walls and low roof, and the girl, again partially mistress of herself, recognised the nature of the rock to be limestone. Occasionally the floor exhibited evidences that human hands had been employed in levelling it, and there were marks along the side-walls to show where the passage had been widened; but the opening itself was originally a cave, through which water had run in long past ages—a cave wide enough to allow six men to walk abreast, but with an average height of about seven feet. For twenty feet it ran almost straight in; then they came to a sharp turn to the right, and entered a much narrower passage. The air was so pure and fresh, even after this turn was made, as to lead her to believe there must somewhere be another opening. The vague thought brought with it a throb of hope.

Her view was limited to the slight radius illumined by the lantern, and even within that small area, her own shadow, and those of the three men, helped render everything indistinct. The side walls appeared to be of solid rock; she perceived no evidence of entrances into any side chamber, only that her eyes twice caught glimpses of what seemed like narrow slits at about the level of her head. She could not be certain as to their purpose, or ascertain exactly what they were, only they bore resemblance to an opening cleft in the rock, either for ventilation, or to permit of observation from without of some interior cell. Near each of these was a strangely shaped bracket of wood fastened in some manner to the side wall, apparently intended for the support of a light, as the ceiling above exhibited marks of smoke.

They had turned the sharp corner, and advanced a few feet beyond when the man with the lantern stopped suddenly, and held it up to permit the light to stream full on the exposed wall to the right. Another of these odd slits in the rock was visible here, and the girl was able to perceive more clearly its nature—beyond question it was an artificial opening, leading into a space on the farther side of the wall. Cateras pushed past her, his body interfering with her view, and bent down, fumbling along the rock surface.

"Hold the light closer," he demanded. "Aye, that's it. 'Tis some trick to find the thing—— Ah! now I have it."

It seemed like a bit of wood, so resembling the colour of the rock as to be practically imperceptible to the eye in that dim light—a bit of wood which slid back to reveal a heavy iron bolt, shot firmly into the stone. This the Mexican forced back, and an opening yawned in the side wall, the rays of the lantern revealing the interior of a black cave. Cateras stepped within.

"Bring the woman," he commanded shortly, "and you, Merodez, see first to the light."

Silva thrust her forward, his grip no light one, while the other struck a match and applied it to the wick of a lamp occupying a bracket beside the doorway. As this caught the full interior was revealed beneath the sickly glow, a cell-like place, although of a fair size, unfurnished except for a rude bench, and one three-legged stool, the floor of stone, and the sides and roof apparently of the same solid structure. It was gloomy, bare, horrible in its dreariness—a veritable grave. The girl covered her face with her hands, appalled at the sight, unnerved at the thought of being left alone in such a place. Cateras saw the movement, and laughed, gazing about carelessly.

"Some boudoir, *señorita*," he said meaningly. "Well, we will see what can be done for you later. Perhaps a few hours in such a hole may work a miracle. When I come again you will be glad to see even me. That's all, lads; there's plenty of oil, and you can bring along some blankets with the evening meal."

He stopped, standing alone in the narrow opening, the light of the lantern without bringing his face into bold relief. The girl had sunk helplessly onto the bench, her head bowed within her hands. The Mexican eyed her frowningly.

"Quite tamed already," he said sarcastically. "Bah! I have done it to worse than you. Look up at me."

She lifted her eyes slowly, her lips pressed tightly together. She was conscious of depression, of fear, yet as her glance encountered his, a sudden spirit of defiance caused her to stand erect.

"There are some women with whom you are not acquainted, Señor Cateras," she said quietly, desperation rendering her voice firm. "And possibly I may prove one of them. I am your prisoner it seems, yet I advise you not to go too far, or I may prove to be a dangerous one. In the first place it might be well for you to remember that, helpless as I seem at present, I have friends—whatever befalls me will be known."

"How known?" his white teeth gleamed. "Do you think what goes on here is published to the world? If I should tell you the history of this secret valley it would take some of the defiance out of you, I imagine."

"Then you reckon wrong, I am not afraid of you, and I believe in my friends. All I ask now is that I be left alone."

"Which will bring you to your senses. I have seen that tried out here, and know how it works. All right, I'll leave you to think it over; then I'll come back for an answer. Until then, *señorita, adios*."

The fellow lifted his hat, and stepped back into the passage, his manner insolent. She remained motionless, contempt in her eyes, but in truth hopeless and crushed. Silva closed the door silently, although her ears caught the click of the bolt when it was shot home.

No sound of their retreating footsteps reached her through the thick wall. The stillness of her prison seemed to strike her like a blow. For a moment she stood staring at the bare wall, her lips parted, her limbs trembling from the reaction of excitement; then she stepped forward, and felt along the smooth surface of rock.

The door fitted so closely she could not even determine its exact outlines. Baffled, her glance wandered about the cell, seeking vainly for any sign of weakness, and then, giving way utterly to her despair, the girl flung herself on the bench, covering her eyes to shut out those hideous surroundings. What should she do? What could she do? What possibility of hope lay in her own endeavours? From what source could she expect any outside help?

After those first moments of complete despair, there came greater calmness, in which her mind began to grapple with the situation. Life had never been an easy problem, and discouragement was no part of her creed. She sat up once more, her lips pressed tightly together, her eyes dry of tears.

In spite of Cateras's cowardly threats these outlaws would never dare to take her life. There was no occasion for them to resort to so desperate a deed. Besides this Mexican was only an under officer of the band, and would never venture to oppose the will of his chief. Her fate rested not on his word, but upon the decision of Pasqual Mendez, and, if that bandit was associated with Bill Lacy, as undoubtedly he was, then as the prisoner of the American, she was certainly safe until the latter expressed his own wish regarding her.

And why should Lacy desire to take her life? Most assuredly he did not, or the act would have been already accomplished. The very fact of her having been transported such a distance was sufficient evidence of his purpose. The conspirators merely suspected her mission in Haskell; they were afraid she knew more of their plans than she really did. The telegram, stolen by Miss La Rue, had convinced the leaders that she might prove dangerous if left at large, and they had determined to hold her helpless until their scheme had been worked out and they were safely beyond pursuit. That was undoubtedly the one object of her capture. Lacy had no knowledge that Mendez's band was at the rendezvous; he supposed them to be on a cattle raid to the south, with only a man or two of his own left as guard over Cavendish.

Cavendish! Her mind grasped clearly now the fact that the man was not dead. It had not been his body found in the Waldron Apartments, but that of some other man substituted for purposes of crime. Cavendish himself had been lured westward, waylaid in some manner and made prisoner, as she and Westcott had suspected.

Through the co-operation of Lacy he had been brought to this desert den, where he could be held indefinitely, with no chance of discovery—killed if necessary. She had heard of such places as this, read of them, yet never before had she realised the possibility of their real existence. It all seemed more like a delirium of fever than an actual fact. She rubbed her eyes, gazing about on the rock walls, scarcely sure she was actually awake. Why, one might ride across that desert, and pass by within a hundred yards of its rim, and never even be aware of the existence of this sunken valley. Perhaps not a dozen men outside this gang of outlaws had ever gazed down into its green depths, and possibly no others knew of that narrow, winding trail leading down to its level. Yet these men must have made use of it for years, as a place to hide stolen cattle, and into which to retreat whenever pursuit became dangerous.

Those huts without were not newly built, and this underground cavern had been extended and changed by no small labour. What deeds of violence must have happened here; what scenes of unbridled debauchery this desert rendezvous must have witnessed. She shuddered at the thought, comprehending that these cells had never been chiselled without a purpose, and that she was utterly helpless in the hands of a band of thieves and cutthroats, to whom murder meant little enough, if it only served their ends. Mendez, no doubt, was brute and monster, yet it was Juan Cateras whom she really feared—he was cruel, slimy, seeking to hide his hatefulness behind that hideous smile; and he had already chosen her for his victim. Who would save her—Mendez? Lacy? God, she did not know: and somehow neither of these was the name which arose to her lips, almost in the form of prayer; the name she whispered with a faint throb of hope in its utterance—Jim Westcott.

The big miner was all she had to rely upon; he had been in her mind all through the long ride; he arose before her again now, and she welcomed the memory with a conscious throb of expectation. Those people back there could not conceal for long her absence from him; if he lived he would surely seek her again.

Her womanly instinct had read the message in the man's eyes; she was of interest to him, he cared; it was no mere ordinary friendliness which would bring him back; no! not even their mutual connection with the case of Frederick Cavendish. Her eyes brightened, and a flush of colour crept into her cheeks. She believed in him, in his courage—he had appealed to her as a man.

Suddenly she seemed to realise the yearning of her own heart, her utter faith in him. He would come, he must come; even now he might have discovered her sudden disappearance, and suspected the cause. He would never believe any lies they might tell—that she had departed without a word, without a message—he would find out the truth somehow; he was not the kind to lie down, to avoid danger when it confronted duty—and, besides, he cared. She knew this, comprehended without question; there had been no word spoken, yet she knew.

Once she had accepted this knowledge with a smile, but now it thrilled her with hope, and set her heart throbbing strangely. Not that she dreamed love in return, or permitted it to even enter her mind; yet the very thought that this man would, if necessary, wade into the very waters of death for her sake, was somehow sweet and consoling. She was no longer alone; no longer hopeless and unnerved—deep down in her consciousness she trusted him.

"If"—how often that recurred; how it brought back memory of Lacy, of Enright, of Beaton, of the La Rue woman. What else could they have remained behind for, except to hide and close the trail? It was Westcott they would guard against; he was the only one they now had any cause to fear. They suspected his connection with her, his knowledge of their purpose; they knew of his presence the night before at the shaft-house of Lacy's mine; they would "get" him, if they could, and by no such simple methods as they got her. If she could only have warned him; if he was only placed on guard before they were ready to act—"if"——

Suddenly the girl's slender body grew taut, and her thin white, delicate hands clutched the granite wall back of her, and into her grey eyes crept the light of terror, a terror that was new and strange to her, a nameless clutching fear that her varied experiences in the city had never brought her, an insidious, terrible fright for her bodily safety. Her delicate ears, strained under their spun-brown covering of hair—there was no doubt of it; she heard footsteps in the passageway. Juan Cateras with his leering, lustful smile was coming back.

CHAPTER XXV
IN THE DARK PASSAGE

The uncertainty was of scarcely an instant. The open slit above the door was a perfect conveyer of sound, and a voice pierced the silence. It was the voice of Juan Cateras, vibrant with anger.

"You sleepy swine," he ejaculated fiercely, "and is this the way you keep watch? Come out of that!" the command punctuated by the scuffling of feet. "Damn you, Silva, but I will teach you a lesson for this when I return. Now go to the hut and stay there until I come. This is a matter where Mendez shall name the penalty. Get you gone, you sleepy dog."

He either struck or kicked the man, hurrying the fellow down the passage to the echo of Spanish oaths. Apparently no resistance was made, for the next instant the key turned in the lock and the door opened. Cateras, smiling, seemingly unruffled by this encounter, stepped within, calmly closed the door behind him, and then turned to greet the lady. She met his bow with eyes of firm resolve, though her heart ached.

"Why do you come, *señor?*" she asked so quietly that the man in surprise halted his step forward.

"To keep my word," and his white teeth gleamed in an effort at pleasantness. "I am always truthful with your sex; and I told you I would return shortly."

"Yet why?" she insisted, anxious only to keep him away as long as possible, and yet enchain his interest. "If I am prisoner here, I am not your prisoner. Do you come, then, to serve me?"

"Can you doubt that, *señorita?*" still endeavouring to retain the mask he had first assumed. "Because circumstances make me defy the law—a mere love of adventure, no more—is no reason why I should be devoid of heart and sympathy." He took a step nearer. "Since leaving here I have questioned the men who brought you, and learned why you were made prisoner. I care nothing for this Bill Lacy—nothing," and he snapped his fingers derisively. "Why should I? But, instead, I would be your friend."

"You mean your purpose is to aid me to escape?"

He bowed low.

"It would be my great happiness to do so. There is danger, yet what is danger to Juan Cateras? 'Tis only part of my life. The *señorita* is an

American, and to her one of my race may not appeal, yet I would prove my devotion with my life."

"Your devotion, *señor*!"

"Is not the word expressive! Though I have seen you but once before, my heart is already devoted to your interest. I am of a Southern race, *señorita*, and we do not calculate—we feel. Why, then, should I conceal my eagerness? It is love which causes me to thus defy all and offer you freedom."

"Love!" she laughed. "Why, that is impossible. Surely you only jest, *señor*."

The smile deserted his lips, and with a quick, unexpected movement he grasped her hand.

"Jest! You would call it a jest. You will not think so for long. Why, what can you do? No; stop shrinking back from me. It will be well that you listen. This is no parlour where you can turn me away with a word of scorn," and his eyes swept the bare walls. "I come to you with a chance of escape; I will take the risk and pledge you my aid. I alone can save you; there is no other to whom you can turn. In return I but ask my reward."

She hesitated, her eyes lifting to his face.

"You promise me your assistance?"

"Within the hour."

"How? What plan have you?"

"That I will not tell; you must trust me. I am the lieutenant of Pasqual Mendez," a touch of pride in his voice. "And my word alone will open the way. You will come?"

"Wait; I must know more. You say it is love which prompts your offer, *señor*. I cannot understand; and even if this be true, I must be frank and honest in my answer—I do not return your love."

"Bah! That is nothing. I know women; they learn love quickly when the way opens. I am not so ill to look at, *señorita*. A kiss now will seal the bargain! I will wait the rest."

"You ask no pledge, then, of me?"

"Only your consent to accompany me, and the kiss. Beyond that I take the gambler's chance. Only you must say yes or no; for it will require time for me to clear the road."

"It must be to-night?"

"The sooner the better; they tell me Lacy will be here himself soon, and after he comes the one chance is over with. You will give the kiss?"

"Do not ask it, *señor*!"

"Oh, but I will—aye, more, I'll take it. A dozen will do no harm, and no scream from those lips will be heard. You may as well be nice, my beauty."

She was against the wall, helpless, and the grip of his hands was like steel. She made no sound, although struggling to break free. His breath was on her cheek; his eyes burning with lust gazing straight into her own.

Slowly, remorselessly, he bent her head backward until she feared her neck would snap. A sob started in her throat, but she silenced it with the will of a superwoman. Into her terror-stricken mind leaped the sudden conclusion that resistance with this beast was futile; she must outwit him with her brains. Suddenly relaxing herself, she slipped to the granite floor on her knees.

"Please, please," she begged. "I give in, *señor*, I give in."

But as she spoke her right hand closed about a square jagged bit of rock.

"So, my pretty," sneered Cateras, "you have learned that Juan Cateras is not a man to trifle with. It is well." And, releasing his grip upon her, he allowed the girl to rise.

As she stood there in the half light, her grey eyes flashing, her young bosom rising and falling, she was a vaguely defined but alluring figure. So Juan Cateras thought, and he took a step nearer, his thick, red lips curling with lust, eager to claim their rich reward. As they came closer Stella Donovan stiffened.

"Look, *señor*," she whispered—"behind you!"

The Mexican in his eagerness was off his guard. He turned to look, and at that instant the girl drew back her sturdy arm and then brought it forward again with all her vigour. *Cluk*! She heard the rock sound against her oppressor's head, heard a low moan escape his lips, and saw him sink slowly to the floor at her feet.

The next instant she was beside him, in terror lest she had killed him; but a hurried glance, supplemented by her fingers which reached for his pulse, assured her that she had only stunned her assailant. Her heart beat less rapidly now, and she again had control of her mental processes. With deft hands that worked speedily in the darkness she unstrapped from around his waist the belt with its thirty-six cartridges and revolver, then pulled from his pocket the keys, not only to her cell, but, she judged, to others.

The feel of their bronze coldness in her hot hands brought a quick message to her brain; beyond a question of doubt, the missing Cavendish was concealed in one of the dark, dank cells in the immediate vicinage, if not actually in this same passage, then in another one perhaps not greatly distant. The speculation gave her determination and decision.

Reaching beneath her outer skirt, she jerked loose her white petticoat, and then began tearing it into long strips which she knotted together. This done, she bound Juan Cateras's hand and foot, and, with some difficulty, turned him over on his face after first thrusting into his half-open mouth a gag, which she had fashioned from stray ends of the providential petticoat.

Then leaping to her feet and strapping the ammunition belt and revolver about her waist, she stole on tiptoe to the doorway and peered out; the silent, cavernous passage was empty.

Lithely, like a young panther, she slipped out of the cell and began making down the passageway to a spot of light which she judged to be its opening. She had scarcely gone ten feet, however, before she stopped short—somewhere in the dark she heard a voice.

Flattening herself against the sides of the passage, she thought quickly; to return to the cell in which lay Juan Cateras would be unwise, for he might break the bonds, which were none too strong, and, in his fury at having been so easily duped, subject her to unknown but anyway horrible indignities, if not death itself. But what other course was there?

As she stood there a fraction of a second against the wall, knowing not which way to turn, the girl wished with all her heart that big Jim Westcott, strong, cool, collected, the master of any situation requiring force, tact, and acumen, were there by her side to take her arm and guide her out of this terrible predicament. But Jim was elsewhere—where, she could hardly guess.

What was to be done? Her temples throbbed as the voices sounded nearer. Then it came home to her—why not try one of the other cells? Possibly she would be lucky enough to find an empty one; the chances were, she felt, that most of them were.

Suiting action to the thought, she stepped quietly from the niche in the wall, moved noiselessly along its surface, and came at length to another dungeon similar to She one she had occupied, except that it had no window in its oaken door. Fumbling with the bunch of keys, she took the first one around which her fingers fell and thrust it hurriedly into the lock. Would it open the haven to temporary safety? She struggled with it—turning it first to the left and then to the right. The footsteps were sounding nearer and nearer every minute, the voices were growing louder.

Frantic, she gave the key a final desperate twist, and as a sigh of relief escaped her lips the door swung open. Slipping through the aperture, she closed it softly after her and, panting from excitement and her exertions, turned and faced the recesses of her hiding-place.

It was black, pitch-black, except for a long ray of light that struggled in between the heavy door and its casing, but as Stella Donovan stood there in the gloom she was aware that she was not the only occupant of the cell. She crouched back, gripped in the hands of another fear, but the next moment her alarm was lessened somewhat by the sound of a soft, well-modulated voice.

"Who's that?" it said faintly.

Then followed the repeated scratching of a wet match, a flame of yellow light, which was immediately carried to a short tallow candle, and in the aura of its sickly flame Stella Donovan saw the face of a man with long, unkempt beard and feverish eyes that stared at her as though she were an apparition.

CHAPTER XXVI
THE REAPPEARANCE OF CAVENDISH

As her eyes became more accustomed to the light she saw that the stranger was a man of approximately thirty, of good robust health. His hair was sandy of colour and thin, and his beard, which was of the same hue, had evidently gone untrimmed for days, perhaps weeks; yet for all of his unkempt appearance, for all the strangeness of his presence there, he was a gentleman, that was plain. And as she scrutinised him Miss Donovan thought she beheld a mild similarity in the contour of the man's head, the shape of his face, the lines of his body, to the man whom, several weeks before, she had seen lying dead upon the floor of his rooms in the Waldron apartments.

Could this be Frederick Cavendish? By all that had gone before, he should be; but the longer she looked at him the less certain she was of the correctness of this surmise. Of course the face of the man in the Waldron apartments had been singed by fire so that it was virtually unrecognisable, thus making comparisons in the present instance difficult. At any rate, she dismissed the speculation temporarily from her mind, and resolved to divulge nothing for the time, but merely to draw the man out. Her thoughts, rapid as they had been, were interrupted by the fellow's sudden exclamation.

"My God!" he cried in a high voice, "I—I thought I was seeing things. You are really a woman—and alive?"

Miss Donovan hesitated a moment before she answered, wondering whether to tell him of her narrow escape. This she decided to do.

"Alive, but only by luck," she said in a friendly voice, and then recounted the insults of Cateras, her struggle with him, and capture of his cartridge belt and revolver, and how finally she had left him bound and gagged in the adjoining cell. The man listened attentively, though his mind seemed slow to grasp details.

"But," he insisted, unable to clear his brain, "why are you here? Surely you are not one of this gang of outlaws?"

"I am inclined to think," she answered soberly, "that much the same cause must account for the presence of both of us. I am a prisoner. That is true of you also, is it not?"

"Yes," his voice lowered almost to a whisper. "But do not speak so loud, please; there is an opening above the door, so voices can be heard by any guard in the corridor. I—I am a prisoner, although I do not in the least know why. When did you come?"

"Not more than two hours ago. Two men brought me across the desert from Haskell."

"I do not know how I came. I was unconscious until I woke up in that cell. I was on the platform of an observation car the last I remember," his utterance slow, as though his mind struggled with a vague memory, "talking with a gentleman whom I had met on the train. There—there must have been an accident, I think, for I never knew anything more until I woke up here."

"Do you know how long ago that was?"

He shook his head.

"It was a long while. There has been no light, so I could not count the days, but, if they have fed me twice every twenty-hours, it is certainly a month since I came."

"A month! Do you recall the name of the man you were conversing with on the observation car?"

He pressed his hand against his forehead, a wrinkle appearing straight between his eyes.

"I've tried to remember that," he admitted regretfully, "but it doesn't quite come to me."

"Was it Beaton?"

"Yes. Why, how strange! Of course, he was Edward Beaton, of New York. He told me he was a broker. Why, how did you know?"

She hesitated for an instant, uncertain just how far it was best to confide in him. Unquestionably, the man's mind was not entirely clear, and he might say and do things to the injury of them both if he once became aware of the whole truth. Besides, the meeting him there alive was in itself a shock. She had firmly believed him dead—murdered in New York. No, she would keep that part of the story to herself for the present; let it be told to him later by others.

"It is not so strange," she said at last, "for your disappearance is indirectly the occasion of my being here also. I believe I can even call you by name. You are Mr. Cavendish?"

"Yes," he admitted, his hands gripping the back of the bench nervously, his eyes filled with amazement "But—but I do not know you."

"For the best of reasons," she answered smilingly, advancing and extending her hand—"because we have never met before. However mysterious all this must seem to you, Mr. Cavendish, it is extremely simple when explained. I am Stella Donovan, a newspaperwoman. Your strange disappearance about a month ago aroused considerable interest, and I chanced to be detailed on the case. My investigations led me to visit Haskell, where unfortunately my mission became known to those who were responsible for your imprisonment here. So, to keep me quiet, I was also abducted and brought to this place."

"You—you mean it was not an accident—that I was brought here purposely?"

"Exactly; you were trailed from New York by a gang of thieves having confederates in this country. I am unable to give you all the details; but this man Beaton, whom you met on the train, is a notorious gunman and gambler. His being on the same train with you was a part of a well-laid plan, and I have no doubt but what he deliberately slugged you while you two were alone on the observation platform. As I understand, that is exactly his line of work."

"But—but," he stammered, "what was his object? Why did those people scheme to get me?"

"Why! Money, no doubt; you are wealthy, are you not?"

"Yes, to an extent. I inherited property, but I had no considerable sum with me that day; not more than a few hundred dollars."

"As I told you, Mr. Cavendish, I do not know all the details, but I think these men—one of whom is a lawyer—planned to gain possession of your fortune, possibly by means of a forged will; and, in order to accomplish this, it was necessary to get you out of the way. It looks as though they were afraid to resort to actual murder, but ready enough to take any other desperate chance. Do you see what I mean?"

"They will rob me! While holding me here a prisoner they propose robbing me through the courts?"

"That is undoubtedly their object, but, I happen to know, it has not yet been fully accomplished. If either of us can make escape from this place we shall be in time to foil them completely."

"But how," he questioned, still confused and with only the one thought dominating his mind, "could they hope to obtain possession of my fortune unless I was dead?"

"They are prepared to prove you dead. I believed so myself. The only way to convince the courts otherwise will be your appearance in person. After they once get full possession of the money they do not care what becomes of you. Living or dead, you can never get it back again."

He sank down on the bench and buried his face in his hands, thoroughly unnerved. The girl looked at him a moment in silence, then touched his shoulder.

"Look here, Mr. Cavendish," she said firmly, "there is no use losing your nerve. Surely there must be some way of getting out of here. For one, I am going to try."

He looked up at her, but with no gleam of hope in his eyes.

"I have tried," he replied despondently, "but it is no use. We are buried alive."

"Yet there must be ways out," she insisted. "The air in that passage was perfectly pure; do you know anything about it?"

"Yes; it leads to the top of the cliff, up a steep flight of steps. But it is impossible to reach the passage, and since these Mexicans came I have reason to believe they keep a guard."

"They were not here, then, at first?"

"Only for a few days; before that two rough-looking fellows, but Americans, were all I saw. Now they have gone, and Mexicans have taken their places—they are worse than the others. Do you know what it means?"

"Only partially. I have overheard some talk. It seems this is a rendezvous for a band of outlaws headed by one known as Pasqual Mendez. I have not seen their leader; but his lieutenant had charge of me."

"Miss Donovan," he said with gravity, "we are in the hands of desperate men. We will have to take desperate measures to outwit them, and we will have to make desperate breaks to obtain our freedom."

The girl nodded.

"Mr. Cavendish," she said with womanly courage, "you will not find me wanting. I am ready for anything, even shooting. I do hope you're a good shot."

Cavendish smiled.

"I have had some experience," he said.

"Then," the girl added, "you had better take the revolver. I never fired one except on the Fourth of July, and I would not want to trust to my marksmanship in a pinch. Not that we will meet any such situation, Mr. Cavendish—I hope we do not—but in case we do I want to depend upon you."

"I am glad you said that, Miss Donovan; it gives me courage."

The girl handed the revolver over to him without a word and then held out the cartridge belt. He snapped open the weapon to assure himself it was loaded and then ran his fingers over the belt pockets.

"Thirty-six rounds," adjusting the belt to his waist; "that ought to promise a good fight. Do you feel confidence in me again?"

"Yes," she answered, her eyes lifting to meet his. "I trust you."

"Good. I am not a very desperate character, but will do the best I can. Shall we try the passage?"

"Yes. It is the only hope."

"All right then; I'll go first, and you follow as close as possible. There mustn't be the slightest sound made."

Cavendish thrust his head cautiously through the door, the revolver gripped in his hand; Miss Donovan, struggling to keep her nerves steady, touched the coat of her companion, fearful of being alone. The passage-way was dark, except for the little bars of light streaming out through the slits in the stone above the cell doors. These, however, were sufficient to convince Cavendish that no guards were in the immediate neighbourhood. He felt the grip of the girl's fingers on his coat, and reached back to clasp her hand.

"All clear," he whispered. "Hurry, and let's get this door closed."

They slipped through, crouching in the shadow as the door shut behind them, eagerly seeking to pierce the mystery of the gloom into which the narrow corridor vanished. Beyond the two cells and their dim rays all was black silence, yet both felt a strange relief at escaping from the confines of their prison. The open passage was cool, and the fugitives felt fresh air upon their cheeks; nowhere did any sound break the silence. Stella had a feeling as though they were buried alive.

"That—that is the way, is it not?" she asked. "I was brought from below."

"Yes; it is not far; see, the passage leads upward. Come, we might as well learn what is ahead."

They advanced slowly, keeping closely against the wall, and testing the floor cautiously before venturing a step. A few yards plunged them into total darkness, and, although Cavendish had been conducted along there a prisoner, he retained small recollection of the nature of the passage.

Their progress was slow but silent, neither venturing to exchange speech, but with ears anxiously strained to catch the least sound. Stella was conscious of the loud beating of her heart, the slight rasping of Cavendish's feet on the rock floor. The slightest noise seemed magnified. The grade rose sharply, until it became almost a climb, yet the floor had evidently been levelled, and there were no obstructions to add to the difficulty of advance. Then the passage swerved rather sharply to the right, and Cavendish, leading, halted to peer about the corner. An instant they both remained motionless, and then, seeing and hearing nothing, she could restrain her impatience no longer.

"What is it?" she questioned. "Is there something wrong?"

He reached back and drew her closer, without answering, until her eyes also were able to look around the sharp edge of rock. Far away, it seemed a long distance up that narrow tunnel, a lantern glowed dully, the light so dim and flickering as to scarcely reveal even its immediate surroundings; yet from that distance, her eyes accustomed to the dense gloom, she could distinguish enough to quicken her breathing and cause her to clutch the sleeve of her companion.

The lantern occupied a niche in the side wall at the bottom of a flight of rude steps. Not more than a half-dozen of these were revealed, but at their foot, where the passage had been widened somewhat, extended a stone bench, on which lounged two men. One was lying back, his head pillowed on a rolled coat, yet was evidently awake; for the other, seated below him, with knees drawn up for comfort, kept up conversation in a low voice, the words being inaudible at that distance. Even in that dim light the two were clearly Mexican.

"What shall we do?" she asked, her lips at Cavendish's ear. "We cannot pass them—they are on guard."

"I was wondering how close I could creep in before they saw me," he answered, using the same caution. "If I was only sure they were alone, and could once get the drop, we might make it."

"You fear there may be others posted at the top?"

"There is quite likely to be; the fellows are evidently taking no chances of surprise. What do you think best?"

"Even if you succeeded in overawing these two, we would have no way of securing them. An alarm would be given before we could get beyond reach. Our only hope of escape lies in getting out of here unseen."

"Yes, and before Cateras is discovered."

"He gave no orders to the guard to return?"

"No; but he will be missed after a while and sought for. We cannot count on any long delay, and when it is found that he has been knocked out, and we have disappeared, every inch of this cave will be searched. There is no place to hide, and only the two ways by which to get out."

"Then, let's go back and try the other," she urged. "That opens directly into the valley and is probably not guarded. What is happening now?"

A grey gleam of light struck the steps from above, recognised instantly as a reflection of day, as though some cover had been uplifted connecting this underground labyrinth with the clear sky. A dim shadow touched the illumined rocks for a brief moment, a moving shadow uncertain in its outlines, grotesque, shapeless: and then the daylight vanished as suddenly as it dawned. There was a faint click, as though a door closed, while darkness resumed sway, the silence unbroken, but for the scraping of a step on those rude stairs. The two guards below came to their feet, rigid in the glow of the lantern, their faces turned upward. Then a man came slowly down the last few steps and joined them.

CHAPTER XXVII
A DANGEROUS PRISONER

He was tall and thin, wearing a wide cloak about his shoulders, and high hat with broad brim. Even at that distance it could be seen that his long hair was grey, and that a heavy moustache, snow-white, made more noticeable the thin features of his face. The man was Mexican, no doubt of that, but of the higher class, the dead pallor of his skin accented by the black, deep-seated eyes. He looked at the two men closely, and his voice easily reached the ears of the listeners.

"Who posted you here?"

"Juan Cateras, *señor*," answered one.

"Not on my order. Dias is watching above. Did the lieutenant give you a reason?"

"The prisoners, *señor*."

"The prisoners! Oh, yes; those that Lacy had confined here. Well, they will not be here for long. I do not believe in prisoners, and because I do business with that dog is no reason why he is privileged to use this place to hold his victims. I have just despatched a messenger to Haskell to that effect, and we'll soon be rid of them. Where is Cateras?"

"In the valley, *señor*! he went back down the passage with Silva after posting us here."

"And the prisoners?"

"Occupy the two inner cells. Merodiz here says one of them is a girl."

"A girl!" the tall man laughed. "That then will account for the unusual interest of Juan Cateras, and why he preferred being left in charge. A girl, hey, Merodiz! You saw the witch? What sort was she?"

"An American, *señor*, young, and good to look at," the other man explained. "Her eyes as blue as the skies."

"Good! 'tis not often the gods serve us so well. I forgive Cateras for failure to report such a prize, but from now on will see that he takes his proper place. She was here when we came?"

"No, *señor*; the two Americanos brought her; it was Silva and I who put her in the cell."

"At Cateras's order?"

"Yes, *señor*."

"In what cell?"

"The second in the passage; the man who was here when we came has the one this way."

"Caramba! this is all pleasant enough. I will pay my respects to the lady, and there is no time like the present."

He turned away, thumbing his moustache, quite pleased with his conceit, but one of the men stopped him with a question.

"We remain here, *señor*?"

"Yes, you might as well," his lips smiling, "and if the Señor Cateras passes, you can tell him that I visit the fair American. It will give him joy."

The girl drew Cavendish back hurriedly, her mind working in a flash of inspiration.

"Quick," she breathed in his ear. "There is a niche where we can hide a few yards back. If he follows the other wall he might pass, and not notice."

"But he goes to your cell; 'tis Pasqual Mendez."

"I know, but come. He must not go there. I will tell you my plan."

They were pressed back within the slight recess before the Mexican turned the corner, and she had hastily breathed her desperate scheme.

"It can be done," she insisted, "and there is nought else possible. We dare not let him enter, and find Cateras, and to kill the man will serve no good end. You will not? Then give me the revolver. Good! Be silent now."

Mendez came down the black passage evidently in rare good humour, humming a tune, with one hand pressed upon the wall to better guide his movements. So dark it was, even the outlines of his form were indistinguishable, yet, as he felt no need for caution, it was easy enough to trace his forward progress. The girl stood erect, the revolver gripped in one hand, the other pressing back her companion into the recess. She had lost all sense of fear in the determination to act; better risk all than surrender without a struggle. Mendez fumbled along the wall, stumbled over some slight projection and swore; another step, and his groping hand would touch her. He never took the step, but was whirled against the side wall, with the cold barrel of a revolver pressed against his cheek. A stern, sibilant whisper held him motionless.

"If you move I fire, *señor*; raise your hands—quick!"

He responded mechanically, too profoundly astounded to dream of resistance. It was the sound of the voice which impressed him.

"Santa Maria! A woman?"

"Yes, *señor*, a woman; the same you sought, but I have found you first."

He chuckled.

"A good jest surely; how came you here?"

"Not to discuss that, *señor*," quietly. "Nor is this to be laughed over. If you would live, do as I say. Mr. Cavendish, see if the man bears weapons."

"Only a belt with a knife."

"Keep the knife; it may come handy for some purpose. Now bind his hands with the belt. Cross your wrists, *señor*."

He had lost his temper, no longer deeming this a joke.

"You damn vixen," he growled savagely. "This play will soon be done; do you know who I am?"

"The Señor Pasqual Mendez, but that means nothing," she answered. "This revolver will kill you as surely as any one else. Do what I say then, and talk no more—cross your wrists behind."

He did so, and Cavendish strapped the stout belt about them, winding it in and out until he had sure purchase. He drew it so tightly the fellow winced.

"It hurts, *señor*," she said, satisfied. "Well, to hurt you a little is better than what you planned for me. Now lead on. No, listen first. I know who you are and your power here. That is why we took this chance of making you prisoner. We are desperate; it is either your life, or ours, *señor*. You are an outlaw, with a price on your head, and you realise what chances one will take to escape. Now there is just one opportunity given you to live."

"What, *señorita*?"

"That you accompany us down this passage into the valley as hostage. You will compel your men, if we encounter any, to furnish us horses."

"But the men may not obey. I cannot promise; Señor Cateras——"

"Señor Cateras will not be there," she interrupted sharply. "We have already seen to Señor Cateras. The others will obey you?"

"They may; I cannot promise."

"Then it will be your own loss; for if there be a shot fired, you will get either a bullet or a knife thrust. I would try no sharp tricks, Señor Mendez. Now we go on."

Mendez smiled grimly in the dark, his mind busy. He had seen much of life of a kind and felt no doubt but this young woman would keep her word. She had become sufficiently desperate to be dangerous, and he felt no desire to drive her to extremes. Besides he was helpless to resist, but would watch for opportunity, trusting in luck.

"I am to go first?" and his voice assumed polite deference.

"Beside Mr. Cavendish," she replied, "and I will be behind."

"This gentleman, you mean?"

"Yes; and there is no need for any more acting. This is the revolver pressing against your back, *señor*. I could scarcely miss you at that distance."

They advanced in silence, through the faint gleam of light which illumined the passage through the stone slits over the cell doors. Only then did Mendez venture to pause, and glance back at his captor.

"Pardon, *señorita*," he said gallantly, "but I would have view of the first lady who ever took Pasqual Mendez prisoner. The sight robs me of all displeasure. In truth it is hardly necessary for you to resort to fire-arms."

"I prefer them," shortly. "Go on!"

The darkness swallowed them again, but the way was clear, and, once around the sharp turn, a glimmer of distant daylight made advance easier. There was no sign of any guard visible, nor any movement perceptible in the open vista beyond the cave entrance. The girl touched Mendez's arm.

"Wait; I would ask a question, or two first, before we venture further. I was brought in this way, yet my memory is not clear. There are two log houses before the cave?"

"Yes," he answered readily, "one somewhat larger than the other—the men occupy that; the other is for myself and my officers."

"Besides Cateras?"

"No, not at present; at times I have guests. It would be pleasurable to entertain you, and your friend."

"No doubt. You expect Lacy?"

"You know that also? How did you learn?"

"I heard you talk to the men at the other end. It is true, is it not?"

"I have sent for him; it was yesterday."

"And he could be here now?"

"Not before night; it is a hard ride; why ask all this?"

"I have reasons. Now another thing; where are your men?"

His eyes wandered to the gleam of daylight.

"There will be one or two in the bunk-house likely; the others are with the cattle up the valley."

"But none in your cabin?"

He shook his head.

"And you say Lacy cannot get here before dark? How late?"

He hesitated over his reply, endeavouring shrewdly to conjecture what could be the object of all this questioning, yet finally concluding that the truth would make very little difference.

"Well, *señorita*, I may as well tell you, I suppose. It is the rule not to enter this valley until after dark. I expect the Americanos to arrive about ten o'clock."

"The Americanos?"

"*Si*, there will be three in the party, one of them a man from New York, who has business with me."

Miss Donovan's decision was rapidly made, her mind instantly grasping the situation. This man would be Enright, and the business he had with Mendez concerned Cavendish, and possibly herself also. She glanced again into the stern, hawklike face of the Mexican, recognising its lines of relentless cruelty, the complete absence of any sense of mercy. His piercing eyes and thin lips gave evidence enough that he was open to any bargain if the reward should be commensurate with the risk. The man's age, and grey hair, only served to render more noticeable his real character—he was a human tiger, held now in restraint, but only waiting a chance to break his chains, and sink teeth in any victim. The very sight of him sent a shudder through her body, even as it stiffened her purpose.

Her clear, thoughtful eyes turned inquiringly toward Cavendish, but the survey brought with it no encouragement. The man meant well, no doubt, and would fight valiantly on occasion; he was no coward, no weakling—equally clear his was not the stuff from which leaders are made. There was uncertainty in his eyes, a lack of force in his face which told the story. Whatever was decided upon, or accomplished, must be by her volition; she could trust him to obey, but that was all. Her body straightened into new resolve, all her womanhood called to the front by this emergency.

"Then we will make no attempt to leave the valley until after dark," she said slowly. "Even if we got away now, we would be pursued, and overtaken, for the desert offers few chances for concealment. If we can reach that smaller cabin unseen we ought to be safe enough there for hours. Cateras will not bother, and with Mendez captive, his men will not learn what has occurred. Is not this our best plan, Mr. Cavendish?"

"And at night?"

"We must work some scheme to get horses, and depart before those others reach here. There will be plenty of time between dark and ten o'clock. If we leave this man securely bound, his plight will not even be discovered until Lacy arrives. By that time, with any good fortune, we will be beyond pursuit, lost in the desert. Do you think of anything better?"

That he did not was evidenced by the vacant look in his eyes, and she waited for no answer.

"Here," she said, thrusting the revolver into his hand, "take this, and guard Mendez until I return. It will only be a moment. Don't take your eyes off him; there must be no alarm."

She moved forward through the gloomy shadows toward the light showing at the mouth of the cave. The rocks here were in their natural state, exactly as left by the forces which had originally disrupted them, the cavern's mouth much wider than the tunnel piercing the hill, and somewhat obstructed by ridges of stone.

Sheltered by these Stella crept to the very edge of the opening, and was able to gain a comprehensive view of the entire scene beyond. Within the cave itself there was no movement, no evidence of life. Quite clearly no guard had been posted here, and no precautions taken, although doubtless the only entrance to the deep valley was carefully watched.

A glance without convinced her that no other guardianship was necessary to assure safety. The valley lay before her, almost a level plain, except for the stream winding through its centre, and all about, unbroken and precipitous, arose the rampart of rocks, which seemed unscalable.

She rested there long enough to trace this barrier inch by inch in its complete circle, but found no opening, no cleft, promising a possible exit, except where the trail led up almost directly opposite, and only memory of her descent enabled her to recognise this. Satisfied that the top could be attained in no other way, her eyes sought the things of more immediate interest. The two cabins were directly before the entrance, the smaller closely in against the cliff, the larger slightly advanced. Neither exhibited any sign of life; indeed the only evidence that the valley contained human occupants was the distant view of two herders, busily engaged in rounding up a bunch of cattle on the opposite bank of the stream. These were too far away, and too intently engaged at their task, to observe any movement at this distance.

Her study of the situation concentrated on the small cabin immediately in front. It was low, a scant story in height, but slightly elevated from the ground, leaving a vacant space beneath. It was built of logs, well mortised together, and plastered between with clay. The roof sloped barely enough to shed water, and there were no windows on the end toward the cliff, or along the one side which she could see from where she lay. The single door must open from the front, and apparently the house had been erected with the thought that it might some time be used for purposes of defence, as it had almost the appearance of a fort. The larger building was not entirely unlike this in general design, except that small openings had been cut in the log walls, and a rude chimney arose through the roof. Both appeared deserted. Confident there could be no better time for the venture, Stella signalled with her hand for the others to join her.

They advanced slowly, Cavendish holding the revolver at the Mexican's head, the latter grinning savagely, his dark eyes never still. Bitter hate, desperate resolve, marked his every action, although he sought to appear indifferent. The girl's lips were compressed, and her eyes met his firmly.

"The way is clear," she said, "and, listen to my warning, *señor*. We are going straight along the north side of your cabin there, until we reach the door. For about twenty feet we shall be exposed to view from that other cabin, if any of your men are there. If you dare utter a sound, or make a motion, this man will shoot you dead in your tracks—do you understand?"

His look was ugly enough, although he compelled the thin lips to smile.

"Quite clearly—yes; but pardon me if I doubt. You might kill me; I think that, yet how would it serve you? One shot fired would bring here a dozen men—then what?"

"I thank you, *señor*; there will be no shot fired. Give me the revolver, Mr. Cavendish; now take this knife. As we advance walk one step behind Mendez. You will know what to do. Now, *señor*, if you wish to try an experiment—we go now."

There was not a sound, not a word. Not unlike three shadows they crossed the open space, and found shelter behind the walls of the hut. The girl never removed her eyes from the other cabin, and Cavendish, a step behind his prisoner, poised for a quick blow, the steel blade glittering in uplifted hand, saw nothing but the back of the man before him. The latter shrugged his shoulders and marched forward, his eyes alone evidencing the passion raging within.

Without pausing they reached the door, which stood slightly ajar. Stella pushed it open, took one swift glance within and stepped aside. The other two entered, and she instantly followed, closing the door, and securing it with a stout wooden bar. Her face was white, marked by nervous emotion, her eyes bright and fearless. With one swift glance she visioned the interior; there were two rooms, both small, divided by a solid log partition, pierced by a narrow door-way.

The back room was dark, seemingly without windows, but this in which they stood had an opening to the right, letting in the sunlight. It was a mere slash in the logs, unframed, and could be closed by a heavy wooden shutter. She stepped across and glanced out. The view revealed included a large portion of the valley, and the entrance to the other cabin. There was no excitement, no evidence of any alarm—their crossing from the mouth of the cave had escaped observation. Thus far at least they were safe.

Her heart beat faster as she turned away, satisfied with the success of her plan. Nothing remained now but to secure Mendez, to make it impossible for him to raise an alarm. If he could be bound, and locked into that rear room. She looked at the two men—the Mexican had slouched down into a chair, apparently having abandoned all hope of escape, his chin lowered on his breast, his eyes hidden beneath the wide brim of his hat. He was a perfect picture of depression, but Cavendish appeared alert enough, the deadly knife still gripped in his hand, a motionless, threatening figure. Feeling no trepidation, she crossed toward the other room, noting as she passed that Mendez lifted his head to observe her movements. She paused at the door, turning suspiciously, but the man had already seemingly lost interest, and his head again drooped. She stepped within.

CHAPTER XXVIII
WITH BACK TO THE WALL

It was dingy dark once she had crossed the threshold, yet enough of light flickered in through the doorway to enable her to perceive the few articles of furniture. The room itself was a small one, but contained a roughly constructed wooden bed, two stools, and a square table of unplaned boards. A strip of rag carpet covered a portion of the floor, and there was a sort of cupboard in one corner, the door of which stood open, revealing a variety of parcels, littering the shelves. Against the wall in a corner leaned a short-barrelled gun, a canvas bag draped over its muzzle.

She had no opportunity to observe more. To her ears there came the sound of a blow in the room she had just left, a groan, the dull thud of a body striking the floor, accompanied by a Spanish oath, and a shuffling of feet. She sprang back into the open doorway, startled, certain only of some catastrophe, her fingers gripping hard on the revolver.

Cavendish lay writhing on the floor, the chair overturned beside him, and the Mexican, with one swift leap forward, cleared the body, and reached the window. Even as she caught this movement, too dazed for the instant to act, the injured man struggled up on one elbow, and, with all the force he possessed, hurled the knife straight at the fleeing figure. It flashed through the air, a savage gleam of steel, barely missing Mendez's shoulder, and buried itself in a log, quivering from the force of impact. With a yell of derision, his hands still bound, the desperate fugitive cast himself head-first through the opening. Without aim, scarcely aware of what she did, the girl flung up her weapon and fired. With revolver yet smoking she rushed forward to look without. Rolling over and over on the ground, his face covered with blood, Mendez was seeking to round the corner of the cabin, to get beyond range. Again she pulled the trigger, the powder smoke blowing back into her face, and blinding her. When she could see once more, he was gone, but men were leaping out through the door of the bunk-house, shouting in excitement.

One of these caught sight of her, and fired, the bullet chugging into the end of a log, so closely it caught a strand of her hair, but, before another shot could follow, she had seized the shutter, and closed the opening, driving the latch fast with the revolver butt. She was cool enough now, every nerve on edge, realising fully the danger of their position. All the blood of a fighting race surged through her veins, and she was conscious of no fear, only of a wild exultation, a strange desire to win. As she turned she faced Cavendish, only vaguely visible in the twilight caused by the closed window. He was still seated on the floor, his expression betraying bewilderment.

"Are you hurt?"

"No—not—not much. He knocked all the wind out of me. I—I'm all right now."

"Get up then! There's fighting enough ahead to make you forget that. What happened?"

"He—he kicked me, I guess. I—I don't exactly know. I heard you go past us into that other room, and—and just turned my head to see. The next I knew I was on the floor, so damned sick—I beg your pardon—I thought I was going to faint. Did I get him with the knife?"

"No, it's over there, and I am afraid I didn't touch him either; it was all so sudden I got no aim. Do you hear those voices? There must be a dozen of the band outside already."

He looked up at her, his glance almost vacant, and she could but perceive how his chin shook.

"What shall we do?"

"Do!" she gripped his shoulder. "Are you a man and ask that? We will fight! Did you imagine I would ever surrender myself into the hands of that devil, after what has happened? I would rather die; yes, I will die before he ever puts hand on me. And what about you, Mr. Cavendish? Are you going to lie there moping? Answer me—I thought you were a man—a gentleman."

The words were like a blow in his face, and under their sting he staggered to his feet; scarlet blazed in both his cheeks.

"You have no right to say that to me," he said angrily. "I'm not that kind."

"I know it," she admitted, "but you lose your nerve; this isn't your game. Well, it isn't mine either, for the matter of that. Nevertheless it has got to be played, and we're going to play it together. Those fellows will be at that door presently—just so soon as Mendez tells them who are inside here. They'll try us once, and, if we can beat them back, that will give us a breathing spell."

She paused, glancing swiftly about, listening to the increasing hubbub without.

"There is no other way they can break in except through this door, unless, perhaps, they smash that shutter. Two of us ought to hold them for some time."

"But we have only one weapon—that knife is no use."

"There is a sawed-off shotgun back yonder; go get it, and hunt for some cartridges. They may be in the cupboard—quick now; that's Mendez's voice, and he'll be savage."

There was a shouting of commands without in Spanish, punctuated by oaths, the meaning of which the girl alone understood. She leaned forward, her eyes on the door, the cocked revolver held ready. She had meant what she said to Cavendish; to her mind death was far preferable to any surrender to that infuriated Mexican; she expected death, but one hope yet buoyed her up—Westcott. Odd that any memory of him should have come to her at that moment—yet it did; as though he spoke, and bade her believe in his coming. She had thought of him before, often in the past two days, but now he was real, tangible; she could almost feel the strong grip of his hand, and hear the sound of his voice. It was exactly as though the man called to her, and she responded. A dream, or what, it brought her courage, hope.

He would come; she had faith in that—and he would find she had fought to the end, even if he came too late. She buried her face in her hands, stifling a sob that shook her body, yet when she lifted the head again, there was no glimmer of tears in her eyes, and her cheeks were crimson. She waited motionless, scarcely seeming to breathe—the statue of a woman at bay.

All this was but for a moment, a moment of swift thought, of equally swift decision. The next Cavendish stood beside her, grasping the shotgun, no longer a victim of weakness, his eyes meeting hers eagerly.

"I could only find twelve cartridges," he exclaimed, "but I know how to use those."

He took a step forward, and held out his hand.

"Forgive me, Miss Donovan," he pleaded. "Really I do not know what makes me like that, but you would make a man out of anybody."

Her firm, slim fingers met his eagerly, her eyes instantly glowing in appreciation.

"Of course I forgive you," she exclaimed. "Your fear is no greater than my own. I am a woman, and dread this sort of thing. All that gives me courage is the knowledge that death is preferable to dishonour," her voice lost its firmness, "and—and my faith in a man."

"You mean in possible rescue?"

Her eyes lifted to his face.

"Yes, Mr. Cavendish. It may prove all imagination, yet there is one—a real man, I am sure—who must know of my plight before this. If he does, and lives, he will come to me. If we can only defend ourselves long enough there will be rescue."

He hesitated, yet something told him this was no time to fear asking all.

"Surely you are not married? Of course not; then he———"

"Is merely a friend; no, there has been no other word spoken between us, yet," her voice trembling slightly, "there are secrets a woman knows instinctively without speech. I know this man cares—enough to come. Isn't that strange, Mr. Cavendish, when we have only met three times?"

"No," he said gallantly, "not to any one who has known you. I believe you might even trust me. Where is this man?"

"In Haskell; but please do not ask any more—there! They are coming."

A blow struck the outer door, and was repeated, evidently dealt by the butt of a gun; then the two, standing silent and almost breathless within, heard Mendez's voice. There was no mistaking his slow, carefully chosen English.

"*Senorita*, and you also, Señor Cavendish," he called his words intended to be conciliatory. "It is of no use that you resist. We are many and armed. If you surrender, and not fight, I pledge you protection."

The girl glanced at Cavendish.

"You answer him."

He stepped closer to the door.

"Protection from whom?" he asked briefly.

"From my men; I am Pasqual Mendez."

"But you propose holding us prisoners? You intend delivering us up to the man Lacy as soon as he arrives?"

"Yes," he admitted, "but I hold no animosity—none. The *señorita* need not fear. I will intercede for you both with the Senor Lacy, and he will listen to what I say. You may trust me, if you unbar the door."

"And if we refuse?"

"We shall break in, and there will be no promise. I ask you now for the last time."

Cavendish turned his head slightly to regard his companion.

"What shall I say?" he whispered.

"The man lies; he will keep no promise once we are in his power. Besides they have not yet found Cateras. When they do there will be no thought of mercy."

"Then we fight it out?"

"I shall; I will never give myself into the hands of that creature."

"Señor," and Cavendish stepped aside to the protection of the logs, "we will not surrender. That is our answer."

"Fools!" he called back, his voice rising harsh above the growling of others. "We will show you. Silva, Felipe, quick now; do what I told you. We will teach these Americano dogs a lesson. No, stand back! Wait until I speak the word.'"

A faint glimmer of light through one of the log crevices caught Cavendish's attention, and he bent down, his eye to the crack, one hand grasping the barrel of his gun. Stella watched him motionless and silent, her face again pale from strain. A moment he stared out, without speaking, the only noise the movement of men beyond the log walls, and the occasional sound of a voice in Spanish.

"I can count about a dozen out there," he said finally, his words barely audible, and his eye still at the slight opening. "All Mexican except two—they look American. Most of them are armed. You must have pricked Mendez, for he has one arm in a sling, and the cloth shows bloody. Ah! Wait! The fellows have searched the cells and discovered Cateras. Do you hear that yell? It will be a fight to a finish now. Here come two men with a log—that's their game then; they mean to smash in the door."

He straightened up, casting a swift glance about the apartment. All hesitancy, doubt, had left him, now that the supreme test had come. He was again capable of thinking clearly, and acting.

"Miss Donovan," he burst out, "we can never hope to hold back those men here—in this room. There must be fifteen of them, and our ammunition is scanty. We shall be in bright light as soon as the door is battered down, and then, if they crush in the window also, we shall surely be attacked from two sides."

"What will be better?" she asked.

"The back room; it is dark, with no windows, and there are strips nailed between the logs. We can force that heavy wooden bed across the door, and hide behind it. We ought to hold them there as long as our cartridges last, unless they set the cabin afire. Good God! They have begun already.

Three more blows like that and the door goes down. Come; it's our only chance."

It was the work of a moment; it had to be. The inner room was so dark they had to feel their way about blindly, yet those splintering crashes on the outer door, interspersed by the shouts of the men, spurred both to hurried effort. Nor was there much to be done. The heavy bed was thrown upon its side, and hauled and pushed forward until it rested against the door jambs, the mattress and blankets so caught and held as to form protection against bullets. Breathless the two sank to their knees in the darkness behind, their eyes on the brightening daylight of the room beyond. Already a hole had been stove through the upper panel of the door, the surrounding wood splintered. Some one fired once through the jagged opening, and an exultant yell followed from without.

"No firing!" the voice was Mendez's rising sharply above the other sounds. "I don't want the girl shot, you fools. Take that other log around to the window. They'll surrender fast enough once we're inside. Now, another one. Here, five of you swing her!"

Stella touched Cavendish's sleeve.

"Show me how to load, please," she urged feverishly. "I've fired two shots already."

His gun rested across the rude barricade, and he left it there, seizing the revolver from her hand.

"You have never handled one before?"

"No; not like this. Oh, I see; you press that spring. I can do that. You have the belt with the revolver cartridges—fasten it about my waist; quick! The door is almost down."

"Rest your barrel on the edge of the bed," he muttered, gripping the shotgun again, "and aim at that door. The instant you see one of those devils, give it to him."

With a crash the remaining wood gave way, the end of the log, used as a battering ram, projecting into the room. Over the shattered door, now held only by one bent hinge, a half dozen forms swarmed inward, the quick rush blocking their passage.

Cavendish pulled trigger, the deep boom of his shotgun echoed instantly by the sharper report of the girl's revolver. She fired twice before the swirling smoke obstructed the view, conscious only that one man had leaped straight into the air, and another had sprawled forward on hands and knees. Cavendish pushed home a fresh cartridge, and the smoke cloud lifted just enough to permit them to perceive the farther doorway. A Mexican lay curled up in the centre of the floor, his gun a dozen feet away; another hung dangling across an over-turned stool, but the opening was vacant. Just outside, a fellow, wounded, was dragging himself out of range.

"Great Scott!" exclaimed Cavendish, excitedly. "Every shot counted. Here, load up quick. They'll try the window next. Get down!"

The warning was not an instant too soon, the hasty volley largely thudding harmlessly into the thick mattress, although a bullet or two sang past and found billets in the logs behind. Cavendish returned the fire, shooting blindly into the smoke, but the girl only lifted her head, staring intently into the smother, until the cloud floated away through the door. The attackers had again vanished, all semblance of them, except those two motionless bodies.

She had not before been conscious of any feeling; all she had done had been automatic, as though under compulsion; but now she felt strangely sick, and faint. An unutterable horror seized her and her hands gripped the edge of the bed to keep her erect. She could seem to see nothing but the ghastly face of that dead man hanging over the stool, and she closed her eyes. Yet this reaction was only momentary. She had fired in defence; in a struggle for the preservation of life and honour. Under spur of this thought she once more gained control.

But how still it was! Even the sound of voices had ceased; and out through the open door there was no sign of movement. The light seemed dimmer, also, as though the sun had sunk below the opposite cliffs, and night was slowly descending upon the valley. What could be happening out there? Were those men planning some new attempt? Or had they decided it was better to wait for a larger force? The silence and uncertainty were harder to combat than the violence of assault; she struggled to refrain from screaming. Cavendish never moved, his gun flung forward across the improvised barricade, the very grip of his hand proving the intensity of nervous strain. Something caused him to glance toward her.

"Looks as though they had enough of it," he said grimly, "and have decided to starve us out."

"Oh, do you think so? I heard a noise then."

He heard it also, his glance returning instantly to the front, his form stiffening into preparation. For a moment neither could determine the meaning of the sounds. Then he cocked his gun, the sharp click echoing almost loudly in the stillness.

"Trying the window this time," he murmured, "Do you hear that? Be ready."

Nothing happened; even the slight noise in the outer room ceased; there was not a sound except their own breathing. The two knelt motionless, peering over the edge of the bed into the dim twilight, seeing nothing, each with finger on trigger—tense, expectant. Then, without warning, the flying figure of a man leaped across the doorway into the security of the opposite wall. It was done so quickly neither fired, but Cavendish licked his parched lips with a dry tongue.

"I'll get the next one who tries that trick," he muttered, "It will be easier than partridge shooting."

A minute—two passed, every nerve on edge; then a second flying form, almost a blur in the gathering gloom, shot across the narrow opening. The shotgun spoke, and the wildly leaping figure seemed to crumble to the floor—its lower half had reached shelter, but head and shoulders lay exposed, revealing grey hair and a white moustache. Cavendish sprang erect, all caution forgotten.

"It's Mendez," he cried. "I got the arch-fiend of them———"

A rifle cracked and he went plunging back, his body striking the girl, and crushing her to the floor beside him. There was no cry, no groan of agony, yet he lay there motionless. She crept across and bent over him, almost dumb with fear.

"You—you are shot?" she made herself speak.

"Yes; they've got me," the utterance of the words a struggle. "It's here in the chest; I—I don't know how bad; perhaps if you tear open my shirt, you—you might stop the blood."

She could see nothing, not even the man's face, yet her fingers rent the shirt asunder and searched for the wound. It was not bleeding greatly, and she had no water, but not knowing what else to do, she tore a strip from her skirt and bound it hastily. He never moved, or spoke, and she bent her head closer. The wounded man had lost consciousness.

Alone, in the dark, she crept back on her knees to her place behind the barricade. Her hand touched the empty gun he had dropped, and she reloaded it slowly, only half comprehending its mechanism. The revolver, every chamber filled, rested on the upturned edge of the bed; her lips were firmly pressed together. Quietly she pushed forward the barrel of the shotgun, and waited.

CHAPTER XXIX
A NEEDLE IN A HAYSTACK

The little marshal of Haskell had the reputation of being as quick of wit as of trigger finger. Startled as he was by that sudden apparition appearing before them in the dark road, and at being addressed by a woman's voice, the mention of the name Cassady gave him an instant clue. There was but one Cassady in camp, and that individual's reputation was scarcely of a kind to recommend him in the eyes of the law. If any woman sought that fellow in this out-of-the-way spot, it was surely for no good purpose. Brennan caught his breath, these thoughts flashing through his brain. He leaned forward over his saddle horn, lowering his voice confidentially, and managing to achieve a highly meritorious brogue.

"Sure, Oi'm Cassady," he admitted grouchily. "How iver come yer ter guess thot?"

"I was sent here to meet you," she explained hurriedly, as though eager to have her task done. "I thought maybe it wasn't you, with another man along. Who is he?"

"His noime's Crowley; just a friend o' moine; mebbe yer know the lad?"

"No; certainly not. Does he go along with you?"

"Fer only a bit o' ther way"; he lowered his voice to even greater intimacy. "Shure, it's a parfectly still tongue the b'y has in the cheek o' him."

She laughed nervously.

"Well, I'm glad of that; and we'll not stand here discussing the matter. Do you know who I am?"

"Divil a thought have Oi."

"You were expecting to meet Mr. Enright, weren't you? That was what Bill Lacy told you. He was to explain to you just what you were to do."

Brennan mumbled something indistinctly, now thoroughly aroused to the situation.

"Well, Mr. Enright couldn't come, and Lacy is over across the creek yet, hunting down Ned Beaton's murderer. I am Miss La Rue," she hurried on, almost breathlessly, "and I've brought you Lacy's note, which you are to give to that Mexican—Pasqual Mendez. You understand? You are to give it to him, and no one else. Lacy said you could kill your horse, if necessary, but the note must be there by daylight to-morrow. Here—take it."

Brennan thrust it into an inner pocket, and cleared his throat. There was no small risk in asking questions, yet, unless he learned more, this information might prove utterly useless. The note to Mendez meant little until he discovered where that bandit was to be found. He felt his flesh prickle in the intensity of his suppressed excitement.

"Shure now, miss," he said insinuatingly. "Mr. Lacy must hev' sint more insthructions 'long with ye then them. All ther word thet iver come ter me wus ter saddle oop, ride down here an' mate this man Enright. I don't aven know fer shure whar ol' Mendez is—likely 'nough he be in Mexico."

"In Mexico!" indignantly. "Of course not. Lacy said you knew the trail. It's a place they call 'Sunken Valley'—out there somewhere," and Brennan could barely distinguish the movement of her arm desert-ward. "It's across that sand flat."

"Shoshone?"

"Yes; I couldn't remember the name. That's all I know about it, only Lacy said you'd been there before."

"Shure, miss," assured the marshal softly, clearly realising that he had already gone the limit, and that any further questioning must lead inevitably to trouble. "If it is Sunken Valley I'm ter ride ter, thet's aisy."

"Then it's good night."

She vanished up the side-trail, as though the wind had blown away a shadow. Except for the slight rustling of dried leaves under her feet, the two men, staring blindly through the darkness, could not have told the direction in which she had gone. Then all was silence, the mystery of night. Brennan gathered up his reins, straightening his body in the saddle. He glanced back toward the dim shade of his companion, chuckling.

"Some bit of luck that, Jim."

"Doesn't seem to me we know much more than we did before," Westcott answered gloomily. "Only that this chap Mendez is at a place called Sunken Valley. I never heard of it; did you?"

"No; I reckon it's no spot the law has ever had any use for. I've supposed all along them Mexican cattle thieves had a hidden corral somewhar in this country; but nobody has ever found it yet. Right now, thanks to this Miss La Rue, I've got a hunch that we're goin' to make the discovery, and put Bill Lacy and ol' Mendez out of business. But there's no sense of our gassin' here. We got a right smart bit o' ridin' to do afore daylight."

They advanced cautiously as far as the bridge, but at that point Brennan turned his pony's head southward, and spurred the reluctant animal up the steep bank. Without question Westcott followed, and the two horses broke into a trot as soon as they attained the more level land beyond. They were slightly above the town now, and could gaze back at the glittering lights in the valley below. The sound of men's voices failed to reach them over the soft pounding of the ponies' hoofs on the prairie sod, but suddenly the distant crackling of a half dozen shots pierced the silence, and their eyes caught the sparkle of the discharges, winking like fireflies in the night. Before they could draw up their mounts, the fusillade had ended, and all beneath them was unbroken gloom.

"Must be rushing the rock," commented Westcott.

"More likely saw something and blazed away at it, just as they did at that log," and Brennan laughed. "Anyhow they haven't discovered we have vanished yet. With an hour more we'll be where trails are unknown."

"In the desert?"

"That is the only safe hiding place around here. Besides we're carrying a message to Mendez."

"Without the slightest knowledge of where that party is."

"Well, hardly that, Jim. I may not know exactly, but I've got a glimmer of a notion about where the cuss hangs out, an' I'm going to have a hunt for it. There's five thousand dollars posted down in Arizona for that fellow, dead or alive; an' I need the money. Besides, I reckon this yere Miss Donovan, an' yer ol' partner—what's his name?—sure, Cavendish—will be mighty glad to see us. You're game for a try, ain't yer?"

"I shall never stop until I do find them, Dan," said the other earnestly, the very tone of his voice carrying conviction. "Every cent of reward is yours; it will be satisfaction enough for me to know those two are safe."

"That's how I figured it. Now let's trot on; we ain't gaining nothing by sittin' our saddles here. We can talk while we travel."

There was a few moments of silence, both men evidently busied with their thoughts; then Westcott asked:

"What is your idea, Dan?"

The marshal rode steadily, humped up over his saddle-horn, his eyes on the uncertainties in front.

"I ain't really got none," he admitted doggedly, "less it be a blind trust in Divine Providence; still I got a medium strong grip on a few things. That Capley girl told you that Matt Moore drove out on the ridge road?"

"Yes; I asked her about that twice."

"Well, he likely was headed for this yere Sunken Valley. That's point number one. But he never followed the ridge road very far, for it skirts the desert. He must have turned off south—but where?"

"Near the lone cottonwood is my guess."

"Why?"

"Because there is a swale there of hard sand, which is easily followed, and leaves no trail. On either side for miles the sand is in drifts, and no two horses would ever pull a wagon through it. This hard ridge, which is more rock than sand, goes straight south to Badger Springs, the only place to get water. I was there once, three years ago."

"You've hit it, old man," exclaimed the other confidently. "That's exactly how I had it doped out. He'd have to use that swale, or go ten miles farther east. I never was at Badger myself, but I've travelled that ridge road some, with my eyes open. Then, I take it, that our course is already laid out pretty straight as far as them springs. Beyond there the general lay of the land may help us, and I aim to reach that point along about daylight. Accordin' to Miss La Rue—she's that blond female I seen at the hotel, ain't she—Cassady was expected to reach this place where Mendez is about dawn, if he had to kill his hoss to do it. That would mean some considerable of a ride, I reckon."

"And yet," put in Westcott, with increasing interest, "would seem naturally to limit the spot to within a radius of ten miles from Badger Springs."

"Likely enough—yes; either south, southeast, or southwest; what sort o' country is it?"

"Absolutely barren; a desolate waste as far as the eye can see, except that range of mountains away to the south, fifty miles or more off. It would be a dead level, except for the sand-hills; that's all the memory I've got of it."

"Well, thar's allers some landmark to a trail, an' I used ter be a pretty fair tracker. Speed yer hoss up a bit, Jim; we've got to ride faster than this."

"How about the note she gave you?"

"We'll wait a while to read that. I don't want to strike no light just yet. Maybe it had best be kept till daybreak."

The men rode steadily, and mostly in silence, a large part of the way side by side. The animals they bestrode were fairly mated, quite capable of maintaining their gait for several hours, and needing little urging. The night air was cool, and a rather stiff breeze swept over the wide extent of desert, occasionally hurling spits of loosened sand into their faces, and causing them to ride with lowered heads. The night gloom enveloped them completely; their strained eyes were scarcely able to trace the dim outlines of the ridge road, but the horses were desert broke, and held closely to the beaten track, Before they arrived at the lone cottonwood, Westcott's pony, which carried by far the heavier load, began to show signs of fatigue. They drew up here, and the marshal dismounted, searching about blindly in the darkness.

"Too damn dark," he said, coming back, and catching up his rein. "A cat couldn't find anything there; but there's firm sand. Wait a minute; I've got a pocket compass."

He struck a match, sheltering the sputtering blaze with one hand. The light illuminated his face for an instant, and then went out, leaving the night blacker than before.

"That's south," he announced, snapping the compass-case shut, "and this blame wind is southeast; that ought to keep us fairly straight."

"The ponies will do that; they'll keep where the travelling is good. Shift this bag back of your saddle, Dan. You ride lighter, and my horse is beginning to pant already; that will ease him a few pounds."

The transfer was made, and the two men rode out into the rear desert, urging their animals forward, trusting largely to their natural instinct for guidance. They would follow the hard sand, and before long the scent of water would as certainly lead them directly toward the spring. With reins dangling and bodies crouched to escape the blast of the sharp wind, neither spoke as they plunged through the gloom which circled about them like a black wall.

Yet it was not long until dawn began to turn the desert grey, gradually revealing its forlorn desolation. Westcott lifted his head, and gazed about with wearied eyes, smarting still from the whipping of the sand-grit. On every side stretched away a scene of utter desolation, unrelieved by either shrub or tree—an apparently endless ocean of sand, in places levelled by the wind, and elsewhere piled into fantastic heaps. There were no landmarks, nothing on which the mind could concentrate—just sand, barren, shapeless, ever-changing form, stretching to the far horizons. The breeze slackened somewhat as the sun reddened the east, and the ponies threw up their heads and whinnied slightly, increasing their speed. Westcott saw the marshal arouse himself, straighten in the saddle, and stare about, his eyes still dull and heavy.

"One hell of a view, Jim," he said disgustedly, "but I reckon we can't be a great ways from that spring. We've been ridin' right smart."

"It's not far ahead; the ponies sniff water. Did you ever see anything more dismal and desolate?"

"Blamed if I see how even a Mex can run cattle through here."

"They know the trails, and the water-holes—ah! there's a bunch o' green ahead; that'll likely be Badger Springs."

Assured they were beyond pursuit, the two unsaddled, and turned the ponies out to crop the few handfuls of wire grass which the sweet water bubbling up from a slight depression had coaxed into stunted growth. There was no wood to be had, although they found evidence of several camp-fires, and consequently they were obliged to content themselves with what they could find eatable in their bag. It was hardly a satisfying meal, and their surroundings did not tend toward a joyful spirit. Except for a few sentences neither spoke, until Brennan, having partially satisfied his appetite, produced the note given him by Miss La Rue, and deliberately slashed open the sealed envelope.

"In the name of the law," he said grimly, hauling out the enclosure. "Now we'll see what's the row. Holy smoke! it's in Spanish! Here, Jim, do you read that lingo?"

"I know words here and there," and Westcott bent over the paper, his brows wrinkling. "Let's see, it's not quite clear, but the sense is that Mendez will be paid a thousand dollars for something—I can't make out what, only it has to do with prisoners. Lacy says he'll be there to confer with him some time to-night."

"Where? At Sunken Valley?"

"The place is not mentioned."

"Lacy write it?"

"Yes; at least he signed it; there's a message there about cattle, too, but I can't quite make it out."

"Well, we don't care about that. If Lacy aims to meet Mendez to-night, he ought to be along here soon after nightfall. How'd it do to hide in these sand-hills, and wait?"

"We can do that, Dan, if we don't hit any trail," said Westcott, leaning over, his hand on the other's knee, "but if we can get there earlier, I'd rather not waste time. There's no knowing what a devil like Mendez may do. Let's take a scout around anyhow."

They started, the one going east, the other west, and made a semicircle until they met, a hundred yards or so, south of the spring, having found nothing. Again they circled out, ploughing their way through the sand, and all at once Brennan lifted his hand into the air and called. Westcott hurried over to where he stood motionless, staring down at the track of a wagon-wheel. It had slid along a slight declivity, and left a mark so deep as not yet to be obliterated. They traced it for thirty feet before it entirely disappeared.

"Still goin' south," affirmed the marshal, gazing in that direction. "Don't look like there's nothin' out there, but we might try—what do you say?"

"I vote we keep moving; that wagon is bound to leave a trail here and there, and so long as we get the general direction, we can't go far wrong."

"I reckon you're right. Come on then; let's saddle up."

It was a blind trail, and progress was slow. The men separated, riding back and forth, leaning forward in the saddles, scanning the sand for the slightest sign. Again and again they were encouraged by some discovery which proved they were on the right track—the clear print of a horse's hoof; a bit of greasy paper which might have been tied round a lunch, and thrown away; impresses in the sand which bore resemblance to a man's footprints; a tin can, newly opened, and an emptied tobacco-pouch. Twice they encountered an undoubted wheel mark, and once traces of the whole four wheels were plainly visible. These could be followed easily for nearly a quarter of a mile, but then as quickly vanished as the wagon came again to an outcropping of rock. Yet this was assured—the outfit had headed steadily southward.

This was desperately slow work, and beyond that ridge of rock they discovered no other evidence. An hour passed, and not the slightest sign gave encouragement. Could the wagon have turned in some other direction? In the shadow of a sand-dune they halted finally to discuss the situation. Should they go on? Or explore further to the east and west? Might it not even be better to retrace their way to the springs, and wait the coming of Lacy? All in front of them the vast sand plain stretched out, almost as level as a floor. So far as the eye would carry there was no visible sign of any depression or change in conformity. Certainly there was no valley in that direction. Beyond this dune, in whose shelter they stood, there was nothing on which the gaze could rest; all was utter desolation, apparently endless.

Brennan was for turning back, arguing the uselessness of going further, and the necessity of water for the ponies.

"Come on, Jim," he urged. "Be sensible; we've lost the trail, and that's no fault o' ours. An Apache Indian couldn't trace a herd o' steers through this sand. And look ahead thar! It's worse, an' more of it. I'm for stalking Lacy at the springs." He stopped suddenly, staring southward as though he had seen a vision. "Holy smoke! What's that? By God! It's a wagon, Jim; an' it come right up out of the earth. There wasn't no wagon there a second ago."

CHAPTER XXX
ON THE EDGE OF THE CLIFF

For a moment both men suspected that what they looked upon was a mirage—its actual existence there in that place seemed impossible. Yet there was no disputing the fact, that yonder in the very midst of that desolation of sand, a wagon drawn by straining horses was slowly moving directly toward them. Westcott was first to grasp the truth, hastily jerking the marshal back to where the tired ponies stood with drooping heads behind the protection of the dune.

"It's the same outfit coming back," he explained. "The Sunken Valley must be out there—just a hole in the surface of the desert—and that's how that wagon popped up out of the earth the way it did. I couldn't believe my eyes."

"Nor me neither," and the marshal drew one of his guns, and held it dangling in his hand. "I'm a bit flustered yet, but I reckon that's about the truth. Get them ponies round a bit more, an' we'll wait and see what's behind that canvas."

The distance must have been farther than it seemed, or else the travelling difficult, for it was some time before the heavy wagon and straining team drew near enough for the two watchers to determine definitely the character of the outfit. Westcott lay outstretched on the far side of the dune, his hat beside him, and his eyes barely able to peer over the summit, ready to report observations to the marshal crouched below.

"It's Moore's team, all right," he whispered back, "and Matt is driving them. There isn't any one else on the seat, so I guess he must be alone."

"We can't be sure of that," returned Brennan, wise in guarding against surprises. "There was another fellow with him on the out trip, and he might be lying down back in the wagon. We'd better both of us hold 'em up. I can hear the creak of the wheels now, so maybe you best slide down. Is the outfit loaded?"

"Travelling light, I should say," and Westcott, after one more glance, crept down the sand-heap and joined the waiting man below. Both stood intent and ready, revolvers drawn, listening. The heavy wheels grated in the sand, the driver whistling to while away the dreary pull and the horses breathing heavily. Moore pulled them up with a jerk, as two figures leaped into view, his whistle coming to an abrupt pause.

"Hell's fire!" was all he said, staring dumbly down into Brennan's face over the front wheel. "Where in Sam Hill did you come from?"

"I'm the one to ask questions, son," returned the little marshal, the vicious blue barrel shining in the sunlight, "and the smarter you answer, the less reason I shall have to hurt yer. Don't reach for that gun! Are you travelling alone?"

Moore nodded, his hands up, but still grasping the reins.

"Then climb down over the wheel. Jim, take a look under that canvas; Moore, here, is generally a genial sort o' liar, and we'd better be sure. All right—hey? Then dismount, Matt, and be quick about it. Now unbuckle that belt, and hand the whole outfit over to Westcott; then we'll talk business together."

He shoved his own weapon back into its holster, and faced the prisoner, who had recovered from his first shock of surprise, and whose pugnacious temper was beginning to assert itself. Brennan read this in the man's sulky, defiant glance, and his lips smiled grimly.

"Getting bullish, are you, Matt?" he said, rather softly. "Goin' ter keep a close tongue in your head; so that's the game? Well, I wouldn't, son, if I was you. Now, see here, Moore," and the voice perceptibly hardened, and the marshal's eyes were like flints. "You know me, I reckon, an' that I ain't much on boys' play. You never heard tell o' my hittin' anybody just fer fun, did yer?"

There was no answer.

"An' yer never heard no one say," went on Brennan, "that I was afraid ter hit when I needed to. I reckon also yer know what sorter man Jim Westcott is. Now the two ov us ain't out here in this damned Shoshone desert fer the fun of it—not by a jugful. Get that fact into yer head, son, an' maybe it'll bring yer some sense. Do yer get me?"

"Yes," sullenly and reluctantly. "But yer haven't got nuthin' on me."

"Oh, haven't I? Well, you shut up like a clam, and find out what I've got. You drove a young woman out here from Haskell night afore last, for Bill Lacy. Ain't abduction no crime? An' that's only one count. I've had an eye on you for more'n six months, an' Lacy's been makin' a damn cat's-paw out of you all that time. Well, Lacy is playin' his last hand right now, an' I've got the cards." The marshal paused, fully aware that he had struck home, then added quietly: "It allers struck me, Matt, that naturally you was a pretty decent fellow, but had drifted in with a bad crowd. I'm offering you now a chance to get straight again." He threw back his coat and exhibited his star. "Yer see, I ain't just talkin' ter yer as Dan Brennan—I'm the law."

The boy, for he was scarcely more than that in years, shuffled his feet uneasily, and his eyes wandered from Brennan to Westcott. The look of sullen defiance had vanished.

"Whar is Lacy?" he asked.

"Back in town, but he will be at Badger Springs about dark. We've got him corralled this time. Yer better climb inter the band-wagon, son; it's the last call."

"Wotcher wanter ask?"

"Who was with you the out-trip, along with Miss Donovan?"

"Joe Sikes."

"And yer left him back there, guarding the girl?"

"He stayed; them was the orders, while I was to bring back the team; but I reckon he won't need to do no guardin' to speak of, fer we run inter a bunch o' fellows."

"Mendez's outfit?"

"You got the right dope, marshal, so I reckon I ain't spillin' no beans. It was the Mex all right, an' some o' his bunch."

"And Lacy didn't know they were there?"

"I reckon not; leastways he never said so, an' they'd only come a few days."

"How many are they?"

"Maybe a dozen; I don't just know. I saw eight, or ten, round the bunk-house, besides ol' Mendez an' that dude lieutenant of his, Juan Cateras. I ain't got no use fer that duck; I allers did want ter soak him. Then ther' was others out with the cow herd."

"They had a bunch o' cattle?"

"Maybe three hundred head, run in from Arizona. I heard that much, but I don't talk their lingo."

"What was done with the young lady?"

Moore spat vindictively into the sand, digging a hole with his heel. He had talked already more than he intended, but what was the difference?

"Cateras took her," he admitted, "but I don't know whar. I rather liked that girl; she's got a hell ov a lot o' sand, an' never put up a whimper. I tried ter find out whar she was, but nobody'd tell me. Then I had ter pull out."

Westcott interjected a question.

"Did you learn if there was any other prisoner there?"

"Not that I heard of. Who do yer mean?"

"A man named Cavendish."

"No, I reckon not." He turned back to the marshal.

"What are you guys goin' ter do with me?"

"That depends, Matt. When a lad is straight with me, I generally play square with him. All this took place in Sunken Valley?"

"Yep; whar'd you hear it called that?"

"Oh, I know more'n some ov you boys think I do. That name's been floatin' 'bout fer some time. I've even got the spot located—it's straight south thar a ways. But you've been in it, an' I never have. Here's whar you can serve the law, an' so get out of yer own trouble if yer so minded. It don't make a hell ov a lot o' difference to me whether yer speak up or not, but it's liable to ter you. What do yer say?"

"Fire away; I reckon I'm up against it anyhow."

"What's the valley like, an' how do you get into it?"

"Well, I'd say it was just a sort o' sink in the desert, a kinder freak. Anyhow, I never saw nuthin' like it afore. You'd never know it was thar a hundred yards away; it kinder scares me sometimes when I come up to it thro' all this sand. The walls is solid rock, almost straight up an' down, but thar's a considerable stream flowin' down thar that just bursts out a hole in the rock, an' plenty o' grass fer quite a bunch of steers."

"How do they get down into it?"

"'Long a windin' trail on the west side. It used to be mighty rough, I reckon, an' only good fer hikers, but they fixed it up so they can drive cattle down, an' even a wagon if yer take it easy."

"Mendez fixed it?"

"No; I heerd that Bill Lacy sorter handled that job. The Mex can't do nuthin' but steal."

"Then Lacy is the go-between? He sells the cattle?"

"Sure; I s'posed yer knew that. He ships them east from Bolton Junction, an' pretends they come from his ranch over on Clear Water. The Mexicans drive 'em in that way, an' they're all branded 'fore they leave the valley. It's a cinch."

The marshal's eyes brightened; he was gaining the information he most desired.

"And there is no other way to the bottom except along this trail?"

"That's 'bout all."

"Well, could Jim and I make it—say after dark?"

Moore laughed, the reckless boy in him again uppermost.

"Mebbe so; but I reckon ye'd be dead when yer got thar. Thar's allers two Mexes on guard when Mendez is in the valley. He ain't takin' no chances o' gettin' caught that way."

"Where are they?"

"Just below the top, whar they kin see out over the desert. Hell, yer couldn't get within half a mile an' not be spotted. It's bull luck yer run inter me."

Brennan and Westcott looked at each other, both uncertain as to the next step. What were they to do with their prisoner? And how could they proceed toward effecting the rescue of the helpless girl? It was a problem not easy to solve, if what Moore told them was true. The latter shuffled his feet in the sand, lifted his eyes shrewdly, and studied the faces of his captors. He was figuring his own chance.

"You fellows want ter get down inter the valley?" he asked at last.

"Yes," and Brennan turned again quickly, "if it can be done. Of course thar's only two of us, an' it would be sort o' foolish tryin' ter fight a way through, even ag'in' Mexicans. Fifteen ter two is some odds, but 'tain't in my nature, or Jim's here, ter turn round an' leave that girl in the hands o' them cusses—is it, Jim?"

"I never will," replied Westcott earnestly. "Not if I have to tackle the whole outfit alone."

"You won't never have to do that. What's the idea, Moore?"

"Oh, I was just thinkin'," he answered, still uncertain. "She's a good fellow, all right, an' I wouldn't mind givin' her a hand myself, pervidin' you men do the square thing. If I show yer a way, what is thar in it fer me?"

Brennan stiffened, his features expressing nothing.

"What do yer mean? I'm an officer o' the law?"

"I know it; I ain't asking yer ter make no promise. But yer word will go a hell ov a ways if this ever gets in court.

"If I help yer I've got ter be protected frum Bill Lacy. He'd kill me as quick as he'd look at me. Then I'd want yer ter tell the judge how it all happened. If yer got the cards stacked, an' I reckon yer have, I ain't big enough fool to try an' play no hand against 'em. But I want ter know what's goin' ter happen ter me. You don't need ter promise nuthin'; only say yer'll give me a show. I know ye're square, Dan Brennan, an' whatever yer say goes."

The marshal stuck out his hand.

"That's the gospel truth, Matt," he said gravely, "an' I'm with yer till the cows come home. What is it you know?"

"Well," with a quick breath as he took the plunge, "it's like this, marshal; there is just one place out yonder," and he waved his hand to indicate the direction, "on the east rim o' the valley, where yer might get down. Ye'd have ter hang on, tooth an' toe-nail; but both of yer are mountain men, an' I reckon yer could make the trip if yer took it careful an' slow like. Leastwise that's the one chance, an' I don't believe thar's another white critter who even knows thar is such a trail."

"Have you ever been down?"

"Wunst, an' that was enough fer me," he confessed, drawling his words. "Yer see it was this a-way. One time I was out there in that hell hole plum' alone fer a whole week, just a waitin' fer Mendez ter show up so I could ride into Haskell and tell Lacy he'd come. It was so damn lonesome I explored every nook an' cranny between them rocks, an' one day, lyin' out in front o' ther bunk-house, I happened to trace this ol' trail. I got a notion to give it a trial, an' I did that same afternoon. I got down all right, but it was no place fer a lady, believe me, an' I reckon no white man ever made it afore."

"It had been used once?"

"There was some signs made me think so; Injuns, I reckon, an' a long while ago."

Westcott asked: "How can we get there safely? Can you guide us?"

Moore swept his eyes over the dull range of sand, expectorated thoughtfully, and rammed his hands deep into his trouser-pockets. He was slow about answering, but the two men waited motionless.

"If it was me," he said finally. "I'd take it on foot. It'll be a jaunt ov near on to three miles, unless yer want ter risk bein' seen by them Mexes on the main trail. You couldn't go straight, but would have ter circle out an' travel mostly behind that ridge o' sand thar to the left. Goin' that a-way nobody's likely ter get sight o' yer on foot. You couldn't take no hoss, though. Here'd be my plan; lead this yere outfit o' mine an' your ponies back inter them sand dunes whar nobody ever goes. They're tired 'nough ter stand, an' there ain't anything fer 'em to graze on. Then we kin hoof it over ter the place I'm tellin' yer about, an' yer kin sorter size it up fer yerselves. That's fair, ain't it?"

They went at it with a will, glad to have something clearly defined before them, Brennan in his slow, efficient way, but Westcott, eager and hopeful, spurred on by his memory of the girl, whose rescue was the sole object which had brought him there. The team was driven into the security of the sand drifts and unhitched. The saddles were taken from the backs of the ponies, and what grain Moore had in the wagon was carefully apportioned among the four animals. Satisfied these would not stray, the men looked carefully to their supply of ammunition and set forth on their tramp.

This proved a harder journey than either Brennan or Westcott had anticipated, for Moore led off briskly, taking a wide circle, until a considerable ridge concealed their movements from the south. The sand was loose, and in places they sank deeply, their feet sliding back and retarding progress. All three were breathing heavily from the exertion when, under protection of the ridge, they found better walking.

Even here, however, the way was treacherous and deceiving, yet they pressed forward steadily, following the twists and turns of the pile of sand on their right. The distance seemed more than three miles, but at last Moore turned sharply and plunged into what resembled a narrow ravine through the ridge. Here they struggled knee deep in the sand, but finally emerged on the very rim overlooking the valley.

So perfectly was it concealed they were within ten feet of the edge before the men, their heads bent in the strenuous effort to advance, even realised its immediate presence. They halted instantly, awestruck, and startled into silence by the wonder of that scene outspread below. Moore grinned as he noted the surprise depicted on their faces, and waved his hand.

"Yer better lie down an' crawl up ter the edge," he advised. "Some hole, ain't it?"

"I should say so," and Westcott dropped to his knees. "I never dreamed of such a place. Why it looks like a glimpse into heaven from this sand. Dan, ain't this an eye-opener?"

"It sure is," and the marshal crept cautiously forward. "Only it's devils who've got possession. Look at them cattle up at the further end; they don't look no bigger than sheep, but there's quite a bunch of 'em. What's that down below, Matt? Houses, by Jingo! Well, don't that beat hell?—all the comforts of home."

"Two big cabins," explained Moore, rather proud of his knowledge. "Carted the logs in from ol' Baldy, more'n forty miles. One is the bunk-house; the other is whar Mendez stops when the ol' cuss is yere. Creep up a bit an' I'll show yer how the trail runs. Don't be afeerd; nobody kin see yer from down below."

"All right, son, where is it?"

"It starts at the foot o' that boulder," indicating with his finger, "an' goes along the shelf clear to the end; then thar's a drop ov maybe five feet to that outcroppin' o' rock just below. It's wider than it looks to be from yere. After that yer can trace it quite a spell with yer eyes, kinder sidlin' ter the left, till yer come to that dead root ov a cedar. Then thar's a gap or two that ain't over easy, an' a slide down ter another shelf. Yer can't miss it, cause there's no other way ter go."

"And what's at the bottom?"

"Them huts, an' the mouth of a damn big cave just behind 'em. I reckon it's in the cave they've got the gal; there's places there they kin shut up, but I don't know what they was ever made fer. I asked Lacy wunst, but he only laughed."

The two men lay flat, staring down. It was almost a sheer wall, and the very thought of climbing along the almost impassable path pointed out by Moore made Westcott dizzy. He had clambered along the ragged crags of many a mountain in search for gold, but the necessity of finding blindly in the dark that obscure and perilous passage brought with it a sensation of horror which he had to fight in order to conquer. It was such a sheer, precipitous drop, a path—if path it could be called—so thickly studded with danger the mind actually recoiled in contemplation.

"You have really been down there, Moore?" he questioned, half unbelieving.

"Oh, I made it all right," boastfully. "But it's no picnic. I'd hate like hell to risk it at night, but that's the only chance you fellows will have to git down. It would be like trap-shootin' for them Mexes if you tried it now."

They lay there for some time talking to each other, and staring down at the strange scene so far beneath them, and which appeared almost like a painted picture within its dark frame of towering rocks and wide expanse of sand. Except for the rather restless herd of cattle there was little movement perceptible—a herder or two could be distinguished riding here and there on some duty; there was a small horse corral a short distance to their right, with something like a dozen ponies confined within, and a bunch of saddles piled outside the fence. Once a man came out of the bunk-house and went down to the stream for a bucket of water, returning leisurely. He wore the braided jacket and high, wide-brimmed hat of the Mexican peon, and spurs glittered on his boot-heels. Beyond this the cabins below gave no sign of occupancy. Moore pointed out to them the main trail leading across the valley and winding up along the front of the opposite wall. They could trace it a large part of the way, but it disappeared entirely as it approached the summit.

The three men, wearied with looking, and knowing there was nothing more to do, except wait for night, crept back into the sand hollow and nibbled away at the few eatables brought with them in their pockets. Brennan alone seemed cheerful and talkative—Moore had liberally divided with him his stock of chewing-tobacco.

CHAPTER XXXI
WITH FORCE OF ARMS

They were still sitting there cross-legged in the sand when the silence was suddenly punctuated by the sharp report of a revolver. The sound barely reached their ears, yet it undoubtedly came from below, and all three were upon their feet, when a second shot decided the matter.

Westcott was first at the rim, staring eagerly downward. It was growing dusk down there in the depths, yet was still light enough to enable him to perceive movement, and the outlines of the cabins. For a moment all he noticed was a man lying on the ground in front of the small hut, but almost immediately men began to swarm out through the door of the bunk-house, and a horseman came spurring from the field beyond.

The men were armed, several with guns in their hands; all with revolvers buckled at the waist, and they bunched there, just outside the door, evidently startled, but not knowing which way to turn. The figure on the ground lifted itself partly, and the fellow must have called to the others, although no sound of a voice attained the summit of the cliff, for the whole gang rushed in that direction, and clustered about, gesticulating excitedly.

An occasional Spanish oath exploded from the mass with sufficient vehemence to reach the strained ears above, and the watchers were able to perceive the fellows lift the fallen man to his feet, and untie his hands, which were apparently secured behind his back. He must have been wounded also, for one sleeve was hastily rolled up, and water brought from the stream, in which it was bathed. Not until this had been attended to did the crowd fall away, sufficiently to permit the fellow himself to be distinctly seen. Moore's hand closed convulsively on the marshal's arm.

"It's ol' Mendez, as I'm a livin' sinner,", he announced hoarsely. "An' somebody's plunked him. What'd yer make o' that?"

Brennan never removed his gaze from the scene below, but his face was tense with interest.

"Blamed if I know; might be a mere row—hold on, there! Whoever did it is in that cabin; watch what they're up to, now."

The three hung there scanning every movement of those below, too intently interested to talk, yet unable for some time to determine clearly what was impending. Occasionally the sound of a voice reached them, shouting orders in Spanish, and men came and went in obedience to the commands. More guns were brought forth from the bunk-house, and distributed; the single horseman rode swiftly up the valley, and a half-dozen of the fellows lugged a heavy timber up from the corral, and dropped it on the ground in front of the smaller cabin. Mendez, his arm in a sling, passed from group to group, profanely busy, snapping out orders.

"They are going to break in the door with that log!" muttered Westcott between his clenched teeth. "That white-head down there is boiling with rage, and whoever the poor devil, or devils, may be, they'll have to fight."

"Yes, but who are they?" and Brennan sat up. "The whole gang must be outside there; I counted fourteen. Then, did you notice? Mendez had his hands bound behind his back. He couldn't even get up until those fellows untied him. That's what puzzles me."

"It would take more than one to do that job. Maybe we'll find out now—he's pounding with a revolver butt on the front door."

They listened breathlessly, hanging recklessly over the rim of the chasm, and staring at that strange scene below, but the man's words only reached them broken and detached. They got enough, however, to realise that he demanded the unbarring of the door, and that he both threatened and promised protection to whoever was within. It was the language he employed that aroused Westcott.

"Did you hear that?" he asked shortly. "The man spoke English. Whoever's in there doesn't understand Spanish. Were any Americans down there when you left, Moore?"

"Joe Sikes, and a fellow they call 'Shorty,' but they're both outside; that was Joe who bound up ol' Mendez's arm, an' Shorty was helpin' bring up the log."

The eyes of Brennan and Westcott met understandingly.

"Yer don't suppose that girl———"

"Aye, but I do," and Westcott's voice proved his conviction. "There's nothing too nervy for her to tackle if it needed to be done. But she never could have corralled Mendez alone."

"Then there must be another along with her—that fellow yer told me about likely."

"Fred Cavendish! By Jove, it would be like him. Say, boys, I'm going down and take a hand in this game."

The marshal gripped him.

"Not yet, Jim! It ain't dark enough. Wait a bit more an' I'm with yer, old man. It'll be blacker than hell down there in fifteen minutes, an' then we'll have some chance. They'd pot us now sure afore we got as far as that cedar. What is the gang up to now, Matt?"

"They're a goin' ter bust in the door," and Moore craned his head farther out over the edge in eagerness to see. "I reckon they didn't git no answer that pleased 'em. See ol' Mendez hoppin' about! Lord! he's mad 'nough to eat nails. Thar comes the log—say, they hit that some thump; thar ain't no wood that's goin' ter stand agin them blows long. Do yer hear?"

They did; the dull reverberation as the log butt crashed against the closed door was plainly audible. Once, twice, three times it struck, giving forth at last the sharper crackling of splintered wood. They could see little now distinctly—only the dim outlines of the men's figures, Mendez shouting and gesticulating, the fellows grasping the rough battering-ram, a group of others on either side the door, evidently gathered for a rush the moment the latter gave way.

"My God!" cried Westcott, struggling to restrain himself. "Suppose I take a crack at them!"

Brennan caught the hand tugging at the half-drawn revolver.

"Are you mad, man? You couldn't even hit the house at that distance. Holy smoke! There she goes!"

The door crashed in; there was a fusillade of shots, the spits of fire cleaving the dusk, and throwing the figures of the men into sudden bold relief. The log wielders sprang aside, and the others leaped forward, yelling wildly and plunging in through the broken doorway. An instant later three muffled reports rang out from the interior—one deep and booming, the others sharper, more resonant—and the invaders tumbled backward into the open, seeking shelter. Westcott was erect, Brennan on hands and knees.

"Damn me!" ejaculated the latter, his excitement conquering restraint. "Whoever they are, Jim, they're givin' ol' Mendez his belly full. Did yer hear them shots? There's sure two of 'em in thar—one's got a shotgun an' the other a revolver. I'll bet yer they punctuated some o' those lads. Lord! They come out like rats."

Westcott's teeth gripped.

"I'm going down," he said grimly, "if I have to go alone."

Brennan scrambled to his feet.

"Just a second, Jim, an' I'm with yer. Moore, get up yere. Now, what do yer say? Can we count you in on this shindig?"

"Go down thar with yer?"

"Sure! Y're a man, ain't yer? If yer say y're game, I'll play square—otherwise we'll see to your case afore we start. I don't leave yer up yere to play no tricks—now which is it?"

Moore stared over the edge into the black depths.

"Yer want me to show you the way?"

"Yer say you've made the trip wunst. If yer have, yer kin do it again. I'm askin' yer fer the last time."

The boy shivered, but his jaw set.

"I don't give a damn fer you, Dan Brennan," he returned half angrily, "but I reckon that might be the girl down thar, an' I'll risk it fer her."

"You'll go then?"

"Sure; didn't I just tell you so?"

Brennan wheeled about.

"Give him his gun, Jim, and the belt," he commanded briefly. "I don't send no man into a fracas like this unless he's heeled. Leave yer coats here, an' take it slow. Both of yer ready?"

Not until his dying day will Westcott ever forget the moment he hung dangling over the edge of that pit, following Moore who had disappeared, and felt gingerly in the darkness for the narrow rock ledge below. The young miner possessed imagination, and could not drive from memory the mental picture of those depths beneath; the horror was like a nightmare, and yet the one dominant thought was not of an awful death, of falling headlong, to be crushed shapeless hundreds of feet below. This dread was there, an intense agony at first, but beyond it arose the more important thought of what would become of her if he failed to attain the bottom of that cliff alive. Yet this was the very thing which steadied him, and brought back his courage.

At best they could only creep, feeling a way blindly from crag to crag, clinging desperately to every projection, never venturing even the slightest movement until either hand or loot found solid support. Moore led, his boyish recklessness and knowledge of the way, giving him an advantage. Westcott followed, keeping as close as possible, endeavouring to shape his own efforts in accordance with the dimly outlined form below; while Brennan, short-legged and stout, probably had the hardest task of all in bringing up the rear.

No one spoke, except as occasionally Moore sent back a brief whisper of warning at some spot of unusual danger, but they could hear each other's laboured breathing, the brushing of their clothing against the surface of the rock, the scraping of their feet, and occasionally the faint tinkle of a small stone, dislodged by their passage and striking far below. There was nothing but intense blackness down there—a hideous chasm of death clutching at them; the houses, the men, the whole valley was completely swallowed in the night.

Above it all they clung to the almost smooth face of the cliff, gripping for support at every crevice, the rock under them barely wide enough to yield purchase to their feet. Twice Westcott had to let go entirely, trusting to a ledge below to stop his fail; once he travelled a yard, or more, dangling on his hands over the abyss, his feet feeling for the support beyond; and several times he paused to assist the shorter-legged marshal down to a lower level. Their progress was that of the snail, yet every inch of the way they played with death.

Now and then voices shouted out of the gloom beneath them, and they hung motionless to listen. The speech was Spanish garnished with oaths, its meaning not altogether clear. They could distinguish Mendez's harsh croak easily among the others.

"What's he saying, Moore?" whispered Westcott to the black shape just below.

"Something 'bout the log. I don't just make it, but I reckon they aim now to batter in the winder."

"Well, go on," passed down the marshal gruffly. "What in Sam Hill are yer holdin' us up yere for? I ain't got more'n two inches ter stand on."

Fifty feet below, just as Moore rounded the dead cedar, the guns began again, the spits of red flame lighting up the outlines of the cabin, and the dark figures of men. It was as though they looked down into the pit, watching the brewing of some sport of demons—the movements below them weird, grotesque—rendered horrible by those sudden glares of light. This firing was all from without, and was unanswered; no boom of shotgun replied, no muffled crack of revolver. Yet it must have been for a purpose, for the men crouching against the cliff, their faces showing ghastly in the flashes of powder, were able to perceive a massing of figures below. Then the shots ceased, and the butt of the great log crashed against something with the force of a catapult, and a yell rolled up through the night.

At last Moore stopped, and waited until Westcott was near enough for him to whisper in the other's ear.

"There's a drop yere, 'bout ten er twelve feet, I reckon; an' then just a slope to ther bottom. Don't make no more noise then yer have to, an' give me a chance ter git out of ther way afore yer let go."

Westcott passed the word back across his shoulder to Brennan who was panting heavily, and, watched, as best he could on hands and knees, while Moore lowered himself at arm's length over the narrow rock ledge. The boy loosened his grip, but landed almost noiselessly. Westcott, peering over, could see nothing; there was beneath only impenetrable blackness. Silently he also dropped and his feet struck earth, sloping rapidly downward. Hardly had he advanced a yard, when the little marshal struck the dirt, with a force that made him grunt audibly. At the foot of this pile of debris, Moore waited for them, the night so dark down there in the depths, Westcott's outstretched hand touched the fellow before he was assured of his presence.

The Mexicans were still; whatever deviltry they were up to, it was being carried on now in silence; the only sound was a muffled scraping. Brennan yet struggled for breath, but was eager for action. He shoved his head forward, listening.

"What do yer make o' that noise?" he asked, his words scarcely audible.

"I heerd it afore yer come up," returned Moore. "'Tain't nuthin' regular. I figure the Mex are goin' in through that winder they busted. That sound's their boots scaling the wall."

"Ever been inside?"

"Wunst, ter take some papers ter Lacy."

"Well, what's it like? For God's sake speak up—there's goin' ter be hell to pay in a minute."

"Thar's two rooms; ther outside door an' winder are in the front one, which is the biggest. The other is whar Mendez sleeps, an' thar's a door between 'em."

"No windows in the rear room?"

"None I ever see."

"And just the one door; what sort o' partition?"

"Just plain log, I reckon."

"That's all right, Jim," and Westcott felt the marshal's fingers grasp his arm. "I got it sized up proper. Whoever them folks be, they've barricaded inter that back room. Likely they've got a dead range on the front door, an' them Mexes have had all they want tryin' to get to 'em in that way. So now they're crawlin' in through the window. There'll be some hellabaloo in there presently to my notion, an' I want ter be thar ter see the curtain go up. Wharabouts are we, Matt?"

"Back o' the bunk-house. Whar do yer want ter go? I kin travel 'round yere with my eyes shut."

"The front o' Mendez's cabin," said the marshal shortly. "Better take the other side; if that door is down we'll take those fellows in the rear afore they know what's happening." He chuckled grimly. "We've sure played in luck so far, boys; go easy now, and draw yer guns."

They were half-way along the side wall when the firing began—but it was not the Mexicans this time who began it. The shotgun barked; there was the sound of a falling body; two revolver shots and then the sharp ping of a Winchester. Brennan leaped past the boy ahead, and rounded the corner. A Mexican stood directly in front of the shattered door peering in, a rifle yet smoking in his hands. With one swift blow of a revolver butt the marshal dropped him in his tracks, the fellow rolling off the steps onto the ground. With outstretched hands he stopped the others, holding them back out of any possible view from within.

"Quick now, before that bunch inside gets wise to what's up. We've got 'em cornered. You, Matt, strip the jacket off that Mex, an' get his hat; bunch 'em up together, and set a match to 'em. That's the stuff! Now, the minute they blaze throw 'em in through that doorway. Come on, Westcott, be ready to jump."

The hat was straw, and the bundle of blazing material landed almost in the centre of the floor, lighting up the whole interior. Almost before it struck, the three men, revolvers gleaming in their hands, had leaped across the shattered door, and confronted the startled band huddled in one corner. Brennan wasted no time, his eyes sweeping over the array of faces, revealed by the blaze of fire on the floor.

"Hands up, my beauties—every mother's son of yer. Yes, I mean you, yer human catapiller. Don't waste any time about it; I'm the caller fer this dance. Put 'em up higher, less yer want ter commit suicide. Now drop them rifles on the floor—gently, friends, gently. Matt, frisk 'em and see what other weapons they carry. Ever see nicer bunch o' lambs, Jim?" His lips smiling, but with an ugly look to his gleaming teeth, and steady eyes. "Why they'd eat outer yer hand. Which one of yer is Mendez?"

"He dead, *señor*," one fellow managed to answer in broken English. "That heem lie dar."

"Well, that's some comfort," but without glancing about. "Now kick the guns over this way, Matt, and touch a match to the lamp on that shelf yonder; and, Jim, perhaps you better stamp out the fire; we'll not need it any more. Great Scott! What's this?"

It was Miss Donovan, her dress torn, her hair dishevelled, a revolver still clasped in her hand, half levelled as though she yet doubted her realisation of what had occurred. She emerged from the blackness of the rear room, advanced a step and stood there hesitating, her wide-open eyes gazing about in bewilderment on the strange scene revealed by the glow of the lamp. That searching, pathetic glance swept from face to face about the motionless circle—the cowed Mexican prisoners with uplifted hands backed against the wall; the three dead bodies huddled on the floor; Moore, with the slowly expiring match yet smoking in his fingers; the little marshal, erect, a revolver poised in either hand, his face set and stern. Then she saw Westcott, and her whole expression changed. An instant their eyes met; then the revolver fell to the floor unnoticed, and the girl sprang toward him, both hands outstretched.

"You!" she cried, utterly giving way, forgetful of all else except the sense of relief the recognition brought her. "You! Oh! Now I know it is all right! I was so sure you would come."

He caught the extended hands eagerly, drawing her close, and looking straight down into the depths of her uplifted eyes. To him, at that moment, there was no one else in the room, no one else in the wide, wide world.

"You knew I would come?" he echoed. "You believed that much in me?"

"Yes; I have never had a doubt. I told him so; that if we could only hold out long enough we would be saved. But," her lips quivered, and there were tears glistening in the uplifted eyes, "you came too late for him."

"For him? The man who was with you, you mean? Has he been shot?"

She bent her head, the lips refusing to answer.

"Who was he?"

"Mr. Cavendish—oh!"

It was a cry of complete reaction; the room reeled about her and she would have fallen headlong had not Westcott clasped the slender form closely in his arms. An instant he stood there gazing down into her face. Then he turned toward Brennan.

"Leave us alone, Dan," he said simply. "Get that gang of blacklegs out of here."

CHAPTER XXXII
IN THE TWO CABINS

The marshal's lips smiled.

"Sure, Jim," he drawled, "anything to oblige, although this is a new one on me. Come on, Matt; it seems the gentleman does not wish to be disturbed—— Well, neither would I under such circumstances. Here you! line up there in single file, and get a move on you—pronto! Show 'em what I mean, Matt; put that guy that talks English at the head—— Yes, he's the one. Now look here, *amigo*, you march straight out through that door, and head for the bunk-house—do you get that?"

"*Si, señor*, I savvy!"

"Well, you better; tell those fellows that if one of 'em makes a break he's goin' ter be a dead Mex—will yer? Get to the other side of them, Matt; now step ahead—not too fast."

Westcott watched the procession file out, still clasping the partially unconscious girl in his arms. Moore, bringing up the rear, disappeared through the entrance, and vanished into the night without. Except for the three motionless bodies, they were alone. The lamp on the high shelf flared fitfully in the wind, and the charred embers on the floor exhibited a glowing spark of colour. From a distance Brennan's voice growled out a gruff order to his line of prisoners. Then all was still. The eyes of the girl opened slowly, her lids trembling, but as they rested on Westcott's face, she smiled.

"You are glad I came?"

"Glad! Why I never really knew what gladness meant before."

He bent lower, his heart pounding fiercely, strange words struggling for utterance.

"You love me?"

She looked at him, all the fervent Irish soul of her in her eyes. Then one arm stole upward to his shoulder.

"As you love me," she whispered softly, "as you love me!"

"I can ask no more, sweetheart," he breathed soberly, and kissed her. At last she drew back, still restrained by his arms, but with her eyes suddenly grave and thoughtful.

"We forget," she chided, "where we are. You must let me go now, and see if he is alive. I will wait on the bench, here."

"But you said he had been killed."

"I do not know; there was no time for me to be sure of that. The shot struck him here in the chest, and when he fell he knocked me down. I tore open his shirt, and bound up the wound hastily; it did not bleed much. He never spoke after that, and lay perfectly still."

"Poor old Fred. I'll do what I can for him—I'll not be away a minute, dear."

He could see little from the doorway, only the dark shadow of a man's form lying full length on the floor. To enter he pushed aside the uptilted bed, picking up the shotgun, and setting it against the log wall. Then he took the lamp down from the shelf, and held it so the feeble light fell upon the upturned face. He stared down at the features thus revealed, unable for the moment to find expression for his bewilderment.

"Can you come here, dear?" he called.

She stood beside him, gazing from his face into those features on which the rays of the lamp fell.

"What is it?" she questioned breathlessly. "Is he dead?"

"I do not know; but that man is not Cavendish."

"Not Cavendish! Why he told me that was his name; he even described being thrown from the back platform of a train by that Ned Beaton; who can he be, then?"

"That is more than I can guess; only he is not Fred Cavendish. Will you hold the lamp until I learn if he is alive?"

She took it in trembling hands, supporting herself against the wall, while he crossed the room, and knelt beside the motionless figure. A careful examination revealed the man's wound to be painful though not particularly serious, Westcott carefully redressed the wound as best he could, then with one hand he lifted the man's head and the motion caused the eyelids to flutter. Slowly the eyes opened, and stared up into the face bending over him. The wounded man breathed heavily, the dull stare in his eyes changing to a look of bewildered intelligence.

"Where am I?" he asked thickly. "Oh, yes, I remember; I was shot. Who are you?"

"I am Jim Westcott; do you remember me?"

The searching eyes evidenced no sense of recollection.

"No," he said, struggling to make the words clear. "I never heard that name before."

Miss Donovan came forward, the lamp in her hand, the light shining full in her face.

"But you told me you were Mr. Cavendish," she exclaimed, "and Mr. Westcott was an old friend of his—surely you must remember?"

He looked up at her, and endeavoured to smile, yet for the moment did not answer. He seemed fascinated by the picture she made, as though some vision had suddenly appeared before him.

"I—I remember you," he said at last. "You—you are Miss Donovan; I'll never forget you; but I never saw this man before—I'm sure of that."

"And I am equally convinced as to the truth of that remark," returned Westcott, "but why did you call yourself Cavendish?"

"Because that is my name—why shouldn't I?"

"Why, see here, man," and Westcott's voice no longer concealed his indignation, "you no more resemble Fred Cavendish than I do; there is not a feature in common between you."

"Fred Cavendish?"

"Certainly; of New York; who do you think we were talking about?"

"I've had no chance to think; you jump on me here, and insist I'm a liar, without even explaining what the trouble is all about. I claim my name is Cavendish, and it is; but I've never once said I was Fred Cavendish of New York. If you must know, I am Ferdinand Cavendish of Los Angeles."

Westcott permitted the man's head to rest back on the floor, and he arose to his feet. He felt dazed, stunned, as though stricken a sudden blow. His gaze wandered from the startled face of the motionless girl to the figure of the man outstretched on the floor at his feet.

"Good God!" he exclaimed. "What can all this mean? You came from New York City?"

"Yes; I had been there a month attending to some business."

"And when you left for the coast, you took the midnight train on the New York Central?"

"Yes. I had intended taking an earlier one, but was delayed."

"You bought return tickets at the station?"

"No; I had return tickets; they had to be validated."

"Then your name was signed to them; what is your usual signature?"

"F. Cavendish."

"I thought so. Stella, this has all been a strange blunder, but it is perfectly clear how it happened. That man Beaton evidently had never seen Frederick Cavendish. He was simply informed that he would leave New York on that train. He met this Cavendish on board, perhaps even saw his signature on the ticket, and cultivated his acquaintance. The fellow never doubted but what he had the right man."

The wounded man managed to lift himself upon one elbow.

"What's that?" he asked anxiously. "You think he knocked me overboard, believing I was some one else? That all this has happened on account of my name?"

"No doubt of it. You have been the victim of mistaken identity. So have we, for the matter of that."

He paused suddenly, overwhelmed by a swift thought. "But what about Fred?" he asked breathless.

Stella's hand touched his arm.

"He—he must have been the dead man in the Waldron Apartments," she faltered. "There is no other theory possible now."

The marshal of Haskell came out of the bunk-house, and closed the door carefully behind him. He was rather proud of his night's work, and felt quite confident that the disarmed Mexicans locked within those strong log walls, and guarded by Moore, with a loaded rifle across his knee, would remain quiet until daylight. The valley before him was black and silent. A blaze of light shone out through the broken door and window of the smaller cabin, and he chuckled at remembrance of the last scene he had witnessed there—the fainting girl lying in Westcott's arms. Naturally, and ordinarily, Mr. Brennan was considerable of a cynic, but just now he felt in a far more genial and sympathetic mood.

"Jim's some man," he confided to himself, unconsciously speaking aloud. "An' the girl's a nervy little thing—almighty good lookin', too. I reckon it'll cost me a month's salary fer a weddin' present, so maybe the joke's on me." His mind reverted to Mendez. "Five thousand on the old cuss," he muttered gloomily, "an' somebody else got the chance to pot him. Well, by hooky, whoever it was sure did a good job—it was thet shotgun cooked his goose, judgin' from the way his face was peppered. Five thousand dollars—oh, hell!"

His eyes followed the outline of the valley, able to distinguish the darker silhouette of the cliffs outstanding against the sky sprinkled with stars. Far away toward the northern extremity a dull red glow indicated the presence of a small fire.

"Herders," Brennan soliloquised, his thought instantly shifting. "Likely to be two, maybe three ov 'em out there; an' then there's them two on guard at the head o' the trail. I reckon they're wonderin' what all this yere shootin' means; but 'tain't probable they'll kick up any fuss yet awhile. We can handle them all right, if they do—hullo, there! What's comin' now?"

It was the thud of a horse's hoofs being ridden rapidly. Brennan dropped to the ground, and skurried out of the light. He could perceive nothing of the approaching rider, but whoever the fellow was he made no effort at secrecy. He drove his horse down the bank and into the stream at a gallop, splashed noisily through the water, and came loping up the nearer incline. Almost in front of the bunk-house he seemed suddenly struck by the silence and gleam of lights, for he pulled his pony up with a jerk, and sat there, staring about. To the marshal, crouching against the earth, his revolver drawn, horse and man appeared a grotesque shadow.

"Hullo!" the fellow shouted. "What's up? Did you think this was Christmas Eve? Hey, there—Mendez; Cateras."

The little marshal straightened up, and took a step forward; the light from the cabin window glistened wickedly on the blue steel of his gun barrel.

"Hands up, Bill!" he said quietly, in a voice carrying conviction. "None of that—don't play with me. Take your left hand an' unbuckle your belt—I said the left. Now drop it into the dirt."

"Who the hell are you?"

"That doesn't make much difference, does it, as long as I've got the drop?" asked the other genially. "But, if you must know to be happy—I'm the marshal o' Haskell. Go easy, boy; you've seen me shoot afore this, an' I was born back in Texas with a weapon in each hand. Climb down off'n that hoss."

Lacy did so, his hands above his head, cursing angrily.

"What kind of a low-down trick is this, Brennan?" he snapped, glaring through the darkness at the face of his captor. "What's become of Pasqual Mendez? Ain't his outfit yere?"

"His outfit's here all right, dead an' alive," and Brennan chuckled cheerfully, "but not being no gospel sharp I can't just say whar ol' Mendez is. What's left ov his body is in thet cabin yonder, so full o' buckshot it ought ter weigh a ton."

"Dead?"

"As a door nail, if yer ask me. It was some nice ov yer ter come ridin' long here ter-night, Lacy. It sorter helps me ter make a good, decent clean-up ov this whole measly outfit. I reckon I'll stow yer away, along with them others. Mosey up them steps there, an' don't take no chances lookin' back."

"I'll get you for this, Brennan."

"Not if the Circuit Court ain't gone out o' business, you won't. I've got yer cinched an' hog tied—here now; get in thar."

He opened the door just wide enough for Lacy to pass, holding it with one hand, his revolver ready and eager in the other.

A single lamp lit the room dingily, revealing the Mexicans bunched on the farther side, a number of them lying down. Moore sat on a stool beside the door, a rifle in the hollow of his arm. He rose up as the door opened, and grinned at sight of Lacy's face.

"Well, I'll be dinged," he said. "What have we got here?"

Brennan thrust his new prisoner forward.

"Another one of yer ol' pals, Matt. You two ought ter have a lot ter talk over, an' thar's six hours yet till daylight."

The little marshal drew back, and closed the door. He heard the echo of an oath, or two, within as he turned the key in the lock. Then he straightened up and laughed, slapping his knee with his hand.

"Well," he said at last, soberly. "I reckon my place will be about yere till sun-up; thar might be some more critters like that gallivantin' round in these parts—I hope Matt's enjoyin' himself."

CHAPTER XXXIII
THE REAL MR. CAVENDISH

It was a hard, slow journey back across the desert. Moore's team and wagon were requisitioned for the purpose, but Matt himself remained behind to help Brennan with the prisoners and cattle, until the party returning to Haskell could send them help.

Westcott drove, with Miss Donovan perched beside him on the spring-seat, and Cavendish lying on a pile of blankets beneath the shadow of the canvas top. It became exceedingly hot as the sun mounted into the sky, and once they encountered a sand storm, which so blinded horses and driver, they were compelled to halt and turn aside from its fury for nearly an hour. The wounded man must have suffered, yet made no complaint. Indeed he seemed almost cheerful, and so deeply interested in the strange story in which he had unconsciously borne part, as to constantly question those riding in front for details.

Westcott and Stella, in spite of the drear, dread monotony of those miles of sand, the desolate barrenness of which extended about in every direction, and, at last, weighed heavily upon their spirits, found the ride anything but tedious. They had so much to be thankful for, hopeful over: so much to say to each other. She described all that had occurred during her imprisonment, and he, in turn, told the story of what himself and Brennan had passed through in the search for her captors. Cavendish listened eagerly to each recital, lifting his head to interject a question of interest, and then dropping wearily back again upon his blankets.

They stopped to lunch at Baxter Springs, and to water the team; and it was considerably after dark when they finally drove creaking up the main street of Haskell and stopped in front of the Timmons House to unload. The street was devoid of excitement, although the Red Dog was wide open for business, and Westcott caught a glimpse of Mike busily engaged behind the bar. A man or two passing glanced at them curiously, but, possibly because of failure to recognise him in the darkness, no alarm was raised, or any effort made to block their progress. Without Lacy to urge them on, the disciples of Judge Lynch had likely enough forgotten the whole affair. Timmons, hearing the creak of approaching wheels, and surmising the arrival of guests, came lumbering out through the open door, his face beaming welcome. Behind him the vacant office stood fully revealed in the light of bracket-lamps.

As Westcott clambered over the wheel, and then assisted the lady to alight, the face of the landlord was sufficiently expressive of surprise.

"You!" he exclaimed, staring into their faces doubtfully. "What the Sam Hill does this mean?"

"Only that we've got back, Timmons. Why this frigid reception?"

"Well, this yere is a respectable hotel, an' I ain't goin' ter have it all mussed up by no lynchin' party," the landlord's voice full of regret. "Then this yere gal; she wrote me she'd gone back East."

Westcott laughed.

"Stow your grouch, old man, and give us a hand. There will be no lynching, because Lacy is in the hands of the marshal. As to this lady, she never sent you that note. She was abducted by force, and has just escaped. Don't stand there like a fool."

"But where did yer come from? This yere is Matt Moore's outfit."

"From the Shoshone Desert, if you must know. I'll tell you the story later. There's a wounded man under the canvas there. Come on, and help me carry him inside."

Timmons, sputtering but impotent to resist, took hold reluctantly, and the two together bore the helpless Cavendish through the deserted office and up the stairs to the second floor, where he was comfortably settled and a doctor sent for. The task was sufficiently strenuous to require all the breath Timmons possessed, and he managed to repress his eager curiosity until the wounded man had been attended to. Once in the hall, however, and the door closed, he could no longer control himself.

"Now see yere, Jim Westcott," he panted, one hand gripping the stair-rail. "I've got ter know what's up, afore I throw open this yere hotel to yer free use this-away. As a gineral thing I ain't 'round huntin' trouble—I reckon yer know that—but this yere affair beats me. What was it yer said about Bill Lacy?"

"He's under arrest, charged with cattle-stealing, abduction, conspiracy, and about everything else on the calendar. Brennan's got him, and likewise the evidence to convict."

"Good Lord! Is that so!"

"It is; the whole Mendez gang has been wiped out. Old Mendez has been killed. The rest of the outfit, including Juan Cateras, are prisoners."

Timmons's eyes were fairly popping out of his head, his voice a mere thread of sound.

"Don't that beat hell!" he managed to articulate. "Where's the marshal?"

"Riding herd at a place they call Sunken Valley, about fifty miles south of here. He and Moore have got ten or twelve Mexicans, and maybe three hundred head of cattle to look after, until I can send somebody out there to help him bring them in. Now that's all you need to know, Timmons; but I've got a question or two I want to ask you. Come on back into the office."

Miss Donovan sat in one of the chairs by the front window waiting. As they entered she arose to her feet.

Westcott crossed the room and took her hand.

"He's all right," he assured her quickly, interpreting the question in her eyes. "Tired from the trip, of course, but a night's rest will do wonders. And now, Timmons," he turned to the bewildered landlord, "is that man Enright upstairs?"

"The New York lawyer? No, he got frightened and left. He skipped out the next day after you fellers got away. Bill wanted him to go along with him, but he said he was too sick. Then he claimed to have a telegram callin' him East, but he never did. I reckon he must 've got cold feet 'bout somethin'—enyhow he's gone."

"And Miss La Rue?"

"Sure; she took the same train," eager now to divulge all he knew. "But that ain't her real name—it's a kind o' long name, an' begins with C. I saw it in a letter she left up-stairs, but I couldn't make it all out. She's married."

The eyes of Westcott and Miss Donovan met. Here was a bit of strange news—the La Rue woman married, and to a man with a long name beginning with C. The same thought occurred to them both, yet it was evidently useless to question Timmons any longer. He would know nothing, and comprehend less. The girl looked tired, completely worn out, and the affair could rest until morning.

"Take Miss Donovan to a room," Westcott said shortly, "and I'll run upstairs and have another look at Cavendish."

"At who?"

"Cavendish, the wounded man we just carried in."

"Well, that's blamed funny. Say, I don't remember ever hearin' that name before in all my life till just now. Come ter think of it, I believe that was the name in that La Rue girl's letter. I got it yere in the desk; it's torn some, an' don't mean nothin' to me; sounds kinder nutty." He threw open a drawer, rummaging within, but without pausing in speech, "Then a fellow blew in yere this mornin' off the Limited, asking about you, Jim, an' danged if I don't believe he said his name was Cavendish. The register was full so he didn't write it down, but that was the name all right. And now you tote in another one. What is this, anyhow—a family reunion?"

"You say a man by that name was here—asking for me?"

"Yep; I reckon he's asleep up-stairs, for he never showed up at supper."

"In what room, Pete?"

"Nine."

Westcott, with a swift word of excuse to Stella, dashed into the hall, and disappeared up the stairway, taking three steps at a time. A moment later those below heard him pounding at a door; then his voice sounded:

"This is Jim Westcott; open up."

Timmons stood gazing blankly at the empty stair-case, mopping his face with a bandanna handkerchief. Then he removed his horn-rimmed spectacles, and polished them, as though what mind he possessed had become completely dazed.

"Well, I'll be jiggered," he confessed audibly. "What's a comin' now, I wonder?"

He turned around and noticed Miss Donovan, the sight of her standing there bringing back a reminder of his duty.

"He was a sayin' as how likely yer wanted to go to bed, Miss."

"Not now; I'll wait until Mr. Westcott comes down. What is that paper in your hand? Is that the letter Miss La Rue left?"

He held it up in surprise, gazing at it through his glasses.

"Why, Lord bless me—it is, isn't it? Must have took it out o' ther drawer an' never thought of the darned thing agin."

"May I see it?"

"Sure; 'tain't o' no consequence ter me; I reckon the woman sorter packed in a hurry, and this got lost. The Chink found it under the bed."

She took it in her hand, and crossed the room, finding a seat beneath one of the bracket-lamps, but with her face turned toward the hall. It was just a single sheet of folded paper, not enclosed in an envelope, and had been torn across, so that the two parts barely held together. She stared at it for a moment, almost motionless, her fingers nervously moving up and down the crease, as though she dreaded to learn what was within. She felt that here was the key which was to unlock the secret of this strange crime. Whoever the man upstairs might prove to be—the real Cavendish or some impostor—this paper she held in her hands was destined to be a link in the chain. She unfolded it slowly and her eyes traced the written words within. It was a hasty scrawl, written on the cheap paper of some obscure hotel in Jersey City, extremely difficult to decipher, the hand of the man who wrote exhibiting plainly the excitement under which he laboured.

It was a message of warning, he was leaving New York, and would sail that evening for some place in South America, where he did not say. Love only caused him to tell her what had occurred. A strange word puzzled her, and before she could decipher it, voices broke the silence, followed by steps on the stairs. She glanced up quickly; it was Westcott returning, accompanied by a tall, rather slender man with a closely-trimmed beard. The two crossed the room, and she met them standing, the opened letter still in her hand.

"Miss Donovan, this is Frederick Cavendish—the real Frederick Cavendish. I have told him something of the trouble he has been to us all."

The real Frederick Cavendish smiled down into her eyes, while he held her fingers tightly clasped in his own. She believed in him, liked him instantly.

"A trouble which I regret very much," he said humbly. "Westcott has told me a little, a very little, of what has occurred since I left New York so hurriedly two months ago. This is the first I knew about it, and the mystery of the whole affair is as puzzling as ever."

Her eyes widened wonderingly.

"You cannot explain? Not even who the dead man was found murdered in your apartments?"

"I haven't the least idea."

"Fred has told me all he knows," broke in Westcott "but it only extends to midnight when he left the city. He was in his apartments less than ten minutes after his valet retired. He supposed he left everything in good order, with a note on the writing-table instructing Valois what to do during his absence, and enclosing a sum of money. Afterward, on the train, he discovered that he had mislaid the key to his safe but this occasioned no worry, as he had taken with him all the cash it held, and the papers were of slight importance."

"But," she broke in impatiently, "where did he go? How did he escape encountering Beaton and why did he fail to answer your message?"

The eyes of the two men met, and they both smiled. "The very questions I asked," replied Westcott instantly. "In the instructions left Valois was a check for five thousand dollars made to my order, to be forwarded at once. Fred's destination was Sonora, Mexico, where he had some large copper interests. He intended to look after these and return here to Haskell within a week, or ten days. But the war in Mexico made this impossible—once across the border he couldn't get back. He wrote me, but evidently the letter miscarried."

"And Beaton missed him entirely."

"By pure luck. Fred phoned the New York Central for a lower to Chicago, and they were all gone. Enright must have learned, in some way, of his calling that office, and so informed Beaton, who took that train. Later, from his own rooms, Cavendish secured accommodations on the Pennsylvania."

He paused, endeavouring to see out through the window, hearing the hoof beats of an approaching team.

"What's that, Pete?" he asked of Timmons, who was hovering as closely as he dared. "Pretty late, isn't it?"

"Guests, I reckon; the Overland was three hours late; sure, they're stoppin' yere."

CHAPTER XXXIV
MISS DONOVAN DECIDES

Two men came in through the door together, each with a small grip in his hand, which Timmons took from them, and deposited beside the stove. The larger wrote both names in the register, and then straightened up, and surveyed the landlord.

"Any chance to eat?" he asked. "We're both of us about starved."

Timmons scratched his head.

"I reckon there's plenty o' cold provender out thar," he said doubtfully, "an' maybe I could hustle you up some hot coffee, but we don't aim ter do no feedin' at this time o' night. What's the matter with the diner?"

"Hot box, and had to cut her off; be a good fellow, and hustle us up something."

"I'll see what there is," and Timmons started for the kitchen, "but I wouldn't wake Ma Timmons up fer a thousand dollars. She'd never git over it."

The large man, a rather heavy-footed fellow, with scraggly grey moustache, turned to his companion.

"Better luck than I expected at that, Colgate," he said, restored to good humour. "The old duffer seems to be quite human."

His eyes caught sight of Cavendish, and hardened, the grizzly moustache seeming to stiffen. His mouth was close to the ear of his companion, and he spoke without moving his lips.

"Our bird; stand ready."

The three were talking earnestly, and he was standing before them before any of the group marked his approach. His eyes were on Cavendish, who instantly arose to his feet, startled by the man's sudden appearance.

"There is no use making a scene, Burke," the big man said sternly, "for my partner there has you covered."

"My name is not Burke; it is Cavendish."

"So I heard in Denver," dryly. "We hardly expected to find you here, for we were down on another matter So you are not Gentleman Tom Burke?"

"No."

"I know he is not," interposed Westcott. "I have been acquainted with this man for nearly twenty years; he is a New York capitalist."

"And who the hell are you—a pal?" the fellow sneered. "Now, see here, both of you. I've met plenty of your kind before, and it is my business not to forget a face. This man is under arrest," and he laid a hand heavily on Cavendish's shoulder.

"Under the name of Burke? On what charge?"

"Robbery, at Poughkeepsie, New York; wanted also for burglary and assault in Denver. My name is Roberts," he added, stiffly, "assistant superintendent of the Pinkerton agency; the man with me is an operative from the New York office."

Cavendish glanced past Roberts toward Colgate, who stood with one hand thrust in his side pocket.

"You know this man Burke?" he asked.

"I saw him once; that's why I was put on the case. You certainly gave me some hot chase, Tom."

"Some chase? What do you mean?"

"Well, I've been on your trail ever since that Poughkeepsie job—let's see, that was two months ago. You jumped first to New York City, and I didn't really get track of you until the night of April 16. Then a copper in the Pennsylvania depot, to whom I showed your picture, gave me a tip that you'd taken a late train West. After that I trailed you through Chicago, down into Mexico, and back as far as Denver. It wasn't hard because you always signed the same name."

"Of course; it's my own. You say you had a photograph of me?"

"A police picture; here it is if you want to look at it—taken in Joliet."

Westcott grasped the sheet, and spread it open. It was Cavendish's face clearly enough, even to the closely trimmed beard and the peculiar twinkle in the eyes. Below was printed a brief description, and this also fitted Cavendish almost exactly.

"Well," said Roberts, none too pleasantly, "what have you got to say now?"

"Only this," and the miner squared his shoulders, looking the other straight in the eyes. "This man is not Tom Burke, but I can tell you where Tom Burke is."

"Yes, you can?"

"Yes, I can. I cannot only tell you, but I can prove it," he went on earnestly. "This description says that Burke had a small piece clipped out of one ear, and that he had a gold-crowned tooth in front, rather prominent. This man's ears are unmarked, and his teeth are of the ordinary kind."

The two detectives exchanged glances and Roberts grinned sarcastically.

"You'll have to do better than that," he said gruffly. "All right. Is there any mention in that description of a peculiar and vivid scar on the chest of this man Burke? It would be spoken about, if he had any, wouldn't it?"

"Sure; they never overlook them things."

"Good; unbutton the front of your shirt, Fred."

The two stared at the scar thus revealed, still incredulous, yet unable to refute the evidence of its existence. Roberts touched it with his fingers to better assure himself of its reality.

"Darn it all," he confessed. "This beats hell."

"It does," coincided Westcott. "This whole affair has been of that kind. Now I'll tell you where Tom Burke is—he lies buried in the Cavendish family lot in Brooklyn."

He turned to Colgate, who stood with mouth half open.

"You're from New York; ever hear of the Cavendish murder?"

"Only saw a paragraph in the Chicago papers. It wasn't my case, and the only thing that interested me was that the name happened to be the same as assumed by the man I was following—why?"

"Because this gentleman here is Frederick Cavendish, who was reported as killed—struck down in his apartments on the night of April 16. Instead he took the midnight flier West and you followed him. The dead man was Tom Burke; wait a minute and I'll tell you the story—all I know of it, at least."

He told it rapidly, yet omitting no detail of any interest. The two detectives, already half convinced of their mistake, listened fascinated to the strange narrative; it was a tale of crime peculiarly attractive to their minds; they could picture each scene in all its colours of reality. As the speaker ended, Roberts drew in his breath sharply.

"But who slugged Burke?" he asked. "The fellow went in there after swag; but who got him?"

"That is the one question I can't answer," replied Westcott gravely, "and neither can Fred. It doesn't seem to accord with the rest of our theories.

Enright told Lacy he didn't know who the dead man was, or who killed him."

Miss Donovan pushed her way in front of Cavendish, and faced the others, her cheeks flushed with excitement, a paper clasped in one hand.

"Perhaps I can help clear that up," she said clearly. "This is the letter found under Miss La Rue's bed. I have read part of it. It was written by Jack Cavendish just as he was taking a boat for South America. It is not a confession," she explained, her eyes searching their faces, "just a frightened boy's letter. I wouldn't understand it at all if I didn't know so much about the case. What it seems to make clear is this: The La Rue girl and Patrick Enright schemed to get possession of the Cavendish property through her marriage to John; this part of the programme worked out fairly well, but John could not get hold of enough money to satisfy them.

"Enright and the girl decided to put Frederick out of the way, but lacked the nerve to commit murder—at least in New York. Their scheme seems to have been to inveigle their victim away from the city, and then help him to get killed through an accident. In that case the law would award the entire estate to John. They never told John this plan, but their constant demands for money fairly drove the young man to desperation.

"The making of the will, and the sudden proposed departure of Frederick for the West, compelled immediate action, yet even then John was kept largely in the dark as to what they proposed doing. All he knew was that Frederick had made a will disinheriting him; that he left the College Club with this document in his pocket, and intended later to take a night train."

She paused, turning the letter over in her hands, and the men seemed to draw closer in the intensity of their interest.

"Some of what I say I learned from this letter," she went on quietly, "and some I merely deduce from the circumstances. I believe the boy went home half mad, his only thought being to destroy that will. In this state of mind, and fortified by drink, he stole later into Frederick's apartments. I don't believe the boy actually intended to murder his cousin, but he did intend to stun him with a blow from behind, seize the paper, and escape unseen. It was a wild, hare-brained project, but he was only a boy, half drunk, worked into frenzy by Celeste La Rue. He got into the room—probably through the bath-room window—unobserved, but after Frederick had departed. This other man—Burke—was then at the table, running through the papers he had taken from the safe, to see if any were of value. John, convinced the man was his cousin, stole up behind him and struck him down. He had no idea of the force of the blow delivered, and may even have left the apartment without realising that the blow had been a fatal one. Afterward there was nothing to do but keep still, and let matters take their own course."

"And what happened then?"

"Naturally this: the La Rue woman wormed the truth out of him, and told Enright. From that moment the boy was entirely in their hands. While they remained in New York they helped him keep his nerve, but as soon as he was left alone, he went entirely to pieces. He was no criminal, merely a victim of circumstances. At last something happened to frighten him into flight."

The four men straightened up as her voice ceased speaking. Then Roberts laughed, as though ashamed of the breathless interest he had exhibited.

"I guess she's got that doped out about right, Colgate," he said, almost regretfully. "And it's clear enough that we are on the wrong trail. Anyhow this man here isn't Tom Burke, although he would deceive the very devil. What is it, landlord? Am I ready to eat? Just lead the way, and I'll show you." He glanced about at the others. "Any of you missed your supper? If so, we'd be glad to have your company."

"I'll accept the invitation," returned Cavendish. "I was asleep up-stairs, and failed to hear the bell. Perhaps you gentlemen can tell me what steps I'd better take in a case like mine."

The three passed out together, following the guidance of Timmons, and as the sound of their voices subsided into a confused murmur, Westcott glanced into the face beside him.

"You must be very tired, dear."

"I am tired, Jim," she said, "but I mustn't allow it. I have a big job on hand. Farriss will want three thousand words of this and he'll want it to-night so that he can scoop the town."

"Scoop the town?" Westcott repeated.

"Yes, that means my paper gets a story that no other paper gets. And this Cavendish case is going to be my scoop. Will you walk with me down to the station?"

Big Jim Westcott nodded silently and took her arm in his and together they went out into the night.

Each stone, shrub, each dark frowning cliff reminded them of their meeting, and silently, with their hearts full, they walked along until a dilapidated box car hove into view, with one oil-lamp still burning, twinkling evidence that Carson had not retired for the night; and as they came abreast the door they found him dozing.

"Wake up, Carson," cried Jim, tapping him on the shoulder, "wake up and get ready to do a big job on the keys. And keep your ears open, too, old timer, for it's interesting, every word of it—Miss Donovan is going to tell a story."

Carson rubbed his eyes, sat up, gave ample greeting, got up, lit another lamp, and tested his wire.

"East wire free as air, Jim," he said. "You can begin that there story whenever you want."

And so, weary as she was, and with nerves still high-pitched, Stella Donovan began, slowly at first, until she got the swing of her "lead," and then more rapidly; one after another the yellow sheets on which she wrote were fed past Westcott's critical eyes and into the hands of Carson, who operated his "bug" like a madman.

An hour went past, an hour and a quarter—Stella Donovan was still writing. An hour and a half. Westcott saw her face tensing under the strain, saw it grow wan and white, and, reaching down he gripped the fingers that clenched the pencil."No more, Stella," he said firmly, "you've sent four thousand!"

She looked at him tenderly. "Please, Jim," she begged, "just let me add one more paragraph. It's the most important one of all."

The miner released her hand and the girl wrote hurriedly, this time passing the sheets direct to Carson. Heroically the station agent stuck to his task, and as he tossed the first of the sheets aside, an eddying wisp of wind caught it, danced it a moment on the table-top, then slid it over under the very palm of big Jim Westcott's right hand. Slowly he picked it up and read it."So!" he said, with something strangely like a cry in his deep voice, "so you've resigned from the *Star*, and you're going to stay in Haskell?"

The girl looked at him, her lips trembling.

"I never want to be a lady reporter again," she whispered. "Never!"

They were in the open doorway now, and through the lush, warm gloom a belated light twinkled down in Haskell, slumbering like a bad child in the gulch below. And as they stood there watching a fair young moon making its first bow in a purple sky, their lips met in a long tender kiss; when they lifted their eyes again it was to let them range over the eternal misty hills with their hearts of gold in which lay the future—their future.